Always Believe
(*In the Magic of Christmas*)

By Barbara Baldwin
Digital ISBNs
Kindle 9781771458184
Print ISBN 9781771458207

Books We Love
A quality publisher of genre fiction.
Airdrie Alberta

Copyright 2015 Barbara Baldwin
Cover art by Michelle Lee

Chapter One

"Are we home, daddy?"

"Yeah, sweetie, we are," Ryan answered as he turned off the car. He closed his eyes for a second and took a deep breath. Three long days and fourteen hundred miles in the car – he was exhausted. He blinked, finally moving when the porch light flickered on, casting a soft yellow glow across the drive.

He climbed out of the SUV and opened the door to the back seat, then carefully unhooked Emma's seatbelt and folded her blanket around her. "Grab Teddy; here we go." He scooped his sleepy daughter, blanket and teddy bear into his arms, ever mindful of the metal brace on her left leg that kept it stretched out straight.

"I can walk." Her protest, once constant, was now random, and usually at times when she knew Ryan wouldn't listen. Still, he acknowledged her.

"I know you can, but this is faster. Besides, Aunt Mary is waiting."

He shuffled along the cracked sidewalk and up the steps onto the porch of the two-storied old Victorian style house. In the weak porch light, he barely saw the shadowy silhouettes of his aunt's rose bushes that bordered the walk. He wondered if October was too late for the brilliant display of color he recalled.

"A rose's bloom is a promise," Aunt Mary had told him when she started the garden shortly after he had come to live with her. For more than the first time since his parents died all those years ago, he sorely needed a promise of something better. In fact, he needed a miracle.

"Ryan, it's so very good to see you." Aunt Mary met him at the door. "When you called to tell me you were coming, I didn't know if you would arrive today or tomorrow. And this is Emma?" His aunt touched Emma's cheek, but she snuggled closer to Ryan's chest, too drowsy to respond. Even though the doctors had assured him she was getting better, it seemed all she did was sleep.

"Come in, come in. I have Emma's room all ready," Aunt Mary said, holding the door wide enough for him to slip through. She led him across the living room to a set of French doors, which she pushed wide. "I thought she would be happier facing the rose garden than being upstairs with those tiny windows. Fact is, I never use those rooms any more. Too much trouble, you know, climbing the stairs all the time."

Ryan was thankful for her thoughtfulness in putting Emma on the ground floor. Although she maneuvered short distances on crutches, she'd never manage stairs, and she was too weak to go far anyway.

Ryan stepped through the doorway of the guest room with its dark, full sized furniture. His aunt had tried to make it into a little girl's room because pale yellow curtains covered the windows and stuffed animals sat propped against the pillows. He gently tucked Emma under the covers of the big bed, brushing back her hair and kissing her forehead.

"Sweet dreams, sweat pea," he said, like he did every night from the time she was born.

"We're not putting you out, are we?" He followed his aunt through the living room to her cozy kitchen at the back of the house.

"Of course not. There's plenty of room in this rambling old house. I freshened your old room upstairs, if that's all right. I remember you loved to pound up those stairs and then more often than not, slid down the banister." She chuckled in remembrance.

"I don't think you'll catch me on the banister anymore."

"No, but we don't want to give Emma an excuse to repeat your antics, do we?"

"Emma's not well enough to..." His voice faded and he wondered if his daughter would ever be well enough to enjoy the simple pleasures of being a child.

"It'll be all right, Ryan. You bide and watch. We're all going to be just fine." Aunt Mary patted his cheek; like she had all those years ago as he grew up in her house in Snow. Ryan held her hand against his face, appreciating the warmth of it, recognizing that age and time had made it frailer. Still, it was a comfort.

He hadn't known what to do after hearing the doctor's latest prognosis. He had a sick child who may never recover, a stressful job that demanded too much of his time, and Houston had been too far away from family. Within a week, he had sorted and packed the furniture and taken a leave of absence, piling Emma and their clothes into the car and driving north. He needed to be somewhere familiar.

"Nothing's changed in twenty years," he said as he scraped back a chair and sat at the table.

"Why change? We always seemed happy this way." Mary put a large bowl of stew in front of him, accompanied by a glass of milk and a plate of hot biscuits and butter. "Will Emma eat something?"

"If she wakes. The medicine she takes makes her pretty sleepy. Besides, we stopped an hour ago and she drank most of a milk shake. She still doesn't have much of an appetite. At this point, I let her eat when she wants and pretty much what she wants."

"Ryan Diantelli, you know better. That child needs fruits and vegetables and plenty of milk if she's going to get well."

Ryan's gaze darted to the ceiling as the sharp sting of tears threatened. Damn. He was the father. He was supposed to be strong, to know all the answers, to protect and save. Yet he was ready to lose it. How was he going to manage everything life had thrown at him lately?

"I know Emma's very sick, honey, but you never did tell me exactly what she has or what her prognosis is and how we can help." Mary covered his trembling hand as she talked. "If you don't want to talk tonight, that's fine. But Ryan, you know running away isn't going to solve the problem. We have to stand together and fight this."

She was right and he smiled at her continued use of the word we. When he had called and told her Peggy and he had separated because his wife's drinking had worsened and she had gone into detox, Mary had hoped they would reconcile. But when he'd had to call and tell her about the accident that crushed Emma's leg and put his ex-wife in jail, Aunt Mary hadn't minced words telling him exactly what she thought of Peggy's negligence. She was totally protective of those she considered her family and Ryan regretted not having stayed in closer touch during those rough patches. He had thought he had to do it all himself.

"At the time of the accident, not only was her leg crushed, causing a comminuted fracture, but windshield glass cut the skin and bacteria entered the bone, causing osteomyelitis. Usually it can be cured with antibiotics, but Emma's leg isn't healing. The latest tests also showed trauma to the epiphyseal plate – the growth plate -- at the end of the bone." He scrubbed his hands over his face.

"She's stable now, otherwise I wouldn't have considered moving away from her doctors in Houston. They've given me a referral to the children's hospital in Pittsburgh. Once the doctors here examine Emma and recommend treatment, it's still a matter of waiting."

The complexities of Emma's disease were sometimes more than even Ryan could wrap his mind around. "The bottom line is that the fracture in her leg isn't mending."

In the year since the accident, they had had to fight for her life three times, and every time Ryan had damned his ex-wife for letting Emma ride in the front seat instead of the back where she belonged. After each operation, it had taken Emma longer to recover, leaving her weaker and more fragile than before, and leaving Ryan physically drained and emotionally devastated.

Yet Emma had always fought back, her indelible spirit eventually allowing Ryan to smile again. There were times when Ryan was well aware of the reversal in roles. Emma buoyed him and kept him going, instead of the other way around. And now he realized why that was.

"Emma is a lot like you, Aunt Mary." At her look of surprise, he continued, "She never seems to get down. When she was in the hospital, sick as a dog, she would always smile when I came in; always ask me if I had bought her a ticket on the space shuttle yet. It was our joke, and sometimes when I wanted to cry, she was the strong one. For an eight year old, she acts much older."

"Are you saying I'm old for my age?"

Ryan knew she teased. "You will always be ageless to me. But I think Emma's very lucky to have inherited your happy spirit and positive outlook on life."

Ryan helped his aunt straighten the kitchen before he went to the car and brought in their luggage. He had sold the house in Houston and most of the furnishings, putting only a few keepsakes and Emma's furniture in storage. There was a lot left unsettled, but it would sort itself out. Emma was – always would be – his first priority. He had learned that lesson the hard way when he almost lost her, and he wasn't going to let it happen again.

He stood at the kitchen sink listening to the wind howl long after his aunt had gone to bed. He glanced out the window but the night was dark. A stained-glass dragonfly, hung on the window with a suction cup, rattled against the glass on the next gust of wind. Tonight's weather caused him to wonder at the wisdom of moving from Houston to Snow, especially with winter right around the corner.

A sudden burst of rain pelted the window, jarring Ryan from his musings. He watched the water sluice down the pane in a continuous sheet. Sighing, he topped off his cup of coffee, flipped off the switch on the pot and turned toward the living room. He peeked through the bedroom doorway to check on Emma then slouched in an oversized chair next to the small gas fireplace. He stared into the flames as he sipped his coffee.

He missed having someone to talk to and cuddle with on nights like this. He loved Emma to pieces and regardless of his periodic misgivings, he knew they were in the right place for this time of their lives. But he was a healthy male in what should be the prime of his life, and he longed for an adult relationship, even as he felt guilty thinking it was because of Emma that he didn't have one.

He reached into his pocket for his cell phone, flipped it open and hit speed dial.

"'Lo?" The voice was husky and drowsy and Ryan smiled.

"Hey."

"Ryan! Where are you? Are you and Emma all right?"

Ryan smiled at Alexis's questions. She always asked about Emma. She and Ryan had dated for over six months and more often than not, Emma was in the middle of it, by Alexis's request.

"We're okay. We finally made it to Aunt Mary's. I'm exhausted."

"Why are you talking to me then? You should be asleep."

"I miss you. I wanted to hear your voice. Now that I'm here, I'm not sure—"

"Yes you are," she interrupted. "It was the right thing to do. You'll see."

The women in his life always had such positive attitudes. "Alexis, I…"

"Sh, I know. Get some sleep."

When Ryan crawled into bed under the sloping roof of the old Victorian, he chuckled. Aunt Mary hadn't changed a thing, including the single bed that now didn't quite fit his six foot, two inch frame. Regardless, he slept soundly for the first time in too long. He and Emma were home.

* * * *

Laughter. How could such an innocent sound cause Ryan's heart to soar? He followed the chatter to the kitchen, where Emma sat at the table with a bowl of cereal while Aunt Mary peeled apples at the sink. Ryan watched from the doorway as Emma lifted the spoon to her mouth, paused, and then put it back in the bowl. He frowned.

8

Reminding himself not to fuss at her, which only made things worse, he sauntered into the kitchen aiming for the coffee pot. "Morning all."

"Hi, daddy."

"Hey, pet. Did you sleep well?" He snatched an apple slice from the bowl. Predictably his aunt swatted at his hand. He held it out to Emma but she wrinkled her nose and shook her head so he popped it into his mouth and winked.

She giggled.

"You, kiddo," he said after swallowing, "need to get changed so we can enroll you in school."

"No way! It's Friday."

"What does Friday have to do with it?"

"Nobody starts school on Friday. Besides, Aunt Mary said I can help make apple pies."

Ryan turned to his aunt.

"Before you say anything I'm not undermining your authority. I didn't say anything about her helping until after she said she was being home schooled." She raised a brow and together they turned to look at Emma.

"Well, I am," she insisted.

Ryan knew that tone of voice. His daughter used it whenever she wanted something. It had taken him a long time to train his ears not to listen and his heart not to give in to her every whim.

"You're doing school work at home," he replied. "That's not the same thing. You don't have to stay but I think the principal and your teacher would like to know what you look like."

"Fern Potts," Mary said.

"Who?"

"That's who is principal now. Your fifth grade teacher."

"But she's got to be a hundred," Ryan said. "Hell, she was old when I was in her class."

His aunt tsked at his language. "She's only retiring this year. I wonder if she remembers you." She gave him a smile that said you'd better hope not.

"Oh, great," Emma said. "Am I going to be profiled because my dad caused trouble in school?"

"I didn't cause trouble—"

"Ha!" Mary interrupted.

"I was just a little rambunctious," he finished.

When Emma looked as though she'd say more, he pointed a finger at the door. "Go get dressed. If I go to school by myself, I'll ask for the hardest teacher."

"She seems very alert this morning," Mary commented after Emma left the room.

"She usually is in the morning. That's why I want her in school, for at least half a day. Once she takes her medicine at noon, she gets pretty groggy."

"Can't they give her something less strong?"

Ryan poured a cup of coffee before answering. "Not if she's going to make any progress. What's with all the apples anyway?"

He followed his nose to the oven, cracking the door open to inhale the rich cinnamony smell of apple pie.

"Have you been gone so long you've forgotten the Apple Cider Festival?"

"You're kidding? Old man Larsen still has the apple orchard?"

"At least through this year. Every year he says he's moving south but never does. I do know he's not been the same since his wife, Eva, died, and that old orchard just doesn't produce like it once did."

Ryan recalled sneaking to the orchard to steal apples with his friends, but Mr. Larsen never minded. In fact he had help yourself, boys signs posted all over. It was probably a better deterrent than if he'd yelled at them. It simply wasn't fun if the element of danger was gone.

"If the apples are just now ready, why do you have a sink full and already baking?"

"The festival is this weekend. The Methodist Church got the bid for the homemade ice cream stand and when the Women's Auxiliary decided to add pie to the menu, George gave us some of the early variety. Everyone that comes to pick apples enjoys their taste. That's why they come.

10

Having products like pie and apple butter and the recipes makes people buy even more apples."

"Making Larsen even more money," Ryan added, although he was all for entrepreneurship.

"You know how Snow is, Ryan. We help each other. All the different organizations in town have booths for crafts and produce at no cost, and George gives ten percent back to the town's community chest. We all benefit."

Ryan glanced at his watch. It was only nine and he wondered how long his aunt had been up. "So you've retired from the bakery in favor of making pies once a year?"

"Heavens, no. I was there at three, like always. Greta comes in at seven to take over." She tsked again, brushing past him with hot pads in hand. "I don't know what I'll do soon, though, because Greta's daughter is ready to have her babies and Greta's leaving for Boston the minute she does. She always said whenever her only daughter had a baby, she'd be a full time grandma. Since her daughter is having twins, she'll need the help."

Ryan grabbed the bundle of clothes he'd brought downstairs with him. "Well, I'm here now so we'll work something out." He headed for the bathroom to shower. "It's been a long time since I made cookies but I think I can remember how."

His aunt laughed. "You always ate more than you made."

"That too," Ryan replied with a smile.

* * * *

Saturday dawned clear and crisp, the promise of fall heavy in the air. Ryan helped his aunt load the pies, along with paper plates and plastic forks before driving her to Larsen Orchard at the edge of town.

He had truly forgotten how small Snow was; how everything was within walking distance on nice days. Or bike distance, he recalled, having pedaled all over with his friends in his youth. It was a good place to raise a family, he thought as he listened to his aunt greet her friends while he unloaded pies from the back of his car.

"And how's your job with NASA?" A grey-haired lady with a cardinal on her sweatshirt pulled at his sleeve.

Ah, yes, Ryan mentally sighed, if you didn't mind everyone knowing your business. "Just fine." He smiled, not about to add to the gossip mill.

Once the last of the food was unloaded and Ryan had helped arrange the tables, he promised his aunt he'd be back later with Emma. He wanted to wait until it warmed up because at the moment it was a rather chilly fifty-two degrees.

He took a circular route back to the house on Maple Street. The car window was down, the crisp morning air smelling faintly of wood smoke and the ever present coal. Still, it didn't detract from the scenic beauty of the town and surrounding area. Leaves were changing colors; everything from yellow to red to rusty brown lay scattered across the lawns or drifted toward the ground in the breeze. The foothills were visible in the distance to the east, their crests still dark green with the abundance of evergreens covering the slopes. Somehow this area west of the Appalachians had been spared the worst of the forest harvesting and timber was abundant. As he pulled into the drive he heard geese honking overhead. He scanned the sky. They were heading west, probably to Piper Lake.

"Emma?" he called as he came in the front door and closed it behind him. They had left her sleeping but he didn't find her when he peeked into her room.

"Emma?"

"Back here." He followed her voice to the bathroom which was off the side of the kitchen.

She came out dressed, but with her hair wrapped in a towel. She maneuvered quite well on the crutches, he thought, as she swung along to the table where he saw her brace on the floor by her chair. She was only supposed to take it off to bathe and even then she couldn't put pressure on her leg, which made giving her a bath awkward.

"You already took a bath? You know you're not supposed to do that alone." He hadn't intended to shout but the thought of her slipping and falling, hurting herself when he wasn't close by, always made him panic.

"Dad, I'm ten years old," she shouted right back, standing straight and tall, despite the crutches.

"Yeah, so?"

She didn't say anything; simply stared at him with narrowed eyes. She reminded him of his wife – stubborn and defiant – with blonde hair and snapping green eyes. She would be beautiful when she grew up. When she...

Oh, God, he mentally groaned. Don't tell me she's gotten to that age? He studied her from head to toe. She crossed her arms over her chest.

He opened his mouth but she forestalled his question.

"Don't ask. Don't even think what you're thinking."

"How do you know what I'm thinking?"

"Because you're my dad and you think you know all about things."

"I do."

"Even if you do, I don't want to hear about some things from my dad." She scowled.

Ryan suddenly wasn't at all sure what they were talking about. Did he need to have Aunt Mary talk to her? She couldn't be ready for a hormone-sex-boy-girl talk. She was only ten.

She sat on a chair and he bent to slip on her socks. He took her brace, already attached to her shoe, and set it in place, buckling it securely. Once again he realized how hard it was to be a single parent.

"Okay, do it your way, only promise me you'll do it when I'm here in case you need help." He was hoping do it encompassed all the things she might be talking about.

She narrowed her eyes.

"When your Aunt Mary's here," he amended.

"Okay. Now, if you are done embarrassing me, can I finish my hair?"

He tweaked her nose. "Go," he said, shaking his head. As she left the kitchen he called to her, "Get your hair dry if you want to go to the apple festival. I don't want you getting a cold on top of everything else."

"Dad." He heard the exasperation in her voice.

"Hey. I'm the parent. It's my prerogative to give orders."

* * * *

Ryan drove Emma around the town square, and past the lake, pointing out places of interest, or so he thought.

"That's where you rode your bike and went swimming every day," she said. When he pulled into the parking that edged Larsen Orchard, she said, "And this is where you stole apples with your friends."

Ryan laughed. "You know all the stories?"

"About a hundred times." She rolled her eyes.

Ryan didn't say anything else, but unbidden memories came rushing back of childhood years spent picking apples, having rotten apple fights with his friends, and in later years, the annual Apple Cider Days Festival. He didn't, however, remember it being such a huge deal.

Bright colored awnings and tents littered the road on both sides. Cinnamon and popcorn and other scents converged in the crisp autumn air to tantalize his senses.

From where he stood, the orchard wasn't even visible. There were hundreds of people strolling along the roadway, stopping to look at the items for sale, most of which had an apple theme.

"Wow!" Emma exclaimed, stopping to look around. "Do they do this every year?"

"I thought you knew all the stories," he said and they laughed. He shoved his hands in his pockets to keep from picking her up, wanting to help…too much sometimes. "Do you want to go find Aunt Mary?"

"Dad, I'll walk as long as I can walk, then I'll go sit. Quit worrying."

"Wait." He touched her shoulder and maneuvered them around some people to one of the booths. Handing the woman behind the table two dollars, he took one of the souvenir pins and bent to pin it on Emma's shirt.

"What's that?" She looked at the small red apple pin.

"It means you're the apple of my eye and let's everyone know you're special." He grinned.

"Oh, brother. This is one of those cornball things, isn't it? I mean, what happens for the snow festival that you told me about. Do they give everybody a snow pin and tell them they're a flake?"

"Hmm, that might catch on." He laughed, and realized he hadn't been doing that much lately.

A petite blonde popped her head around the corner of the next tent. "Ryan Diantelli, is that you?" She scurried over and gave him a hug.

"Corin Grant?" Even though it had been fifteen years since high school, his friend and classmate looked the same.

"Well, it's Parker now; although that's the only thing that idiot left me before he moved out. My god, I can't believe you're back in town. Visiting Mary?"

"Actually, we moved here, for a while at least."

Corin glanced at Emma. Her smile widened. "Hello?"

Emma stuck her hand out. "Hi, I'm Emma Diantelli. I'm ten."

"Wonderful! My son, Charlie, is ten. I bet you'll be in his class at school."

"My dad won't let me go to school."

Ryan felt his mouth drop open in surprise. "I never said she couldn't go; only that it wasn't the right time now." He shook his head as Corin laughed.

"Don't you just love them at this age? Anytime they can get their parents in a dither, they do it. Hey, look, I have to get back to the booth; we're trying to raise money for a children's drama program, but a bunch of us are meeting over at Butch's Bar-b-que tent about one. Why don't you stop by?"

"You mean you're not the only one from our class still living here?"

15

"More like you're the only one who moved away." She laughed as she walked away and Ryan wondered if the old adage you can't go home again would be true here. It wasn't that he didn't want to see old friends. He only wondered, after being in a high pressure job at NASA, having a marriage fall apart and moving back home, he wouldn't be looked on as an anomaly.

Following after Emma as she made her way carefully along the dirt path, he figured there was only one way to find out, but it meant handling Butch's spicy hot wings for lunch.

"Dad, where's the orchard? Are we going to pick apples?"

"Emma, why did you tell Corin I wouldn't let you go to school?"

"Because if I say I'm home schooled or I can't go because of my leg, all the kids will think I'm different."

"And different is bad?"

His little girl shook her head and sighed. "I have to remember to ask Aunt Mary if you were ever ten years old."

They finally came to a path between the tents that led further off the road and toward the orchard. When they rounded the curve past the last colorful canopy, Ryan was shocked to see what had become of his favorite childhood haunt. Oh, the trees were there and plenty of apples were still high in the branches, but it didn't look the same. Some of the trees had apparently been damaged by storm and branches bowed low to the ground. Others had only a few leafy branches; the rest were bare broken limbs. For an orchard to remain successful, new trees needed to be planted continually, and it didn't look as though George Larsen had done that.

"Hi, I'm Charlie." A young boy came barreling to a stop in front of them. He was about Emma's size, with red hair and freckles. He had one hand clutched in the fur of a dog half as tall as him – a husky from the looks of it. "This is Wolf." He flung his arm around the dog's neck and hugged him. The dog wore a harness attached to a wagon with wooden sides. It had several sacks of apples in it.

Ryan might have wished for a dog all those years ago when he came and picked apples for people. When he was a kid, he had had to lug the heavy sacks back to the barn for weighing. This young man would go far.

"Can I pet him?" Emma asked and at Charlie's nod, she reached out, totally unafraid. When she quit stroking him, the dog nudged her with his head, almost knocking her down. She just laughed.

"You're the new girl at school, aren't you? I saw you in Principal Pott's office yesterday. Who did you get for a teacher? You'd better hope it wasn't old Mr. Jensen. He's the meanest teacher in school."

"I'm in Miss Michaels' class, fifth grade."

"Super, that's my class, too."

Ryan watched the interaction between the two kids, thinking this must be Corin's son. It would be nice for Emma to know someone, because as soon as her leg healed, she'd be attending school full time.

"Did you pick those apples for anyone?" Ryan gestured to the wagon.

"Yeah, Mom always freezes tons of applesauce and apple butter every year. Do you want some apples? As soon as I get these weighed and Wolf hauls them home, I'll come back and pick you some."

Ryan smiled. "Well, you can come back and help, and I know Wolf will be useful, but I'm sure Emma wants to try her hand at picking."

"She can't climb a tree with that brace on her leg," Charlie said with all the tact of a ten year old boy.

"Can, too," Emma chimed in immediately.

"Bet you can't."

She stuck her tongue out at the boy.

Ryan quickly defused the situation. "We'll all help, as soon as you and Wolf get back, we'll be over that way." He pointed to a tree where the branches were low to the ground, figuring Emma could pick without having to climb.

17

"He's stupid," Emma said when Charlie and Wolf had moved on.

Ryan started to reprimand her before recalling how dumb he had thought girls were when he was in fifth grade. And the most stupid were the ones he liked, but they hadn't like him. Ah, no amount of money would make him want to be ten again.

Chapter Two

"I can take care of Emma," Aunt Mary said the next morning at breakfast when Ryan regaled her of his previous conversation with his daughter.

"No, she's my responsibility. I've been taking care of her since Peggy left two years ago."

"Then why did you come home, Ryan?"

That question was a lot easier to answer than some. He smiled at his aunt. "Home, that's why. All I did was work. Between the pressure of the job and Emma's illness, I was losing it. I didn't know how to handle anything anymore. The only thing I realized as a certainty was that I needed to go home. When my investment broker laughingly asked why I even worked – that I could have retired years ago, I had this epiphany. Why not?"

"So here we are." He shrugged. "Is anyone living in that apartment over the bakery? I thought we might stay there and I'll help at the Snickerdoodle."

"You don't have to do that. You can stay here."

"Aunt Mary, don't you see? This is the ideal situation. If we're in the apartment I can work and Emma is right upstairs instead of blocks away. When she's awake or doing her homework, I can bring her down to the bakery."

"I thought you said you didn't need to work."

"I don't, but I do need to keep busy; just not the all-consuming way I did at NASA. I realized last Friday when I registered Emma for school that she can't actually attend until her leg heals. The fifth grade classroom is upstairs even though the cafeteria and music room are downstairs. For a while anyway, this will make it easier for me to help her with her school work."

He gave Mary a hug then put his dishes in the sink. "You said Greta would be leaving soon and besides, it's time you started taking it easy."

She laughed. "What would I do if I wasn't at the bakery?"

"Bridge?"

She scoffed.

"Bingo?"

She wrinkled her nose.

"Poker?"

Her brows shot up. "I doubt the American Legion gentlemen would let me in their games. They tend to think a woman's place is at home."

Ryan knew better. The women in Snow were the driving force behind the town's success. They were the strength and hope that kept the town going in good times and bad.

Carston Mine, which employed a large majority of work eligible men in town, at one time had owned everything from the company store to the school. Over several generations of miners and mine owners, the town had gradually broken away and re-established itself with privately owned businesses that weren't controlled by Carston. The majority of those businesses were run by women.

From what he had heard when he met Corin for lunch at the Apple Cider Festival, Carston was running out of coal. That led to a host of problems, one of which was the utilities company, which of course was fueled by coal. There was talk that Carston was going to raise coal prices yet again and quite a few people were up in arms over the maneuver.

It was one thing to raise prices on a commodity that was sold out of state to the highest bidder. It was another entirely to charge your own residents a rate higher than what outsiders were charged. Carston knew there was no option in terms of turning elsewhere for electricity. All the major power grids circumvented Snow because for years, the coal mine had generated the electricity to fuel the town. Now, what would become of Snow?

"Speaking of the American Legion," his aunt interrupted his thoughts, "are you going to the meeting there tomorrow?"

Ryan focused on what his aunt had said. "What meeting?"

"Harold Carston continues to think Snow is totally controlled by the mine, but we have a city council and a mayor." She snorted. "Some days I do wonder if he doesn't control them. Anyway, some of us have put enough pressure on the city council that they have called a meeting to discuss the energy crisis."

Ryan smiled at his aunt's language. "Some of us? You're right in the middle of this, aren't you?"

She just shrugged.

Ryan had read his history books on coal mining around Snow and the rest of Pennsylvania. Back in the late 1870's a few men controlled not only the coal industry but law in the towns and the very lives of those who worked in the mines. He remembered reading about the Molly Maguires, supposedly started to resist deplorable mine conditions, and the violence that surrounded the industry at that time as factions faced off. Thankfully things were different today.

"You make it sound dire. Besides, there aren't any coal kings anymore who control everything in their reach."

"You'd be surprised," his aunt replied. "Most people in Snow come from generations of miners. They know who butters their bread, so to speak, and are individually afraid of speaking out. Together, maybe we can make a difference."

"And I'm an outsider; there's no sense in getting involved," Ryan said.

"You grew up here and now you're living here again. You're not an outsider."

"Regardless, I have other things to worry about at the moment. I'm sure Snow isn't going to run out of coal tomorrow."

* * * *

Ryan spent most of the morning at the apartment over the bakery. He had the heat and electricity turned on, made a list of furniture they would need, and after borrowing his aunt's vacuum, did a lickety-split job of cleaning. He wasn't the best housekeeper, and in Houston had a lady who came in twice a week to do some cleaning and cooking.

Here, he would have to become more independent from the services readily available in the city. He was sure he could find someone to cook and clean, but because of the size of Snow, he also knew everyone in town would know about it within a week. The real trouble would begin as matchmaking mothers offered their daughters to help him.

He sat on the top step of the stairs to the apartment, sipping a cup of coffee from the bakery and going over his list. He and Emma could do this; he was sure of it, and he would have more time to spend with her while still helping his aunt. He stared down the stairwell. If only Emma's leg would heal; if only....

He mentally gauged the width of the stairway. The stairs were inside the building, wide and deep, and the landing at the top was at least five foot square, with the apartment door to the left. What if he put a chair lift in the stairway; the electric kind that slid up and down on a rail attached to the wall?

The first time he had taken Emma to the physical therapist, he had been given all kinds of brochures for equipment and apparatus that would make it easier for a handicapped (he hated that word) person to maneuver through a house. Since their house in Houston had been a single story ranch style, Ryan had scarcely bothered with one particular flyer, but he did remember the chairlift. He pulled his phone out of his pocket and called the hospital in Houston, who connected him with Emma's doctor.

Within minutes, he had called the company, and was referred to a rep in the Pittsburgh area who said he would be happy to come to Snow and look at the project.

Ryan walked through the bakery, waving at Greta on his way out the door. He paused, buttoning his coat when the wind hit him. He looked at the cloud laden sky, wondering if it would snow even though it was only October. The annual snow festival that drew thousands to the little town didn't officially start until November or early December, but the first heavy snow was always cause for celebration.

That was another reason moving to the apartment was a good idea. Snow had that name for a very good reason. He remembered school being closed for weeks at a time when enough snow fell that it buried cars and came almost to the tops of windows. As a kid he hadn't minded missing school, and had made money shoveling walks and digging cars out once the roads were finally cleared.

Now, as the parent of a child, he worried about getting stranded at the bakery with Emma at Mary's house; getting stuck in a snow drift while driving, or a hundred other scenarios that probably would never happen. Still, he worried. At least this way, he and Emma would be in the same building; easily within reach any time of day.

"Looks like snow."

He turned to find Corin exiting the Wonderland Bookstore, which sat right next to the bakery. "Might," he replied.

"Charlie says Emma's really not going to school," Corin commented as she tucked her hair under her stocking cap before tugging on her mittens. "I thought she was just giving you a hard time."

Ryan chuckled. "I swear. It's only been a day and everyone in town already knows our story."

Corin shrugged. "Hey, it's Snow. What can I say?"

Ryan knew she was right. Everybody knew everything. "The logistics of a second floor classroom will keep her from attending until her leg is better, but I've talked to the principal and she's agreed to let Emma do her work at home. I'll go to school and get her assignments weekly and take in her work."

"Charlie can do that, if you want," Corin said.

"He wouldn't mind? I'm fixing the apartment upstairs, so we'll be living here."

"They're in the same class and he always comes to the bookstore after school." She sighed. "He's too old for a sitter, but I hate leaving him home alone, you know?"

Ryan nodded. "I definitely know that drill."

"I was going to pop over to Blitzen's for a latte. Want to come?"

They turned to walk along the square, turning north at the corner. "Man, some things never change, do they?" Ryan asked as they passed Jolly Pots, the Evergreen Gazette newspaper office, and Candy Cane Lane, stores with holiday names that had been around for as long as he could remember.

"They do; and they don't," Corin cryptically stated as he held the door to Blitzen's open and followed her inside. The warmth of the store carried the fragrant smell of roasting coffee and Ryan breathed deep. After placing their orders at the counter, they sat at a corner table out of the flow of traffic.

"We never had a chance to visit at the apple festival," Ryan opened the conversation. "Bring me up to date." He and Corin had been friends throughout their school years, but they had been wise enough in high school not to date. Dating can kill a good thing, Corin had reminded him on more than one occasion. And for the two of them, it had worked.

Ryan had had a confidant to explain the female mind when he was having girl trouble, and he had cautioned her against dating certain guys when he heard scuttle-butt in the locker room about who was going to try and make points with whom that weekend. But from the little she had said over the weekend, he hadn't been here when she needed him.

"I'm sorry about you and Parker," he said, even though he hadn't known the guy. He was actually sorry that Corin was raising her son alone.

She shrugged off his concern. "It happened long after you left for college; and with a guy not from around here, so you couldn't have beaten him up after school for me." She gave him the smile he had always remembered, and he wondered again why some people remained friends but never lovers.

"I could have beat him up in a bar fight instead."

Corin laid a hand on his arm. "It is so good to see you back in town, Ryan. I've missed you."

Ryan got the impression Corin didn't want to talk about her ex. They had once been best friends, but high school was a long time ago. Hopefully their friendship renewed, even if on a different level because of past history.

They didn't stay long at the coffee shop. Corin ran the bookstore alone, so had put a "be right back" sign in her window and couldn't be gone long.

"Please say you'll go to the meeting at the Legion," Corin insisted as they strolled back the way they had come. "Your input might sway the outcome."

"Corin, I don't know anything about coal mining, or what has happened to Snow over the past twenty-some years. Besides, I'm an outsider; like they're going to listen to me."

"You're not, Ryan. You've worked for NASA, for God's sake. You're an expert."

He snorted. "Designing space craft is not exactly the same as figuring out the town's energy problem. I had a whole different department at NASA that worked on the fuel aspects. I was just the shell man." His job had entailed creating a vehicle to house and transport all the equipment astronauts needed in space or at the space station. He never had to worry about how it got there; that was someone else's problem.

They came to a halt in front of the bookstore. Ryan looked at his watch, realizing he should get back to his aunt's and check on Emma. "Better go. If your offer is still good, I'll call the school and ask them to send Emma's homework with Charlie."

"Of course it is. But Ryan, if you're going to live in Snow, sooner or later you'll have to take sides. Whether you like it or not, it's us against them."

As Ryan climbed into his car, he had to wonder exactly who the us and them were.

* * * *

Charlie had already talked their teacher, Miss Michaels, into letting him bring Emma's books and homework assignments to the house. By the time Ryan came in the back door, the two were ensconced at the kitchen table with cookies, milk and math books.

"Hi, Mr. D," Charlie said around a mouthful of cookie. "I brought Emma her homework but she won't let me show her how to long divide."

Ryan watched Emma roll her eyes. He knew his daughter wouldn't brag, so he'd have to do it for her. "Sorry, Charlie, but Emma knows long division already." His daughter gave him a smile for keeping it simple. The actuality of it was, his ten year old did high school algebra – often in her head -- and it looked as if a visit with her teacher was in order, since they apparently hadn't looked at her records before placing her. They probably wouldn't agree to let her take algebra, but he might purchase the book and continue teaching her himself, which is what he had done when he discovered her unusual ability. Given what he now understood about Emma not wanting to be labeled different, it was up to her as to what she told Charlie.

"Let's work on something else," Emma said, closing her math book and putting it aside. "What do we have to do with our spelling words?"

Charlie made a face. "I hate spelling. Miss Michaels always makes us write a story."

"That should be easy for you. Your mom owns the bookstore," Emma replied.

"That doesn't mean I like to read," Charlie grumbled.

Ryan moved past the table to where his aunt was taking another batch of cookies from the oven. "You don't get enough baking at the store?"

"That's business. These are for the children, and for the meeting tonight." His aunt leveled her gaze at him and Ryan knew what she was asking without saying a word.

"I need to be here for Emma."

"I called Corin when Charlie showed up after school and she said he could stay here while we all attend the meeting. Besides, it shouldn't last more than an hour."

Ryan looked over at the table where the two youngsters were avidly listening, even though they were pretending to do homework. He supposed...

"Is that alright with you, sweet pea?"

Charlie snickered.

"Dad," his daughter groaned at his use of her nickname, her cheeks bright red.

He looked from one to the other. Just this past weekend she had said Charlie was stupid. Now she was...

He narrowed his gaze as he thought back over the years. Corin and he had formed a lasting bond by the middle of fifth grade. Why did he think his daughter and Charlie wouldn't do the same? Why was he panicking because his daughter didn't seem to need him anymore?

* * * *

The meeting room at the Legion was packed by the time Ryan found a place to park and followed his aunt inside. They had settled the kids in front of the television at home and popped a movie into the DVD player. While Ryan wasn't totally comfortable leaving them, the phone was within reach and Emma knew his cell number by heart. She had promised to take her medicine, and Ryan knew she would, even though the stuff was vile tasting. Emma knew it would make her well.

Now, as he wove between the crowds to find his aunt one of the last folding chairs against the back wall, he studied those around him. He could tell every time a miner entered the room. It wasn't their physical appearance; broad shouldered with work-worn faces. And it had nothing to do with gender because Ryan noted a few women enter who he was sure weren't wives of the miners.

They were, for the most part, clean shaven men in flannel and jeans, sturdy woolen coats and stocking hats, which they tugged off upon entering the room. There was a hardened look about them, and to a man, their hands were large and calloused.

What actually set them apart was that they traveled in packs. Not one entered the room alone. Most often, three, five or six came in at once, surveyed the room and as a group selected to sit near other miners, or stand together at the back. They conversed quietly among themselves.

Ryan thought he saw familiar faces – perhaps parents of some of his classmates, but when he bent near and asked his aunt, he was shocked to learn they were his classmates.

"Working in the mines ages you, but it's all they've ever known," she whispered. "That's why I wanted something better for you. No, that's the wrong word. Someone has to do the job your uncle and others do. Different. That's the word I wanted." She continued to point out people, refreshing Ryan's memory with their names.

Uncle Paul had died long ago; Ryan had almost forgotten he was a miner. He wondered how his aunt felt about all that was going on.

"What side are you on?"

"Oh, I don't take sides. I want what's best for Snow, that's all."

Ryan looked around the room again. The miners were strong in number and united in their beliefs. He knew it came from years of working together, living together and when necessary, striking together. Although he knew it improbable, he hoped they would be on the same side. They would be a formidable force.

Chapter Three

As mayor, Mark Cox called the meeting to order, pounding a gavel on the table that was set on a platform to raise it above the rest of the chairs, which were in neat rows with an aisle through the center. It took several minutes for the sound to quiet the murmuring crowd.

Ryan glanced around at the crowd that filled the small meeting room. If body language were any indication, this meeting could prove dangerous. Most of the men who stood against the walls had their arms crossed over their chests, a sure indication that they wouldn't like whatever was said.

The majority of people seated appeared to be separated into two factions – a younger, twenty to thirty-something crowd taking many of the seats in front and down the middle. The older group -- mostly women -- were no doubt married to the miners standing against the wall and would not open their mouths unless the building caught fire. That sounded terribly chauvinistic for a man his age, but he had grown up in Snow, and knew how things worked. Mine families stuck together. He actually took time to wonder why a meeting had even been called.

Mayor Cox cleared his throat. "While I'm gratified at the turnout for this meeting, there was no need." He glanced to both sides, where other members of the City Council – all men – nervously avoided his gaze. "I have word that the cost of mining the coal is increasing, and Mr. Carston has informed me that he will be increasing energy rates to the town effectively immediately."

The words hadn't left his mouth before a murmur swept the crowd, swelling in volume although individual words couldn't be deciphered. Ryan watched Shelby Hall, owner of the Evergreen Gazette, rapidly take notes of who was saying what.

One younger resident stood and pointed a finger at the contingent along the wall. "This is your fault. You and your damn unions."

A miner straightened from the wall. "We're not getting any more wages than we did three years ago. If Carston's raising the rates, it's so he can pocket more."

Ryan looked quickly around, but the mine owner was conspicuously absent. Even so, he was surprised that a miner would speak against him.

The yelling and accusations quickly escalated and even though Cox banged his gavel, it couldn't be heard.

"Oh, dear," Aunt Mary whispered next to him. "Ryan, do something."

He coughed, looking at his aunt. "Me? I've been here less than a week. Even if I could be heard above this din, nobody's going to listen to me."

"I thought this was going to be a discussion meeting," a young man shouted above the crowd. "What the hell is there to discuss if Carston already increased the rates?"

More murmurs, but at least they were at a level where a person could be heard.

"I think we should quit paying him," said another.

"You willing to go without heat and electricity? What about your kids and the school?" This from a miner.

"There's got to be another way," Corin stood to have her say. She was short but her blue eyes snapped as she turned full circle, catching gaze after gaze, making sure she had the room's attention. "We should be looking at alternative energy sources. What about using the river to generate electricity?"

Carl Williams, from the Parks Department and the City Council, spoke. "The snow run off into Prospect River has been less and less over the years. Some years, it's been enough to feed Piper Lake and keep it at a decent level, but y'all know this past summer, there was hardly a trickle coming down the mountain. There sure isn't enough of a steady flow to run a power plant."

"Well, what about solar power. It's not like the sun doesn't shine," Corin fired right back.

There were plenty of affirmative murmurs before a voice from the back called out. "You're talking about putting those gigantic panels all over town and on top all the houses? They're an eye sore!"

"Like that mine isn't?" Corin spun around to face her opponent. Ryan craned his neck but couldn't see who had spoken.

"Coal's supported this town for more than a hundred years. We got no right looking elsewhere."

"The coal's running out. Carston doesn't want you to know that, but why do you think they're charging you double what they should to fuel your homes and businesses?"

The arguing continued, but small groups and individual people were beginning to file out of the room. Mayor Cox banged his gavel once again, apparently calling an end to the meeting although nobody paid him any attention.

Ryan caught Corin's eye and waited for her to reach him and his aunt. Her cheeks were flushed with color and her eyes glittered in anger. She was hopping mad and he couldn't tell if it was from the increase in rates or the fact no one was willing to listen to alternatives.

"Did you honestly think to change this place?" His lips quirked in a grin.

She let out a sigh. "I don't know why I continue to try. There's just no getting through some of those thick heads and stubborn attitudes."

They left the Legion and Ryan offered Corin a ride back to the house since she had walked and Charlie was over with Emma.

"I'm going to write an editorial," Corin said as they entered the living room where the two children were watching television. "If the mine would cut back two hours per shift, the majority of people could stand a little hit to their wages and the whole town wouldn't have to suffer. It's not like we'd be asking him to cut shifts completely and put men out of work."

"Oh, boy," Charlie muttered, "Mom's on her bandwagon again."

"Did you get your homework done, young man?" his mother changed the subject. "It's time to head for home."

"Do you think writing an editorial is going to do any good?" Ryan had more questions because like it or not, he felt drawn into the town's problems. "Is anyone going to pay any attention?"

"Probably not," Corin said, "but someone has to speak out against Mr. Carston. I know we should be grateful because the mine does mean jobs, but no one person should have that kind of control over a town. Besides, if I were to guess, Snow makes more money with the tourist business and our festivals. At least he can't take those away."

* * * *

The rest of October flew by as Ryan and Emma settled into the apartment above the bakery and Ryan began taking over some of his aunt's duties. She still came in at three in the morning to start the bread dough rising, but more often than not would leave by nine for coffee with friends. Ryan liked the idea that she was enjoying a little bit of freedom.

The stairway chair lift had been installed, and although Ryan had thought Emma would protest using it, she said it was cool. In fact, in the beginning she made a point of waiting for Charlie upstairs every afternoon when he brought her homework. Then she'd ride the lift down with him clomping beside her.

They had made one trip to the Children's Hospital in Pittsburgh. The doctor had run more tests, changed Emma's medicine, and told them that the epiphyseal plate was finally beginning to produce cells. That meant Emma's leg was on the mend, even though she still had to wear her brace.

Life was good, Ryan decided, as he poured cake batter into different sized round pans and carefully slid them into the oven.

"Hey, Dad." Emma swung around the back corner of the bakery from the hallway to the apartment.

"Hi, there. I thought you were upstairs watching TV."

"There's nothing good on." She slowly made her way to the front corner of the bakery, where he had created a study area for her. Actually, the small table and chairs, throw pillows and various toys had accumulated over the weeks as customers came into the bakery. Several people had brought in items and it had become more of a small play area, for which mothers seemed grateful. They could converse with him about their orders, pick out their cake designs or look through the book for holiday treats without having their children tugging on their shirttails.

He watched now as Emma sat in a chair and propped her leg on another chair, tucking a pillow beneath it. She was quite adept on crutches now, and the doctor seemed to think she may not need them at all after the first of the year. Ryan said a prayer every night for that to be the case. Emma took it all in stride, but he had to wonder if she missed making friends at school and hanging out.

Beep-beep. Beep-beep.

"Daddy, it's time," Emma called.

Ryan looked up from the cake he was decorating for Mr. Larsen's eightieth birthday. Emma was punching buttons on his iPhone.

"Time for what, sweetie?"

She rolled her eyes at him. "It's a good thing I'm in charge now." She tapped the phone as she set it beside her notebook.

Ryan laughed as he washed his hands and reached above the sink for Emma's medicine. When they came to Snow, he had little use for the advanced technology of his iPhone when all he did was get up at three and go to bed at nine; if he was lucky.

"Open wide." He tipped the spoon and she grimaced as she swallowed. He followed with a nibbly kiss as if trying to get it from her until she laughed. Her medicine was horrid tasting but she took it four times a day like a trooper and he tried to make it a little less tedious.

He felt his goal in life was to make Emma happy, anyway he could. None of his associates would believe him if he said he'd rather time bread dough rising than a space shuttle countdown, but he would do whatever it took to care for Emma.

"Why don't you have one of those funky songs for your medicine like you do for your friends?"

She wrinkled her nose. "Medicine is no fun so it can't have a fun sound."

She was already texting away. She worked all the capabilities on the iPhone and like many kids her age, the technology came easy. She had downloaded music and pictures off the computer, created a daily medicine reminder and used the calculator for her math homework.

He had rounded the counter again when it actually did ring like a phone, which usually meant it was for him.

"Hi, Uncle Lou," Emma said. "No, he's baking a cake." A pause; a giggle. "Yeah, the Snickerdoodle Bakery."

"Give me that phone." Ryan reached for it but Emma pulled away.

"What? You'll name the next space shuttle the Snickerdoodle? Cool."

Ryan took the phone. "Hey, Lou." He kissed his daughter's forehead and wandered back around the counter as he talked to his boss. He was technically on a leave of absence, but in reality Lou had switched him to a paid consultant in order to continue some projects in which he was the lead.

"Did you get the figures I sent on the Orion project?" Lou asked.

"Yeah, but I haven't had time to compare them yet."

"What are you doing?" His boss sounded exasperated.

"Decorating a cake."

"Emma wasn't kidding?" He definitely sounded disbelieving. "That's more important than a multibillion dollar government project?"

"It is to Mr. Larsen," Ryan replied. "I'll get it done, Lou. Good bye." He tucked the phone in his pocket.

"Dad, can I help you with the Orion project?"

Ryan laughed, shaking off the anger he had felt at Lou's pushing. "I would love that, but I think this is a little harder than algebra."

"Speaking of, when are you going to talk to Miss Michaels?"

"Emma, we discussed that. Once your teacher sees you can do the work and your records get here, I'll talk to her. Otherwise, I sound like any other bragging father."

The door to the bakery banged. Without turning, Ryan knew school was out and Charlie had arrived; just like he did every afternoon.

"Sorry, Charlie," he said. "Miss Vera bought all the sugar cookies for her bridge club. I do have chocolate chip."

"That's okay, Mr. D. I came to give Emma her homework."

Charlie never turned down cookies. Surprised, Ryan glanced their way, but the boy didn't seem to notice, making a beeline to the corner where he bent and whispered something in Emma's ear.

"Dad, Charlie wants to take me for a ride in his wagon." Emma called to him. "Please can I?"

"It's too cold," Ryan automatically replied.

"I can keep her warm, sir. She can sit in the wagon and I'll pile blankets on her. Besides, it's not very cold today."

Ryan looked at the two youngsters. Emma and Charlie had quickly become friends, and he was a good boy. Was he being too over protective? The doctor said Emma could do whatever she felt up to as long as she didn't over do. Ryan opened his mouth to refuse, but one look at his daughter's face stopped him.

"Did you get your work back? Do we have correcting to do on your homework?"

She ginned at him. "I got all the problems right, so you can't use that excuse." His daughter was bright, there was no doubt.

"All right, but only for a short time and I want you bundled up good."

She already had her coat and stocking hat on and was almost out the door with Charlie before he could finish the sentence.

"Charlie."

The youngster turned. "I'll take care of her. I promise."

Ryan watched through the window as Charlie helped Emma into it. His dog, a beautiful husky, was hitched to the wagon by a harness. After tucking a thick blanket around Emma, he said something to the dog and he started forward, easily pulling the wagon behind him. Ryan's heart hammered as he listened to Emma's laughter fade.

* * * *

"I don't believe you, Charlie Parker." Emma snuggled under the blanket as Wolf pulled her along in the wagon.

She liked Charlie, even if he did make stuff up, like telling her he had found Santa Clause. He had red hair, was shorter than she was and wore braces on his teeth. But she liked him anyway, not that she would ever tell him that. After he had made a wisecrack about her leg brace at the Apple festival and she had shown him she could pick apples anyway, he had ignored the fact she couldn't walk or run and had treated her like any other girl. That meant he still liked to tease her.

"Then why'd you come with me?" He grinned.

"To prove you're a liar."

"I'm not; honest." He whistled sharply and Wolf turned left at the corner.

Emma was very impressed with his dog training, not that she would tell him that either.

"Mom said he's rented the empty store right here." Two short soft whistles and Wolf stopped.

They stared through the dirty store window. There wasn't anything inside except for some scraps of lumber and a couple of empty paint cans, turned on their sides.

"Maybe he hasn't started building toys yet," Charlie said in what Emma thought was a rather hopeful tone.

"Even if he is who you say, he builds toys at the North Pole." Emma wasn't sure she believed in magic anymore; not after everything she'd been through.

"He could have other workshops," Charlie countered as he whistled for Wolf to begin walking again. "Maybe his elves work at different places around the world. That would save him having to drag all the toys with him from home."

Emma shook her head.

They turned at the next corner and Emma realized they were heading for the apple orchards on the edge of town. By this time of year, all the leaves were gone, and only bare branches were silhouetted against the sky, some looking like gnarled arms reaching out to snatch you. A few rotten apples were scattered on the ground with the brown leaves. She had heard her dad saying Mr. Larsen might sell the orchard, but she didn't see any signs. In a way she didn't quite understand, she hoped he wouldn't sell. Everyone in Snow believed in the stuff they did – the festivals and the magic that was supposed to happen all the time – but all she'd heard since they moved there were the problems with the mine. Some things needed to stay the same.

"Sh, do you hear that?" Charlie whispered, grabbing hold of Wolf's collar and bringing him to a halt.

"Hear what? There's nothing here, Charlie."

"Quiet," Charlie whispered to Wolf as he crept slowly forward.

Emma wanted to get out of the wagon but knew that would make too much noise, and the wheels were turning quietly on the wet undergrowth. She held her breath as they sneaked behind a gnarled tree that provided them cover but allowed them to see through the criss-cross of branches.

Several rows of trees further on, she could see a man, his back to them, dressed in a red flannel shirt and black pants and suspenders. That didn't look as strange as…Emma blinked and looked again. Where those reindeer?

One of the animals nudged the man with its nose.

"Ho, ho, ho, Donner. I didn't bring you a treat when you have all these delicious apples right at your feet." He laughed again, the sound deep and jolly, and a shiver went through Emma. "Well, okay; at your hooves." The man rubbed the deer's head, right between a huge set of antlers.

Emma tugged Charlie's sleeve and when he turned toward her, she mouthed the word, "Donner?" A grin popped across his face.

They continued watching as the man petted each reindeer in turn. Emma tried to count them, but they were very large and kept milling around. She was sure she'd counted some more than once, because she came up with twelve and Santa only had eight reindeer.

If you believed in Santa, that is. Maybe this man had named his deer Donner because he liked Christmas. Yet when he turned around, Emma sucked in her breath.

He had a snowy white beard that hung clear to the wide black belt around his fat stomach. He had a ball cap on, not a red and white hat like Santa wore, but she could still see his white hair, and the small glasses perched on his nose. His cheeks and nose were red from the chilly wind and he rubbed his hands together like he was trying to warm them.

He couldn't be Santa, Emma thought, because Santa rode in a sleigh all over the world at night in the winter and he never got cold. Did he?

Chapter Four

"He's not." Emma stated firmly as she hobbled into the bakery right at closing time.

Ryan had begun to wonder if he should go looking for the kids. Now he sighed in relief.

Charlie shook his head. "Maybe, but do you know anyone who looks like that and has..." he stopped short when he saw Ryan listening closely.

"Who has what?" Ryan asked, curious about their heated discussion. Emma's cheeks were red, whether from the cold outside or their argument, he couldn't say.

The kids looked at each other and Ryan swore he heard the gears grinding as they manufactured some story.

"Old man Pritchert. I said he was crazy because he has a dog that dances in circles."

Ryan looked at Emma, who solemnly nodded her head, corroborating her friend's story. "You didn't do...anything to make the man mad, did you?" He wasn't sure he believed their story, but as long as they weren't committing vandalism or something, he supposed they could just be doing kids' stuff.

"Dad, we didn't do anything; honest." She unwound her scarf from around her neck, tugged off her hat and coat and plopped onto a chair by the table, lifting her leg to the chair next to her. He scrutinized her face, watching for any signs of pain but saw none.

He debated whether to question them further when the bakery door flew open, the bell clanging like crazy, and Corin stormed in. She had neither coat nor hat but from the look on her face, Ryan figured anger kept her warm.

"Do you see what they have done now?" Her voice was several octaves higher than normal and she was waving a newspaper above her head.

"Whoa, Mom, calm down," Charlie said. He shrugged at Ryan as though saying he had no idea why his mother was acting this way.

His mother ignored him, slamming the paper on the counter in front of Ryan. "We have got to do something."

Ryan slid the paper from beneath her quivering hand and turned it around. He wasn't sure what he was looking for in the Evergreen Gazette, the weekly local paper, but he definitely knew when he found it.

No outdoor holiday lights this year.

"What?" He gazed at the headline in disbelief, then quickly scanned the article below it. "The City Council has voted that due to the increase in energy costs, there will be no outdoor holiday lights around the square, at the city park or on the courthouse. The City Council is encouraging residents to forego outdoor lights this year, and suggesting the use of indoor lights is greatly restricted." He looked up. Emma looked puzzled and he supposed it didn't seem a big deal to her as they hadn't done a lot of Christmassy stuff in Houston. Charlie, on the other hand, looked as outraged as his mother.

"They can't cancel Christmas!"

"They aren't," Emma said. "They're only cancelling the lights."

Charlie turned, his eyes narrowed and hands clinched into fists at his sides. "You're just a dumb girl. You don't know anything. In Snow, it's the same thing!" He turned and slammed out of the bakery, leaving the three of them gapping.

"I'm sorry, Emma." Corin's voice shook. "He's never that rude."

"He's a stupid boy," Emma said, as though that explained everything.

Ryan was about to tell Emma to apologize, but Corin shook her head and a smile slowly replaced her frown. She leaned over the counter. "Did I call you stupid?"

He grinned. "Probably only when I called you a dumb girl."

She laughed outright at that. "I wouldn't go through that stage again for love nor money." She sighed and blew out a breath. "But what are we going to do about that?" She tapped the paper with her finger.

"Corin, I just moved here," Ryan gave his pat answer, wondering how many months he'd get by with that excuse.

She put her hands on her hips, glaring at him over the cookie counter. Yeah, he didn't have any months left with her. "Let me remind you of something, Ryan Diantelli. Snow financially depends on the Snow festival just as much as it does the coal mine. The Snow festival depends on the lights. They can't shut them off, that's all there is to it."

The bakery door burst open again, banging against the wall and Ryan cringed. What was it with people and doors around here? Charlie stood in the doorway.

"Oh, geez. It's already started," Corin muttered almost too low for Ryan to catch. Before he could ask what she was talking about, Charlie gave him the answer.

"It's snowing!"

* * * *

You had to be a lifetime resident of Snow to understand the meaning of those two words. Even though Ryan had spent most of his young life in Snow, he still had a hard time understanding it, and yet his face split into a grin at Charlie's words and he grabbed his coat off a hook by the door.

"Come on, Emma, bundle up. You're going to miss it." He helped her into her coat picked her up and headed outside, standing her near him on the outer edge of the sidewalk.

"Dad, why don't we stand under the awning? It's snowing on us."

"I know," he said with a grin. He tilted his face skyward as fat wet flakes descended. It was going to be a good one, he thought, watching the swirling masses of white quickly cover car tops and the sidewalk. This wasn't a little skiff; this was going to be the full-blown snow that always energized the town.

For most people, falling snow generated instant panic and thoughts of where they buried the snow shovel last spring. But in Snow, chaos of a different sort always erupted. He wondered how long it would take before…aha, things hadn't changed in all the years he'd been gone.

Church bells broke through the stillness, ringing loud and long in the crisp air. The streets were instantly crowded with shop keepers, business men and children. Cars stopped in the middle of the street; drivers and passengers alike spilling out, smiling.

People looked heavenward; spreading their arms wide as though trying to capture the swirling drops of moisture. Others opened their mouths, tongues stuck out to grab the season's first snowflake.

Ryan glanced around and spotted the few strangers in town. They were the ones standing and gapping in wonder. He watched one couple frown as they huddled close together then scurried to their car. He bet they would leave town in a heartbeat, not realizing the fun and joy they were missing.

They hadn't stayed around long enough for anyone to ask them if they'd ever eaten a snowflake. According to legend snowflakes tasted sweeter than spun sugar, felt like angel kisses and smelled like mountain air. He lifted his face again, opening his mouth.

"Dad, what are you doing?" Emma jerked at his hand.

"Try it, Emma. Some believe there's magic in the snowflakes in Snow."

She looked dubious, even as she tentatively stuck out her tongue. "Will they make my leg better?"

Ryan didn't know what waited his daughter and him down the road, but on this particular day, at this particular time, he once again believed in miracles.

* * * *

Ryan knew Corin wouldn't forget the City Council's edict, but for the next several days, the town's excitement over the snowfall took precedence. Regardless of the City's insistence that there was a lack of money for Christmas lights, the budget contained enough for the snow plows and street maintenance. The streets were kept fairly clear and the town workers dumped the snow on corners and in central parking lots close to the center of town. You would have thought it would get dumped close to some drainage ditches near the river or Piper Lake, but not in Snow. And there was a perfectly legitimate reason for that.

As soon as the blizzard tapered off to light flurries, people scurried here and there scooping snow into small wagons, pickups and even wheelbarrows to take to their yards, adding to what they already had in preparation for building their snow sculptures.

Once the first major snow storm swept through the area, the temperature never again got above thirty degrees until the end of February. It was a phenomenon that Ryan had never understood, and when he worked at NASA had even investigated. Anything the residents of Snow created in their yards; on the sidewalks; through the middle of town and across the square, didn't melt. They never had to worry about the snow festival creations melting in the middle of the season, when people from miles around drove through town and of course, stopped to spend money in the stores.

Ryan turned from the apartment window, antsy to get outside and do something after four days practically hibernating. School had been called off, not that it mattered since Emma did her work at home. Since Charlie hadn't been to school, Emma figured she was caught up. Ryan had tried to get her to work ahead, but she insisted that none of the other kids would, and she'd be bored once school resumed.

"You going to be alright here?" He tugged on his coat. Corin had called and a bunch of friends were going to meet at the BAT for a drink. He didn't know who all would be there, but figured most parents were as ready as their kids to do anything that would eliminate the cabin fever. It was only November, and winter in Snow lasted long enough without getting snowbound this early in the season.

"I'll be fine, Dad. You need to get out." She looked over from the television and gave him an I-know-what's-good-for-you smile and he laughed. He wondered at times if their roles weren't reversed. She had been the one who insisted he go when Corin had called. "Oh, here. You might need this." She held out his phone.

"You sure you can get by without it for the evening?" he teased. She used his cell phone more than he did.

"Yeah. Charlie doesn't have one, so I can't text him anyway."

He bent and kissed the top of her head. "Call me if you need anything. I'll be back in time to help you get ready for bed."

"Dad." A long sigh emphasized her exasperation. "I can get to bed myself. I'm getting better."

"I know that." And he did. The doctors had said it, too. It was just... "It's hard for parents to let go sometimes, sweet pea."

"Geez. Does that mean you'll tag along on my honeymoon?"

He laughed. "Is it going to be anytime soon?"

"Yeah. Right." She grabbed the remote and angled it at the TV, flipping through the channels and effectively dismissing him.

Ryan trotted down the stairs and out the back door into the cold night, wondering what the future held. As the door clicked shut behind him, he stood for a minute, sucking in a deep breath of frigid air to clear his mind. He needed to stay positive, and Emma was right. He needed adult companionship and it was up to him to seek it. He climbed into the SUV and started the engine, giving one last look at the upstairs window, where a warm yellow light shone in the dark night.

* * * *

43

Ryan found Corin with a crowd at two tables at the back of the BAT when he walked into the bar a few minutes later. At one time called Arnie's Bar & Tavern, once Arnie sold it, it became just the B & T, shortened even further to the BAT. It was a hangout for people his age, not the twenty-something crowd, or the old timers who frequented the American Legion. He glanced around the group. They had all aged, as he knew he had too, but he recognized the group as people who had gone to school with him; either in the same class or within a year or two of each other.

"Hey, Ryan. Glad you could make it." Corin slid over as he dragged another chair to the table and signaled the bartender. "You remember everyone?"

He looked around the table. "Mostly."

"OK, quick introductions." Corin waved a hand around the table. "Chrissy Carroll, Paige Michaels, Janet and Steve Anderson, and Mitch Farley, who owns Mitch and Jerry's auto repair at the corner on the highway." There was the collective wave and chorus of "hi".

Ryan glanced quickly Mitch's way. There had been a different inflection in Corin's voice when she had introduced him. Was something going on with the two of them? He and Corin had been friends for years but he hadn't had a chance to catch up with her since he'd gotten back.

The waitress plunked a beer in front of him and he tossed some bills on her tray.

"Here's to old times," Steve said, raising his drink to the center. Everyone lifted their glass or bottle and said here, here.

"I, for one, never thought I'd be back in Snow; especially not teaching the children of kids I hung out with," Paige stated as she set her glass on the table.

Ryan choked on his beer, for some reason only now connecting her with the Miss Michaels who was Emma's teacher. He had only met with the principal when he had enrolled his daughter. He turned watery eyes toward the young, pretty brunette.

44

"Oh, please," she said when she saw his expression. "Don't tell me you didn't think our teachers drank."

Ryan supposed that was right, and he certainly wasn't one to judge. "Well, I…"

"But don't tell the kids," Corin interjected. "Even if it's none of their business. Anyway, I called you all here tonight because—"

Groans resounded around the table. Corin had always been the planner, and that apparently hadn't changed in all these years.

"You already rattled the City Fathers' cage with your editorial, 'Rin," Mitch said. "What do you expect us to do; storm the mine offices and hold old man Carston hostage?"

She appeared to seriously think on his suggestion but said instead, "My editorial requesting the mining company make some adjustments is not what made the City Council say we couldn't have Christmas lights. While that problem hasn't been resolved, yet, we do need to create something special for the Snow Festival this year; something that will show everyone how much it means to the residents and to the economy of the town."

"How about ice bars," Mitch said. "I hear they're making millions."

"Like the Woodley sisters would let that happen," Miss Michaels said. Ryan had a hard time thinking of her as Paige.

"Who?" he asked.

"Oh, God, you have to remember Violet and Vera Woodley," Corin stated with such certainty Ryan felt he'd get thrown out of town if he didn't answer correctly. "Vera was married to a banker way back when but after he died Violet moved in with her. Well, they've just been the Woodley sisters ever since. They're in their eighties and considered the epitome of society in Snow, even if they did put the kibosh on legalizing whiskey until 1949, well after the rest of the country had done away with prohibition."

"Geez, they were old when we were kids," Ryan nodded in remembrance. "Or so it seemed."

45

Corin switched subjects, turning to Mitch. "When are you going to rename your garage and gas station with a theme name?"

He snorted. "When it's a cold day in hell."

Janet shivered. "That would be today." She looked at Ryan. "It never gets above thirty degrees once the first snow comes, but that doesn't mean it can't get colder."

"The whole town goes crazy this time of year, and it's not because of the snow or cabin fever," Mitch grumbled, a little too vehement to be talking only about the festival.

Ryan felt the tension around the table and wondered what he was missing. Corin's eyes softened as she looked at Mitch, but when she put a hand on his arm, he jerked away.

"You have to admit the festival brings a lot of money into the town. People come and stay. They eat, drink, and buy stuff. Between this and the Apple Cider Days and Ekalrepip every summer, Snow has managed to survive. But now that Mr. Larsen is talking about selling the orchards, we'll only have two events. We'd better make them count."

"I forgot about Ekalrepip," Ryan stated in surprise. "People still come looking for the swamp monster in Piper Lake?"

"At least that's a man's festival," Mitch said. "Lots of fishing and beer drinking." He and Steve clinked beer bottles and the girls rolled their eyes.

"You're still going to have the Christmas pageant, aren't you, Corin?" Paige asked.

"Of course," she replied. "That reminds me, I need to get the practice schedule to the paper. But that's only one part of the whole thing."

Ryan was amazed that much of what he remembered as a boy still was alive and going strong in Snow. Every kid from kindergarten on up participated in the Christmas Pageant, at one time directed by his teacher, Mrs. Potts. He remembered how it added to the magic of the holiday. He'd have to mention it to Emma…

"I told you to find another place," Mitch's hard words interrupted Ryan's thoughts. Ryan looked between him and Corin. Something was definitely going on with those two.

"It's the only place with a stage."

"What are you talking about?" Ryan felt like he was ten seconds behind on every conversation taking place tonight. Then again, catching up was the reason he had come to this gathering.

"We rehearse and have the program in the old Majestic Theater," Corin said and Mitch's scowl deepened. "It hasn't been a movie theater for years, and the city lets us use it for free." She frowned. "Well, it has been free. I'd better stop by the Mayor's office and see if it's still available."

"The place is old and about to crumble around you." This from Mitch.

Corin's gaze narrowed. "Well, Mr. Know-it-all, why don't you get involved this year and you can protect us all." It was a dare, and while Ryan didn't know what precipitated it he held his breath for the outcome.

Mitch pushed back from the table and stood. "That'll be another cold day in hell." He walked off, a severe limp hampering his stride as he made his way to the door. Ryan turned back to see Corin's eyes water before she looked away from Mitch's retreating back.

Chapter Five

Ryan slept late the next morning and when he walked into the small living room, he found Emma awake but still in her pj's, leaning on her crutches as she stared out the window.

"What's up, mutt?"

"I hate these crutches," she said, not looking at him. "I hate this brace."

"You know it won't be forever; just until your bones start growing." He walked over to stand beside her, wondering at her attitude. She had been taking things in stride, always telling him that next year she would be running around on the playground.

He followed her gaze. The morning was bright and sunny after a week of overcast skies and snow. Their apartment looked over the town square, and he immediately realized why her attitude had taken a downturn.

The center of the square was being transformed into a snow village. Kids were everywhere, rolling snow or building snow walls. The octagonal pavilion in the center of the park square was being swept clean by an older man in a red coat and plaid flannel hat with earflaps. Ryan squinted but couldn't make out the man's features, other than he had a beard and was laughing as the children gathered the snow he swept from the steps.

He put his hand on Emma's shoulder and she leaned into him.

"I want to be like other kids," she said almost too quietly for Ryan to hear. He closed his eyes and prayed that her wish would be granted.

"Come on," he said, shaking her gently. "Let's get dressed and eat some breakfast. You can call Charlie and we'll pick up Aunt Mary and take a drive out to see the lake. I haven't been out there since I was a kid. I wonder if—" he broke off before adding he wondered if they still ice skated there in the wintertime.

"Charlie's probably out there." She nodded in the general direction of the square.

Ryan didn't know how to improve her humor, so he reverted back to a parent's age old threat. "If you don't want to go, I guess you can do your homework. I hear school is back in session tomorrow."

She scrunched her eyes for a second. "Did Aunt Mary use that on you?"

"Well, yeah, she probably did."

"Did it work?"

He laughed. "No, I don't recall many of her threats working."

"Well, there you go." She gave him a sassy grin and headed for her bedroom, her humor restored.

Aunt Mary was ready by the time they drove to her house, and since Ryan had called Corin from the apartment, she had Charlie corralled and they both climbed into the back seat with Emma, one on each side of her as she had her leg propped on the console between the front seats.

Before they headed for the lake, Ryan drove slowly through some of the streets and Charlie quickly gave them a rundown of who lived where and what they were creating for the Snow Festival. Although the Festival itself didn't have a theme, regardless of Corin's attempts to give it one, each residence, or sometimes streets, appeared to have designed their own.

Oak Street, two blocks over from Maple where Aunt Mary lived, appeared to be given to a seafaring theme, as they saw several boats and the beginnings of a rather large ship in one yard.

"I wonder how he's going to do the sails," Ryan murmured as he turned toward the square. "Are apparatus allowed?"

Corin laughed from the back seat. "There are no official rules that I can recall, but most people try to use just snow…and food coloring."

"That's why Winter Time Grocery didn't have any." Ryan had run by the store yesterday because he was out of yellow color and the bakery's delivery truck wasn't due until Tuesday.

"Oh heavens, no, Ryan," Aunt Mary said. "Ron Morton at the hardware store orders in the food coloring for the festival. It takes a lot more than an ounce squeeze bottle to color a sailing ship brown."

They circled the square before heading west of town, turning onto a side road that would lead them to the lake. The road had been scraped fairly clear but the parking lot was still covered with mounds of white. Ryan shifted to four-wheel drive and proceeded cautiously past the swimming area to the campground. He barely saw some tables under the snow here and there.

"The lake's frozen, but from the last report, only an inch or two," Corin said as everyone piled out of the car. He helped Emma slide out and reached for her crutches. He didn't suppose she would let him carry her with Charlie around.

They carefully made their way closer to the edge of the lake, Ryan shuffling and scooping with his feet to clear a wider path for Emma and the ladies. When Charlie realized what he was doing, he walked beside him, not saying anything, and scooped with his boots the opposite direction.

"Goodness, boys," Aunt Mary commented, "you'd think a bulldozer came through here. We're not that wide in the girth." They all laughed, including Emma, and Ryan hoped she wouldn't feel bad that they were simply trying to make it easier for her.

"It's not going to be the same this year without all the lights," Charlie commented, and they all knew his mind was on the festival.

Corin sighed. "I know, Charlie, and I was pretty upset when that article first ran in the newspaper, but with Carston Mines increasing the cost of coal, it's too expensive to run all those lights twenty-four seven during the entire time of the festival."

"Why don't they charge admission?" Emma asked.

Aunt Mary answered. "There are donation boxes around town, and the people who come are often very generous, but it's always been a free festival; a gift from the people of Snow. You can't ask a person to pay for something that has always been given away."

"Always?"

"Don't you remember the story I used to read you?" Ryan remarked at his daughter's question. "About the beginning of the Snow Festival and how back in the depression, when people were out of work and barely had enough food to eat, all the children still decorated the town?"

His daughter shook her head. Ryan turned to Corin.

"What's the name of that?"

"Once upon a Christmas Wish," Corin answered. "It's in a book of Christmas stories called Christmas Quilt Anthology."

"I suppose you have it at the bookstore?" At her nod, Ryan said, "We'll have to get a copy, Emma. The children were the real reason there has never been a charge."

Emma looked over at Charlie. "Maybe we kids need to get together and figure out a plan for this year." She looked back at her dad, shifting the crutches under her arms to stabilize herself. "We need a miracle, don't we, dad?"

He smiled as he tugged her knitted hat lower on her ears. "Yeah, kiddo, we do. Maybe even more than one."

"What's that?" Charlie pointed toward the center of the lake.

They all turned and watched as a chunk of snow was blown along the frozen surface by the wind, gathering wet snow along the way, much the same as when the kids rolled snow to make a snowman. But unlike those snowballs, these were cylindrical in shape, and became hollow on the inside as the weaker layers fell away.

"Why, they're snow rollers," Aunt Mary said. "I had forgotten how often they formed across the lake once it froze."

"Snow rollers?" Emma said. "They look like the jelly rolls Dad makes at the bakery. They just make themselves?"

"They're actually a rare meteorological phenomenon," Ryan replied. "You find them on lakes because the ice underneath keeps the snow from sticking to one spot. The wind moves a chunk of snow along and it collects wet, loose snow along the way."

"Cool," Charlie said.

"Why doesn't the wind make them all the time?" Emma asked.

"The temperature has to be exactly right – near the melting point of ice -- and the wind has to be strong enough to move the snow rollers, but not too strong or it would blow them apart." Ryan answered his daughter, but his mind had gone off on a tangent. "The wind always seems to blow down and along the mountains. Even in the summer, as a kid I remember not being able to go on the lake for the wind advisories."

He turned to Corin. "The other night at the meeting, why didn't anyone mention wind energy as an alternative energy source?"

She shrugged. "I guess because everyone here is bent on using coal like they have for the last hundred years or more. Nobody looks beyond the mountains."

Ryan smiled. "We don't have to look beyond; we only have to look at." He turned to his daughter. "We may just have stumbled across our first miracle, kiddo. Remind me to call Alexis when we get home." Alexis worked for the Department of Energy, and Ryan was beginning to think they might have an answer to Snow's energy crisis.

****

"I need your help," Ryan said when Alexis answered the phone later that night.

"Is it Emma?"

"No. I –"

"Your idiotic ex-wife?" she interrupted. "I never did like her, Ryan. I'm sorry, but that's the way I feel."

"Geez, Lexi, that's ancient history. This is an energy problem."

There was a pause, and Ryan pulled the phone away from his ear to look at the read-out, making sure they were still connected.

"Great. Just what a gal wants – to be needed for her brain."

Ryan laughed. "I thought that's what all twenty-first century women wanted."

"Not from an attractive, single male."

"What?"

He heard her tsk, like his aunt Mary. "Guys just don't get it." A sigh came across the line. "How can I help you, Ryan?"

Ryan was stuck on her earlier comment. "You think I'm attractive?"

This time she laughed. "Don't get a swelled head. Whatever I think, you're way too far away for me to act on it."

While Ryan and Alexis had dated in Houston, their relationship had barely progressed beyond serous friendship. He was always worried about Emma and Alexis understood that. Very early in their relationship, they had both laid all their cards on the table and decided that they would not force anything; they would simply see what developed. Because of that, they had enjoyed each other's company and shared some pretty heated kisses, but nothing more.

Ryan thought he wanted something more from Lexi, even as he felt guilty because his first concern should be Emma. How did single parents balance their lives – giving their kids what they needed yet having time for their own emotional growth?

"I used to ask if you were out in space when you got quiet, and mean it almost literally," Alexis' voice interrupted his thoughts. "Now where are you?"

Ryan sighed. "I've found myself in the middle of a town controversy."

"You've only been there a month. Couldn't you stay out of trouble a little while longer?" He heard the humor in her voice.

"Aunt Mary dragged me to a City council meeting. The coal's running out and they've almost decided to cancel Christmas." That was a little exaggerated, but that's pretty much how the kids felt.

"They wouldn't!" Alexis exclaimed, laughing.

"For the town of Snow, that's not funny. Anyway, we were at the lake today and saw a bunch of snow rollers and –"

"You're kidding? I've never seen them made; just read about them in college."

"Well, if you come to Snow for Thanksgiving, I'll take you to see them for real. It's not quite the phenomenon around here; they happen all the time."

"You're inviting me?"

"Yeah. And while you're here, maybe you can do some wind tests. I think there may be possibilities here."

Another sigh. "Ryan, you could have simply asked me to come and I would have thought you missed me. Once I got there, you could have subtly suggested I look at the area for wind energy. Here I thought you might actually miss me."

"I do miss you, Lexi. I told you that the very first night we got here. And for the record, I also told you I wasn't very good at the dating game the first time we went out. What do you expect from a man whose major conversations in life have been through a headset with someone millions of miles in space or with a ten year old?"

"We should do something about that." Her voice had gone all soft and whispery and Ryan closed his eyes, her face coming into view in his mind's eye. Short, with long blonde hair and green eyes, Alexis was a bundle of energy and attacked projects like it was a personal contest and she was going to win. The thing was; she did ninety-nine percent of the time. As they said good-bye, Ryan had to wonder what she had in mind for him.

****

54

Another heavy snowfall hit the next day, and it wasn't until Wednesday that Ryan had time to take Emma over to the Wonderland Bookstore. Aunt Mary was minding the store as she said the Woodley sisters had placed their annual Christmas order and no one, not even Ryan, was supposed to know what they ordered, or the recipes used to make it. Besides, his aunt had told him, he needed a day off.

Corin had decorated the inside of her small store to look like fairyland with stars hanging from the ceiling and murals painted on the walls. Short stairways ran up the walls to reading lofts, full of plump pillows or chairs just the right size for young children.

"Hey, you two. Thanks for the great time Sunday. Can you believe this snow?" Corin came from behind the counter to greet them. Two other customers turned to see who had entered the store, then returned to their browsing.

"What happened to the holiday music that was always played around the square?" Ryan had noticed the unusual quiet when he and Emma had walked next door.

Corin shrugged. "Another casualty of the energy crisis, I guess."

"Alexis is coming for Thanksgiving," Emma said. "She'll fix everything."

Corin raised a brow at Ryan, who shrugged. "A friend of mine works for the Department of Energy. I asked her to come and do some wind tests."

"She's really dad's girlfriend," Emma whispered.

"And you asked her here to work?" Corin raised a brow in disbelief. "How are you ever going to have a woman in your life when you do dumb things like that?"

"Who said I wanted a woman in my life?" Ryan retorted.

"You're a man." Corin turned and led Emma to the holiday shelves, showing her not only the book with the story about Snow, but also some junior readers she thought his daughter might enjoy.

When she returned to where she'd left Ryan standing, he was ready for her. "What's with you and Mitch, speaking of woman-man things?"

She narrowed her gaze. "What do you know? What have you heard?"

Ryan laughed. "Don't get defensive. For a male, I can be pretty observant."

His long time friend let out a sigh. "It's a long story but Mitch hasn't been the same since he came back from Iraq and Jerry didn't."

Ryan would have asked more, but the door flew open and Charlie burst in, tugging at his hat. Did he ever quietly walk into a room, Ryan wondered.

"I saw crazy old man Pritchert snitching grapes at the grocery," he said.

"Charlie," his mom immediately gripped his shoulders to get his attention. "It's Mr. Pritchert."

He looked at her, a quizzical expression on his face. "Does it make a difference if Mr. Pritchert was snitching grapes?"

Ryan's laugh was cut short when Corin glared at him.

"No, it doesn't and Mr. Pritchert shouldn't have snitched."

"Who's Mr. Pritchert?" Emma handed Ryan a couple of books when she came to stand by them.

"Remember when I told you he's this crazy old man—"

"Charlie," his mom warned.

Charlie made a face which Ryan decided to ignore. "Mr. D., can I take Emma for a ride? The snow's off the walks and it's not too cold. And I already have Wolf hitched to the sleigh."

"Please, Daddy," Emma chimed in, already tugging on her mittens.

Ryan watched Charlie's changing expressions. He was up to something. Ryan had been ten years old once and knew all the angles.

"If you promise not to take her to snitch grapes." He gave Charlie his most serious expression.

"I won't," he said, heading for the door, Emma close behind. "Mom would blister my butt."

"Lordy, what am I going to do with that boy?" Corin shook her head as the door slammed shut behind the two kids.

Ryan stepped to the window and watched Charlie help Emma into his home-built sleigh, sliding her crutches in beside her, and carefully tucking a blanket around her. "I think you're doing just fine, Corin."

****

"Where are we going, Charlie?"

"You'll see," he said no more as he led the dog with a hand on his neck until they rounded the corner and proceeded up the alley. "There, look." He nodded to the house across the alley behind the square. "That's where Mr. Pritchert lives. Remember me telling you about him?"

Emma looked at the house beside the greenhouse. "Besides what you told your mom?"

"Just keep watching. Maybe something will happen." Charlie had slowed the sleigh when they got close to the end of the snowy alley.

Suddenly the door to the house opened and Mr. Pritchert stepped onto the porch, a gun in his hands and a small dog yipping at his heels.

"Charlie!"

"It's only a BB gun. Watch." Charlie giggled.

Emma scrunched down in the sleigh. She didn't know this man and wasn't too happy about being close by when he had a gun, even if it was a toy. The dog had darted down the steps and was dancing around in circles beneath a bird feeder. Instead of birds, a fat squirrel sat on the edge picking at the bird seed.

"Take that!" the old man yelled and Emma heard a poof as he shot at the squirrel. The squirrel chattered wildly and jumped from the feeder, surprising the dog that stood still for a second before running off after it.

"Get 'em, Harley!" the man yelled.

Emma watched as the squirrel ran up a tree at the curb and disappeared. She let out the breath she had been holding now that the squirrel was safe.

Harley skidded to a stop, scattering snow everywhere. He looked around, not seeing the squirrel but spying Wolf. Tongue hanging, he made a mad dash across the street to dance in circles in front of Wolf, who seemed to ignore him.

"Hi, Harley," Charlie said as he patted the dog. Harley stuck his nose under Emma's hand on the side of the sleigh. She gave him a tentative pat, not used to animals other than Wolf.

"Harley, get back here," the man yelled and the dog, hearing his name, danced around in circles again.

Emma laughed. "Is that all he does?"

"Just about," Charlie answered. "Go on home now, Harley. You'll have to get that squirrel another day."

The dog raced off across the street and Emma and Charlie continued on their way.

"It's not very nice of them," Emma said. "About the squirrel, I mean."

Charlie looked at her and shrugged. "I told you he was a crazy old man. Besides, that old BB gun doesn't shoot a BB five feet, and Harley isn't near as quick as that squirrel." He whistled softly and Wolf stopped at the curb, waiting. Charlie looked both ways before whistling again and they crossed the street.

"Wolf sure is trained good."

Charlie petted his dog's head. "Yeah, Mitch helped me train him. He's the best."

Emma didn't know if he meant the dog or Mitch, who was someone she hadn't met.

"Here. This is what I wanted to show you." They had stopped in front of the vacant store he had taken her to weeks before. "Remember Mom saying a man named Mr. Nicholas rented it and it's going to be a toy store?"

He had Wolf pull the sleigh close to the window so Emma could see.

There was only a dim light inside. "There aren't any toys in there," she said, disappointed. Only scraps of wood and boxes lay scattered around on the floor.

As they watched, the back door opened and a man walked in, carrying a large canvas bag slung over his shoulder. He wore a red plaid shirt with black suspenders, and his face was partially hidden with a beard. He had on a green winter hat with ear flaps.

"It's the man with the deer," she whispered.

"This is going to be Santa's workshop," Charlie said in awe.

"It's not Santa Clause. Your mom said Mr. Nicholas rented it."

Charlie turned to her, a wide grin on his face. "Santa Clause -- also known as Saint Nicholas."

Chapter Six

Emma looked over to where her dad was bagging cookies for some lady. In the time they'd been in Snow, she'd come to know most of the regular customers in the store by name. This was a lady she hadn't seen before, and she was looking at Dad and giggling. Emma didn't like it.

"Dad, can I call Alexis?"

When her dad looked at her with an eyebrow raised, she added, "I'm sorry. I didn't mean to interrupt," even though she did, and she was happy to see the lady take her change and leave.

"What was that all about?" Dad asked the minute the door closed.

"What? I need some information for a report for school."

"And you chose that exact minute to ask?"

When she didn't say anything else, her dad looked at her and shrugged. "Go ahead."

Emma wanted her dad to be happy. He had been better since they moved to Snow, but she still thought some days he looked too sad. She knew he worried about her, so she tried to make the best of her leg and the brace. Still, he needed someone to make him happy, like married people were; only not that woman who just left.

"Don't you like Lexi anymore?"

He looked at her in surprise. "Of course I do."

"But you left her in Houston."

"Emma, I did what I thought was best at the time. You know that."

She did know. He had brought her back to Snow, where he'd grown up, and where Aunt Mary could help with her. Even though he didn't say anything, she thought maybe he missed his job.

"And besides, Alexis and I talk almost every night."

60

It was her turn to look surprised, and she wondered if he said that so she wouldn't think it was her fault. "When?"

"When you're in bed asleep, Miss Nosey." He looked at his watch. "You'd better call her now if you want to catch her at work."

Emma scrolled through the numbers and punched a button.

"Ryan, hi," Lexi said when she connected.

"No, this is Emma."

"Well, that's even better. How are you, darling girl?" Unlike some woman her dad had dated since her mom left, Lexi always made Emma feel special.

"I'm fine. I had a good report from the doctor. He said my leg is getting better."

"That's wonderful news."

"I have to write a report for school and I need your help."

"Sure. What's it about?"

"Well, everybody in Snow is worried about the coal running out and not having any electricity. They got in a big argument last week and now the town is saying nobody can turn on Christmas lights and that's important because Snow has this festival and everybody makes snow people all over the place."

"Uh…Which worries you -- not having snow people or the Christmas lights?" Lexi asked.

"The Christmas lights, of course. The snow people don't have anything to do with old Mr. Carston charging the town more for his coal to make electricity."

"I see."

"I was thinking about writing a report on saving electricity to use on the Christmas lights. Charlie says they have to have the lights because people come to Snow from all over the state just to see the snow people." Emma and Charlie had talked about this and even though she hadn't lived in Snow long, she understood how important it was to him.

"Who's Charlie?"

"He's my friend. Can you help me?"

61

"Sure, sweetie," Alex said. "Let's see. The problem is finding a way to save electricity so the town won't run out before the Christmas lights go on, right?"

"Yeah."

"Well, the best way is to consider time-of-use-metering."

"What's that?" Emma wrote the words on her notebook.

"Hmm. Think about Snow. During the day, all the businesses and schools are open and that means the lights and the furnaces are on and everybody's using a lot of electricity. A lot of times, people are asked not to use extra things at home, like their washer and dryer, or ovens and dishwashers. Things like that."

"But don't people have to cook and wash their clothes?" Emma was confused.

"Of course they do. But time-of-use-metering means that during peak times – like the middle of the day – electricity is more expensive. If people wait and do some of their chores at night – like setting their water heater to heat water at midnight instead of two in the afternoon –the electricity doesn't cost as much therefore it saves money."

Emma thought about this. "Yeah, but it's cold here and people have their furnaces on and stuff like that at night. Plus it gets dark so early that you wouldn't be able to see after five o'clock if you didn't turn on the lights."

Lexi laughed. "You're right. Winter is a little different."

"What about if people turned off their lights early; like at nine instead of at eleven or twelve? Would that save a lot?"

"It would depend on how many people did it, I guess."

Emma had an idea. She wondered if she and Charlie could make it happen. "How about if the whole town did it?"

"Even turning lights off an hour earlier than normal would save a lot of electricity. What if I email you a list of things that save and you can pick ones right for Snow?"

"Okay. Thanks. Do you want to talk to Dad?" She didn't wait for a reply but held out the phone. "Dad, Lexi wants to talk to you."

Ryan dusted off his hands as he came around the counter and took the phone from his daughter, who was grinning from ear to ear. "What was that all about?" He turned his back and headed for the rear of the shop.

Alexis laughed and the sound reminded Ryan of how much he missed her. "I'm not sure if it was an excuse to make you talk to me, or if she's actually going to get the whole town to shut off their lights."

"The whole town, huh?" Ryan looked back to where his daughter had her head bent, writing in her notebook. "I heard her mention Charlie, so it's hard telling. The two of them hit it off from the day we got here."

"I'm glad she's making friends," Alexis said. "What about you?"

"I'm doing okay," Ryan replied.

"That's not what I meant."

"I miss you. Does that answer your question?"

"I miss you, too. Any chance Lou's going to get you back sometime soon?"

"Afraid not, but you are coming for Thanksgiving, aren't you?"

"Of course," she answered without hesitating. "Should I pack a flashlight in case Emma manages to write an A-plus report?"

Ryan laughed. "I'm sure we can find one if we need it. Personally, I can think of several things more fun to do in the dark."

"Mmm, that does sound nice." Her voice, soft and sexy, reminded Ryan even more of everything he had left behind in Houston. It wasn't as important as Emma's health, of course, but he longed for an adult relationship. His first responsibility was being a parent but as every day passed, Emma seemed to rely on him less and less. In the blink of an eye, she'd be going off to college and where would he be?

"Hey, you still there?"

The bell over the door jingled.

"I'm here but have to go." They said good bye and with a sigh Ryan pasted a smile on his face as he greeted his customer. Thanksgiving couldn't get here fast enough.

* * * *

The days flew by with more snow and more days off school until Ryan wondered if moving back to Snow had been such a great idea. He tried to keep Emma busy, but she insisted there was no sense getting too far ahead of the rest of the class.

Charlie would come over every afternoon, whether there was school or not and Ryan finally consented to installing a video game box on the TV in the apartment, to keep them occupied. He was very cautious as to what games he let them play, and refused to connect to the internet to game with others. There were too many weirdoes out there for his peace of mind.

Emma still hobbled around on her crutches, but they were gradually decreasing the dosage on her medicine. She was scheduled to see the doctor right before Thanksgiving, and Ryan had convinced Alexis to arrange her flight on the same day.

"There's no sense in making two trips to the city," he had told her the night before, "and there's no sense in you renting a car either."

She had sighed. "We really do need to work on your relationship skills," she had said and when he questioned what he had said wrong this time, she patiently explained. At least Ryan hoped she was being patient. "Simply tell me you would love to pick me up at the airport."

"But I did," he had reiterated.

"Only as part of a list of other things you have to do."

Now, when Ryan recounted the conversation to Corin over a cup of coffee at Blitzen's, she actually agreed with Alexis. "You guys don't get it. We don't feel special if we're part of a whole list of things."

"It wasn't a whole list. It was two things."

64

"Ryan."

"Okay, I get it. A woman wants to feel she's the only thing in a man's life."

"Exactly."

"You do know that's impossible, even in a perfect world."

Corin smiled. "Yes, we know. But we still like to think it."

"Tell me about Mitch," Ryan said, wanting to get the conversation off himself. "We got interrupted the other day."

Corin looked at her half empty cup, her mouth scrunching in thought.

"Come on, Corin. We're friends. I've spilled my guts to you more times than I can count. Maybe I can help."

She snorted. "Ryan, we were just discussing your impossible relationship, and you think you can help me with mine?"

He shrugged. "Well, you gave me the woman's perspective. Maybe if I gave you the male's view, we might help each other."

She gave him a tender smile. "Like we did for senior prom? Going together like everyone would think we were a couple?"

"We were a couple; for all of two days." He grinned. "I think I'm glad we decided to be friends instead."

"Me, too."

"Spill it. I'm not asking again."

"Mitch was in the Army and he came back from Iraq all messed up."

"His limp?"

"He has prosthesis, from the knee down. His best friend, Jerry Hall, died in the same explosion that cost Mitch his leg. Mitch thinks it should have been him, and he can't forgive himself. Everyone tells him how lucky he is; that it wasn't an arm or his eyes, but he doesn't see it that way. He simply stays mad at the world."

"I'm surprised his attitude hasn't hurt his business."

"That's not going to happen. He's the best mechanic in town and the only full service gas station within a hundred miles. He may grumble at his customers but they keep coming back."

"Are you saying he keeps Jerry's name on the business, not to honor a friend, but to remind himself daily that Jerry's dead?"

"Yeah, morbid, isn't it?"

Ryan shrugged. "It's a process everyone has to go through. I kept Peggy's pictures out for a long time. I kept telling myself it was for Emma, to help remember her mother, but maybe part of it was because I felt guilty for not being able to help her in some way."

"Sometimes people don't want our help, no matter how much we want to see them get better."

"I finally realized that…and I put the pictures away. But you…why are you so intent on helping Mitch?"

A faint blush stained her cheeks but before she said any more, they were interrupted.

"Hi, Dad. Hey, Corin," Emma hobbled up beside him. "Charlie and I have been over to The Sleigh. Can we have some hot chocolate?"

Ryan pulled his wallet from his pocket and handed her some bills. "Buy Charlie one, too." While the kids got their drinks, he turned back to Corin.

"I'll talk to Mitch. My car's due for an oil change anyway."

Her eyes grew round. "You will say nothing, do you hear me."

He shrugged. "Hey, just thought I'd help. Regardless of what you women think, guys do talk, you know."

The conversation shifted rapidly when the kids got back to the table, unbundling and chattering away.

"How is Pam Farley?" Corin reached over to smooth Charlie's hair but he jerked his head away. "Owning a store means I never have time to go around the square and shop at anyone else's," she added to Ryan. "We used to have business association meetings, but I haven't even been able to make those lately."

66

Charlie shrugged. "She's okay, I guess. I mean she's not sick or anything."

"She was putting her Christmas display in the window and we helped," Emma said. "She has all these neat little houses that are repli…replicas of real houses and we put them on top of cotton to make it look like snow."

"I like the little wooden trucks she had better," Charlie said. "I made my wagon and sleigh. I'll bet I can make some trucks like that."

"They were little, Charlie." Emma put her hands up inches apart. "You can't make little stuff."

Ryan listened to the kids' chatter, thinking back over the years to his and Corin's friendship. He hoped Charlie and Emma would remain lifelong friends, too.

"Dad."

"Hmm?" From the looks he was getting from both Emma and Corin, he had lost the thread of the conversation at a critical point.

"You have to take me to school tomorrow for an important meeting. Miss Michaels said." She slapped a paper onto the table in front of him.

"I thought there wasn't any school today?"

"Charlie forgot to give it to me yesterday."

Ryan glanced over the green half slip of paper. "It doesn't say what the meeting is about."

"Charlie and I have a plan."

"It's your plan," Charlie said. "We had to write an essay," he explained to Ryan and his mom, "and Miss Michaels read them aloud. We talked about them and everyone got to saying we should do what Emma said."

Ryan looked at his daughter. "What did you say? About what?"

She shrugged, tugging on her coat again. "About the lights; and the Snow Festival. You read me the story about the kids in the depression and how they all got together and made the festival anyway, even when the adults didn't want to."

"And?" Ryan prompted when she stopped.

"Dad." She gave him that look that Ryan swore all females must be born knowing. "Take me to school tomorrow and you'll find out." She gave him a kiss on the cheek before she and Charlie headed for the door.

"Their talk about the festival reminds me how fast the days are going," Corin said after the kids left. "I need to get busy on the Christmas pageant. I hope you'll let Emma participate."

"If it doesn't mean climbing a bunch of stairs."

Corin shook her head. "There are some stairs to the stage, but not many."

"Don't they do a program at school?"

"You know with all the PC stuff going on today, they don't dare sing a religious song, so Miss Christiansen, the music teacher, turned it over to me several years ago. We do a program for the entire town, instead of only parents of kids in school."

"Sounds like you're a miracle worker at organization."

"Oh, I don't know," she said. "It would appear that Emma has inherited some of that from her dad, too."

Ryan's gaze slid to the door where the kids had disappeared. "Yeah, I wonder what that's all about."

* * * *

Ryan watched from the back of the school library as his daughter stood in front of a large group of middle schoolers, outlining her plan. Heat pricked the back of his eyes and he focused hard to keep the tears at bay. When had she grown up?

"The story said that, during the depression, the parents didn't want to bother with building the snow people or having the festival for people to come and see, but the children decided to do it anyway, and a Christmas miracle happened when all the snow food was changed into real food, and all the snow people got real coats and toys and stuff."

"We are making the snow people and forts and stuff," one of the kids near the front said. "That's not the problem.

The problem is the city council won't turn the lights on so everyone can see what's been built, and to add decoration to the displays."

"Yeah, and I don't see a Christmas miracle happening, either," said another.

"Children, I think you need to let Emma finish," Miss Michaels gently corrected the class for interrupting.

Ryan noticed no one mentioned the increased cost of coal from the mine, which increased the cost of the electricity, as the real culprit. These kids, the majority of whom had parents associated with the mine, were very savvy.

"It's not making the snow festival figures that will solve the problem. In the story, it was the children who had a plan and did the work. I think we can do it, too," Emma said. "If all the kids in school get their parents to shut off the lights for only an hour a day, it can save enough to turn on the city lights."

"No television or X-box?" one boy asked.

Emma shook her head. "Not after nine o'clock at night."

"I do my homework at night," another said. "Does that mean I don't have to do any?" All the kids started chattering at his remark.

"Class, while I may adjust the amount of homework between now and Christmas, there is still work to be done, especially with the number of snow days we've had." Groans met her statement. "However, if we can make this plan work, for every day the lights come on around the square, that will be one day of homework you won't have."

"What about the people with no kids in our grade?"

Emma had an answer for that, too. "Miss Michaels said we can write an article for the Evergreen Gazette and ask people to help by turning their lights off at nine."

"Class," Miss Michaels interjected. "We've studied the democratic process and the way all the representatives signed the Declaration of Independence. We have the opportunity to practice that process in Snow. Emma has written a short paper that I've copied for each of you to take home. Once your parents sign up saying they'll help, Emma and Charlie will use those names as part of a petition in the newspaper."

"My dad always told me that if you want one thing, sometimes you have to do without something else," Emma told her class. "If we want the holiday lights in Snow, can't we do without lights for an hour at home?"

"We don't have to unplug the refrigerator, do we?"

Miss Michaels smiled. "No, Charlie. Class, please make sure your parents understand that they don't have to go without heat or hot water or," she smiled at Charlie, "cold food. We're simply asking for lights and televisions to be turned off at nine at night." She looked around at her students as she passed out the papers to take home. "Any other questions?"

A bell rang and there was a quick migration to the door, with the exception of Emma and Miss Michaels. Ryan walked toward them.

"Ryan, hi," Miss Michaels greeted him.

"Yikes, you know my teacher?"

Ryan smiled, not about to tell Emma they met at a bar. "We've met. That was a great presentation. Do you think it'll work?"

Emma shrugged. "We had to do a project relating to the colonies and the fight for independence and all, and I thought that we were kind of like the colonists and the City Council and the mine were kind of like England, bossing us around and making rules for us."

Ryan was impressed, and apparently so was Miss Michaels. "Emma has a unique ability to take a process and apply it to real life. When I read her essay, I thought why not." She shrugged. "So here we are. I'll help Emma transform her original essay for the newspaper article. I think the same thing should be told to everyone in Snow. Maybe it'll raise the patriotism.

"Here, you need one of these, too. We can't have the father of the author of our own Declaration not participating." She handed Ryan a paper. "By the way, I want to have Emma tested for advanced math. Do you know she put together a mathematical table that shows exactly how many people it will take and how much electricity needs to be conserved in order to run the city lights during the entire holiday?" She looked at him. "Or did she have help on that?" It was no mystery that he had worked for NASA.

Ryan looked at Emma, who did the eye roll thing. "I should have mentioned Emma likes math, but I figured once her school records got here, she would be placed where she had left off in Houston."

"We don't do a lot of advanced placement here, especially in middle school. Exactly where should she be placed?"

"She was doing Algebra II last year."

Miss Michaels looked between him and Emma, her mouth dropping open for an instant. "It's probably a good thing she's working at home for a while. I can't imagine what you would have thought, Emma, when I started reviewing long division." She turned to Ryan. "I'll get a Calculus book from the high school for her. There's no sense wasting a talent like that."

They left the library and Ryan walked slowly by his daughter toward his car. "You didn't tell Miss Michaels about your brain?" He teased.

"You always said it wasn't nice to brag."

"And besides, boys don't like brainy girls, do they?" He was recalling his conversation with Lexi.

Emma made a face as he helped her into the car and snapped the seat buckle. "Who likes boys anyway?"

"What about Charlie?"

"He doesn't count. He's a friend."

Ryan started to close the door when a siren pierced the cold wintery air. His stomach instantly dropped to his toes.

"Daddy, what is it?" Emma put her mittened hands over her ears.

"The mine." Ryan slammed the door and hurried around to the driver's side. In all the years he'd been gone, he had never forgotten that dreadful sound because it meant only one thing – a mine disaster.

71

Chapter Seven

Ryan cautiously backed from his parking space and pulled away from the school. Soon, other cars fell in line behind or in front of him, everyone taking the one road that led out of town to the mine. When the whistle blew like now, the entire town shut down. Everyone, whether mine families or not, stopped their lives until the 'all clear' came. Regardless of conflicts between Carston mine and the residents, they all came together in times like this.

"Did something happen?" Emma asked from the back seat.

"I don't know, sweetie. We'll find out. Call Aunt Mary and tell her where we are and see if she's heard anything." Even though Aunt Mary was a widow and not associated with the mine, he knew she kept up with things. If his aunt wasn't already on her way to the immediate care tent, she soon would be. Ever since Uncle Paul died, she had helped others, usually making coffee and sandwiches, but more often by offering comfort and support during the wait.

There was always a wait. Families huddled close to hear the extent of the damage; how many men were trapped; how many were dead. It was the one part of Snow that Ryan hated, and yet in his job with NASA, he'd gone through similar disasters.

Disaster. The word was ugly, and didn't belong in the pristine, snowy small town where neighbor helped neighbor and everyone cared about everyone else.

"Daddy, Aunt Mary said she'd meet us there. They haven't released any reports yet. What does that mean?"

"It means they don't know exactly what happened."

"Is it bad?"

"It might be good." Ryan pulled into the mine parking lot, trying to find a space as close as possible to the main entrance because he didn't want Emma out in the elements.

Mitch pulled in right beside him and Ryan rolled down his window. "See what's going on and let me know," he hollered as the other man hurried toward the main office.

Ryan kept the car running, the heater on high so Emma wouldn't get chilled. Minutes later, a quick knock and the passenger side door opened and Aunt Mary climbed in. "I couldn't get close and then I saw your car. Beats standing in the cold waiting word."

Ryan reached over and grabbed her trembling hand. "You okay?"

"You never get used to it; no matter how many years pass." Her husband, Ryan's Uncle Paul, had died in a cave-in shortly after Ryan came to live with them. "You don't have the radio on."

Ryan flipped to 107.5 without thinking, surprising himself that he remembered the regional number after all these years. A gravelly voice came over the air.

"Carston Mines released a statement that seven men were temporarily trapped in tunnel five-oh-four, but have since been rescued and are in the mining infirmary. No serious injuries have been reported, and operations will resume as normal within hours."

Aunt Mary snorted. "That man. He won't even shut down for a cave-in."

"Is everybody all right, daddy?"

Ryan turned the radio down. "That's what the man says, sweetie."

"Charlie says a lot of the kids in our class have dads who work in the mine. I haven't met them yet, but can we do something?"

Ryan thought about Alexis coming and about the project Emma had started; both ways of helping the town. "We are, honey. Everybody in their own way has to find a way to help."

"Yeah, but conserving energy isn't the same."

"It still means you're helping. Tell Aunt Mary about your project. She'll help too, even if she doesn't have kids."

Emma regaled his aunt on her idea and Aunt Mary responded as Ryan knew she would – with enthusiasm and a promise to make sure her bridge club and friends complied with the declaration when the newspaper published it. By the time they were through visiting, the crowds of people were beginning to disperse.

Mitch stopped by the car. "Appears a few are banged up, but no major injuries."

"Yeah, we heard on the radio." Before Mitch turned away, Ryan added, "Can I drop the car off for an oil change?"

Mitch narrowed his gaze and didn't say anything for a time. "What did Corin tell you?"

Ryan's hope for a conversation went down the drain. "She only said you were the best mechanic in town."

Mitch seemed to think about that for a minute before nodding. "I can fit you in tomorrow morning."

"Great." Ryan didn't have time for more than the one word before Mitch had moved passed the window to his own truck.

Ryan put the SUV in drive and slowly made his way through the parking to where his aunt had left her car.

"I don't know what's to become of that boy." She shook her head. "So much anger isn't good for a body."

Ryan didn't want to get into the particulars with Emma in the back seat, so said a noncommittal, "I hear he has cause." He stopped by his aunt's car.

She grabbed the door handle but turned back. "Sometimes you just have to let go so you can fall down. It's the only way to get back up."

She got out, closed the door and Ryan watched until she got in her car and started the engine. He wasn't sure if she was talking about Mitch, or himself, or maybe even her, because he knew she had had a rough time when Uncle Paul died.

＊ ＊ ＊ ＊

Emma worked that night on her essay. By the end of the week when the parents had – hopefully – returned their compliance forms, she and Miss Michaels would put it together in the form of a petition and submit it to the newspaper. The goal was that more than just the middle school kids and families would get involved.

Ryan watched as her brow furrowed in thought. He was more than pleased that she was making a place for herself in school, even though she wasn't in the actual classroom. He had been taking her for music and library because those rooms were on the main floor and classes were only a couple times a week. But it gave her a chance to meet other kids.

While she studied, Ryan worked on the Orion project that he had promised Lou. The data was all there; all he had to do was crunch numbers and make sure the logistics were correct. The budget was tight, and they couldn't afford a shortfall on the project. He checked his email and got a confirmation from Alexis on her flight, which came in Wednesday afternoon. They would have enough time for Emma's doctor's appointment before the plane arrived.

Ryan closed his eyes in thought. The last doctor's report was good. Emma never said anything about any pain, and had quit taking her medicine, which meant she stayed awake during the day like other kids. That was also a good thing if she was going to start school after winter break. He had talked to her doctor the other day and if there was more improvement this time, he thought she might be able to do away with the crutches. Ryan hadn't told Emma because he didn't want to raise her hopes.

"Time for bed, kiddo." He closed his laptop and stood, stretching and yawning. Three o'clock seemed to come earlier every day.

"Dad, it's only nine. You're getting old."

"There's no doubt about that."

"Can't I watch TV?"

He walked over to where she sat at the table, her papers and books spread across the surface. "Do you have your homework done?" At her look, he amended his question. "Need any help on your project?"

"It's Charlie's and my project."

"What's Charlie doing on it?"

"He's the PR man. I write and he talks to all his friends and the other kids at school to get them to buy into it. He's good at that, but his spelling sucks."

Ryan laughed. "That's probably why spell check was the first thing they added to computer programs."

"Did they really?"

"Probably." He bent to kiss her forehead. "Night, sweet pea. Sweet dreams."

"Night, Dad."

* * * *

Wednesday dawned bright and sunny, although the temperature still hovered right at thirty. Ryan bundled Emma into the back seat and headed for Pittsburgh. The drive was scenic on clear days, as the road wound around and through the foothills. Aunt Mary had suggested he talk to Rich Martin about flying them into the city, but it wouldn't work this trip since they had to get Alexis at the airport.

Rich was a retired freight pilot who had a grass landing strip on his property west of town, and a couple of small planes he flew for pleasure. Once in a while he might be hired, if he wasn't busy restoring old cars, doing woodwork, and brewing beer. He was one of those unique individuals who said what he thought, damn the consequences, and according to Aunt Mary, had been in more than one squabble with the city over the years.

"Are we there yet?" Emma pulled her earphones away from her ears.

He smiled. Yes, talking to Rich about flying them the next time was a good idea. "We've only been driving forty-five minutes. At sixty-five miles an hour, how far have we gone and how far do we have left if it takes two hours and 20 minutes to get to the doctor's office?"

He caught her gaze in the rear view mirror and watched as she mentally did the math. He was still calculating when she said, "We've gone forty-eight and three-fourths miles, and we have one hundred three left to go, rounded up."

"I'll take your word for it," he said with a smile.

The trip went relatively fast with a couple of bathroom and drink breaks. Ryan pulled into the parking lot at the Doctor's office with ten minutes to spare. Emma insisted on walking to the building by herself, which meant they took a meandering route to avoid icy patches and places where the snow hadn't been scraped clear.

The receptionist greeted Emma warmly and she was taken back to have a bone density test. Ryan hoped they didn't have to do another bone marrow because he knew it hurt like the dickens, even if Emma put up a brave front.

It wasn't long before the nurse came and got him, taking him back to the exam room where Emma waited. She was sitting on the exam table, swinging her legs over the side. Her brace and shoes were on the floor.

"Do you want me to help you with your brace?"

"Nope. Nurse Pat said the doctor wanted to see the tests and me first." She kept swinging her feet.

Her left foot was smaller than her right and what he saw of her ankles below her jeans showed the same. Because of the problem with her bone growth, she hadn't been able to put pressure on her leg at all, and that meant no physical therapy or exercise. Ryan's stomach turned at the thought she might never walk and run like a normal child.

"Emma, how's my best girl?" Doctor Wesley came in, closing the door behind him. "Ryan, how's retired life in the small town?" Wesley was young, given his extensive pediatrics and orthopedic background; probably only in his late-thirties. He was also extremely busy and they had been lucky to get a referral to see him.

"If retirement is getting up at oh-dark-thirty to bake cookies, hey it's great." He shook the doctor's hand.

"But I understand you get to spend more time with this girl." He sat on the small stool and rolled over to the end of the exam table. "Let's have a look-see, shall we, Emma?"

He carefully rolled her jeans to her knee and slowly and methodically ran his hands up and down her leg, gently probing with his fingers. Ryan watched Emma's face for signs of discomfort, but she was looking at what the doctor was doing.

"It's good; right?" she asked and Ryan heard the hope in her voice.

"Hmmm." Wesley held her leg at her calf with one hand and slowly rotated her foot. "Does that hurt?"

"No."

The doctor concentrated on her face as he continued the motion. She opened her eyes wide and shook her head.

"Honest. It doesn't hurt at all."

"That's good," Dr. Wesley said. "All the tests show improvement."

"Do I have to keep the brace?"

"A little while longer." At his daughter's crestfallen expression, the doctor added, "Tell Nurse Pat to squeeze you in for another appointment before Christmas."

The doctor gave her knee a pat, shook Ryan's hand and left the exam room. Ryan carefully watched his daughter slip on her shoe and scoot back on the exam table to straighten her leg and buckle the brace. He thought about helping her, but knew from past experience she needed this time to adjust to the idea that she still wasn't healed.

He tucked his hands into his pockets to keep from grabbing her close. Sometimes he thought that he needed Emma more than she depended on him.

She gave an audible sigh, hopped off the table on her good leg, and grabbed her crutches from where they leaned against the chair.

"I'm ready."

He tilted his head as she looked at him. "You okay, noodle?"

She scrunched her mouth for a minute then gave a tentative smile. "I will be if you quit calling me those silly names."

Chapter Eight

"Is Lexi going to stay with us at the apartment?" Emma asked as they made the last turn into the arrival flights lane at the airport.

"No, I got her a room at the Poinsettia Bed and Breakfast around the corner." Ryan would love to have her at the apartment, but didn't feel it appropriate with Emma there. Besides, their relationship hadn't progressed that far. Having been apart for two months, he realized how much he missed her. Now that he knew Emma was healing, he finally felt he had more time to their relationship. Yet how was he supposed to make that happen when she was based in Houston and he in Snow?

They pulled up to the baggage claim area right on time. With security at the airport, Ryan couldn't leave his car and go inside to find Lexi, notwithstanding leaving Emma in the car by herself. But he had barely put the car in park when he saw Alexis walk through the sliding glass doors.

She was bundled in a ski parka with a furry hat and a colorful scarf around her neck. Ryan hopped out of the car and hurried around to the other side.

"Alexis." He waved to catch her attention and when she saw him, she smiled and hurried their way.

Ryan leaned in and gave her a quick kiss. "Hi there."

He opened the back door for the porter to load her baggage. "Are you moving in?" he teased, for she had a large suitcase, a duffle and a wooden travel box that Ryan knew held equipment.

Alexis shivered. "No way. I'm a southern girl, born and raised. If I had known it was going to be this cold, I would have told you to wait until spring."

"Oh, but we can't." Emma twisted around from the rear seat. "We need you to find the wind so we can have Christmas lights in Snow."

Alexis looked over at Ryan, a doubtful expression on her face. Ryan tipped the porter and opened passenger door. "Let's get everyone loaded into the vehicle instead of standing in the cold. We can discuss this on the way home."

"But dad…"

"Emma, Alexis just got here. Do you want to scare her off before we even get her to Snow?"

Once everyone was settled, Ryan pulled into the traffic pattern and they were soon on their way. Emma kept up a steady stream of chatter, telling Alexis about the town, the problems with the lights and the mine and how important it was that she help.

"You can, can't you?" She ended her monologue.

"It sounds like a very exciting project, but we'll have to do lots of tests and collect information, and that's not something that can be done overnight. Even if we do find the right conditions for wind energy, it's definitely not going to be complete by Christmas. I can't perform miracles. Isn't there something the people in town can do to make sure they have holiday lights?"

Ryan glanced in the rear view mirror. "Tell Alexis about your project."

"It's Charlie's and my project." She was always adamant about giving her friend credit. She told Alexis what she and Charlie had come up with and how they were working with their class to get an article in the newspaper.

"What an excellent idea," Alexis said enthusiastically. "Not only are you learning about American history and the democratic process, but you're doing something constructive for the town. On top of that, you're conserving resources, and showing how working together gets things done." To Ryan, she added, "I'm very impressed with this Miss Michaels. Maybe I should see if she wants to become an education specialist on my team."

"Snow's not a backwards little town, regardless of how I made it sound. It's…quaint may not be the right word, but…well, you'll see when we get there."

They stopped midway for a bite to eat and got home as the sun set. The minute the sun dropped behind the mountains, darkness came quickly. "Looks like we'll have to save the tour for tomorrow," Ryan said as he pulled to a stop in front of the Bed & Breakfast. "Emma, hang tight while I get Alexis settled, then we're all going to Aunt Mary's for supper."

He and Alexis got out and he opened the back to grab her suitcase. "If those instruments aren't cold sensitive, we can leave them here instead of hauling them inside."

"They'll be fine," Alexis said. "Unless we have to worry about vandals."

Ryan laughed. "Nobody's going to take a box of stuff they have no idea what to do with. Besides, Snow has almost no crime, unless you consider apple stealing, and Mr. Larsen never turns anyone in."

* * * *

Thanksgiving as usual meant eating too much at Aunt Mary's; board games with Emma and Lexi, and watching old movies. The day after, Ryan and Alexis toured the town and he pointed out all his childhood haunts.

Alexis insisted on getting to know the town, Aunt Mary and renewing her friendship with Emma and refused to discuss the energy problem or what might be accomplished by conducting wind tests. In truth, it all hinged on the outcome of the City Council meeting the first of the week.

Ryan was fine with that, and he enjoyed watching her with Emma. The two very important women in his life seemed to understand each other on a level he couldn't. They would exchange looks sometimes and shake their heads and he wondered if he should worry that they were plotting.

Emma and Charlie's project had taken off with a bang when their petition and a list of all the cooperating families had appeared in the Evergreen Gazette. Usually by Thanksgiving weekend, every house was decorated and all the lights came on, but this year every night fewer and fewer lights could be seen around town. Last night when Ryan drove home from the grocery store, he hadn't seen one set of Christmas lights turned on. People were still decorating, and the town had more and more snow creatures and creations, but everyone was conserving in the hopes that when the important time came – the festival weekends – it would all count.

There was no real official start to the Snow Festival. Traffic gradually became heavier in town with more people wandering around Center Park commenting on the creativity of the snow sculptures. Sales increased as people bought from the unique stores and that was the important part.

"When are you going to find the wind?" Emma questioned first thing Saturday morning when Alexis came over for breakfast. They sat around the small table in the apartment after Ryan made pancakes. He had been up since three at the bakery, but now Aunt Mary was there for the mid-morning to afternoon time.

Alexis looked at Ryan then back to Emma. "I would like to talk to the people first, Emma. I can't go around doing tests without permission. That would be like your dad going into your room and nosing around when you were gone."

"When can she do that, Dad?"

"It happens that Aunt Mary said there was a city council meeting Monday night. We might as well go brave the lion in his den." To Alexis he added, "You should know that people probably aren't going to be happy."

"Why did you ask me to come?"

"Because I missed you?" He raised a brow.

She smiled at him. "That was a very good answer. And the rest?"

"Snow has always been a coal mining town, and regardless of the cost, the increase and the slow disappearance of any new veins, most people in town will refuse to give up what has been their foundation for generations. Even the festivals can't support everyone all year, besides which not everyone is involved in a retail business like that. The majority are still miners."

"In other words, we don't go in with blueprints for wind generators?"

"Definitely not. We'll suggest that they have some tests done; that you're willing to do that and see what happens."

Alexis shrugged. "Usually when I get called in, it's because the people want alternative energy sources. In this case, perhaps we can show them the savings and efficiency and let them come to the conclusion that it's needed."

"That's all we can do," Ryan replied.

"Can I go to the meeting?" Emma stood. "I want to help."

"No. This is a meeting for grown-ups and you can't vote anyway. You and your classmates are already doing more than your share of helping."

****

Corin dropped Charlie off at the apartment Monday and walked over to the city council chambers with Ryan and Lexi. Aunt Mary promised to meet them with members of her church club. Word must have spread that something new was on the agenda, because the place was packed.

It didn't take long for Ryan to determine exactly who was on what side. The miners, once again in their flannels and heavy coats, stood against one wall, arms crossed over their chests, scowls on their faces. As Ryan scanned the group there didn't appear to be a friendly face among them.

Mayor Cox called the meeting to order. "There's only one item on the agenda tonight, folks, and I'm not even sure why. We discussed this before. Regardless of the recent petition in the paper, there's no money in the city coffers to have Christmas lights on for the entire month."

"But the children have asked us to conserve and we're doing it," Corin spoke. "If you drive around at night, you won't see any holiday lights, and house lights are few and far between."

"Individual conservation is saving individual residents money on their electricity. It's not saving the city a dime," the mayor replied.

"Let me get this straight. What you're saying is that Snow isn't short on electricity," Mitch spoke up, "but short on the money to pay for it because of what Carston is charging?"

The mayor squirmed in his seat.

"He knows how important the festival is to this town," Aunt Mary stood as she spoke. "Why did he decide to raise rates right at this time of year? Why not raise rates in the summer when we don't need heat for our homes, or electricity for the festival lights?"

"I don't think Mr. Carston is likely to answer that question."

"Mr. Carston doesn't even live in this town. All he cares about is making money and squeezing the last ounce of coal from that mine; practically killing us in the process." This comment came from a man near the back. Ryan was pretty sure he wasn't a miner, but it seemed to be the perfect opening.

He stood. "Perhaps it's time to look at alternative energy sources."

An audible grumble went through the crowd. "We talked about that last time."

"But we didn't talk about wind energy. I was at the lake the other day and realized the wind always blows in Snow; perhaps enough to create electricity with wind turbines."

"With what?" One of the miners near the door spoke.

Alexis stood beside Ryan, putting a hand on his sleeve. "If I may have a moment, Mr. Mayor?" At the man's nod, she continued. "I'm Alexis Gray with the United States Department of Energy. I'm sure you all have seen pictures of what Ryan mentioned. Wind turbines are built so when the wind blows it turns blades which are attached to a drive shaft. That turns an electric generator to produce electricity. But let me say that I am not here to sell you on building wind turbines."

"Why are you here?" the Mayor questioned.

"My job is to assess areas for the possibility of establishing wind farms. It's my understanding that coal is getting harder to find. It would seem plausible for Snow to begin looking at alternative sources of energy if this is the case. If the town has to start importing coal to generate electricity, you will have to pay fair market price, which will increase the costs of producing that electricity even more than what you're already experiencing."

"Who says we're running out of coal?" An angry voice came from the back of the room.

Alexis turned to answer the unknown speaker, her gaze sweeping the area where the miners clustered. "Even if coal is abundant now, it's a fossil fuel which will eventually disappear; in addition to the fact it releases harmful gases into the atmosphere. Wind power is clean and renewable, and we're not in danger of running out of wind any time soon."

"That all sounds real nice, Miss Gray, but I imagine those wind turbines are pretty expensive. We don't have the money for a wind generator, much less the several it would take to generate enough electricity for our town."

"In 1980, it cost about eighty cents per kilowatt hour to produce electricity with wind turbines," Alexis told the crowd. "On the average today, the cost of wind power is about four to ten cents per kilowatt hour." She paused before adding, "The costs have dramatically dropped as new technology is developed. Can you say the same for the coal industry?"

Murmurs ran through the crowd, but if Ryan thought people would see things their way, he was mistaken.

"You're an outsider," one of the miners said loudly. "You got no right coming in here and telling us how to run our town. This has always been a mining town, always will be."

Ryan stood beside Alexis. "Snow is also known for its festivals. I would bet there's more money generated by tourism than what the town sees in benefits from the mine. With things the way they are, you can't depend on the mine staying open another year. If that happens, where will Snow be? Not only will there be no jobs, there will be no fuel. This is a way to become independent. Alexis has come

86

to see if we have an opportunity at an alternative energy source. Then we won't have to worry about things like this."

"Whichever way the mine closes, those men won't have jobs. How will that help anybody?" The mayor tried to sound open-minded and at the same time stand up for residents. An impossible task as far as Ryan was concerned.

"Wind energy is a relatively new field," Alexis said. "As such, there are numerous job opportunities once a wind farm has been established – technicians, monitors, electricians. There's every possibility that many of your residents can be retrained and employed in this new industry."

"The coal mine's been good to us. My family's fifth generation miners. My loyalties are with them." The man who spoke turned and walked out, followed by a large contingency of miners. Most of those left in the room were the business owners, some retired people, and quite a few widows of miners.

With difficulty, an older lady stood. "Jake's right about the mine being good over the years. He can't be faulted for that. But those times are gone. We have to look ahead, and the future of Snow is in our name. Our Snow festival, our holiday businesses, our holiday spirit. My widow's pension isn't much, Mr. Ryan, but I'm willing to do what needs done to bring those wind generators here. They couldn't disrupt the environment any more than that blasted coal mine does."

Enthusiastic applause met her statement.

Ryan addressed the City Council members, looking every one straight in the eye as he spoke. "As a resident of Snow, all I'm asking is permission for Miss Gray to run tests...tests to determine whether the area around Snow is even feasible for a wind farm."

"What kind of tests?" Tom Brown, the county sheriff, sat with arms crossed at the end of the row, not exactly hostile but close to it.

"To make wind energy feasible requires a minimum wind speed of thirteen miles per hour," Alexis replied. "We need to test for speed, but also for the altitude around Snow where that wind is accessible, and the consistency of that wind. Since generated electricity can't be stored, there needs to be a fairly constant supply."

The members of the council glanced back and forth at each other, none apparently wanting to commit to even such an easy task. Alexis seemed to understand their hesitation.

"It costs the city nothing to run these tests. They involve no more than setting up a meter box and floating some helium balloons aloft at various locations. It isn't anything that will interfere with your Snow Festival, or that will detract from the appearance of the town. In fact, most people don't even notice when they're around."

The Mayor, who was also chairperson for the Council, cleared his throat. "We'll have to have a vote. If you all would please wait outside?" Although a question, Ryan knew it was pretty much a direct order. He and the remaining audience filed out the back door to wait.

Their closed door session lasted only five minutes and Ryan wasn't sure if that was good; or bad.

"First, we want to thank you, Ms Gray for taking the time to come to Snow and present your information."

Ryan's heart sank. She hadn't had an opportunity to present much of anything.

"We held a vote – and just to let you know it was very close – and it's been decided that you can do your tests."

The remainder of the audience – all those in favor of the project -- cheered.

The mayor banged his gavel. "Let me make this clear. We didn't vote to build a wind farm in Snow. We only voted to conduct tests. This council meeting's adjourned."

* * * *

Later that evening, Alexis sat in Ryan's apartment, a few candles lit on the tables and a fire going in the fireplace. "You're quite the boy scout," she laughed as Ryan knelt by the fireplace and checked the saucepan. Since they were conserving electricity, he'd decided to make coffee over the fire. She knew a lot of parents wouldn't get as involved with their children's projects, much less be involved with local politics. After all, who would know if they used the stove or the lights? But as long as she'd known Ryan, he never did things half way.

"Boy scouts don't drink coffee," he replied, dropping the lid back in place and shaking his hand. "Damn, that's hot."

"You expected otherwise?"

"I don't expect anything anymore. Every day comes as a complete and sometimes unwanted surprise." He sounded tired.

Lexi reached over and rubbed the back of his shoulders. "You seem to be handling it well. I mean, who would think to make coffee in a saucepan over an open fire instead of using electricity?"

"You don't want to mess with me if I don't have my coffee."

"Oh, you weren't being the consummate host. It was self preservation?"

Ryan ran a hand over his face. "See? That's what I mean. I don't even know how to romance a lady anymore."

Her heart thudded. "Were you romancing, Ryan?"

He handed her a cup of coffee and in his gaze she saw longing and desire, but also regret. "I probably shouldn't have said that. Right now everything seems too complicated. There's Emma and long hours at the bakery. And what do I do but ask you to visit and immediately embroil you in the town controversy." He gave her a sad, puppy dog look.

"Well, you certainly know how to keep a woman interested."

"That wasn't the original plan, but I…will you hang in there with me long enough for me to get things figured out?"

"Of course I will. I wouldn't be here otherwise." She understood the importance of his daughter's health. And given his disastrous first marriage, she understood his reluctance to commit to another relationship. She would have to show him things could be better.

"Let's work on one problem at a time." She glanced out the window. "I see that even though the town voluntarily goes without electricity, the mine is still operating." A blaze of lights north of town created a glow over the entire hillside.

"Carston Mining has its own generators. I think it probably has backup for the backups."

"Why don't they funnel some of that fuel to the town at a reduced cost?"

"That feud goes back more generations than I can count. There have always been two factions – the miners and the 'others'".

He sat beside her and continued the story. "When I first came to live with Mary and Paul, I was on the mine side because that's where Paul worked. This time, I don't want to take sides."

"You can't bury your head, Ryan. It sounds like you don't have a choice."

"I know. I quit NASA full time to eliminate stress, but I think I traded one kind for another."

"You thrive on digging in and making things happen."

"You're right, of course, but I have to proceed carefully if I don't want to adversely affect Mary's business."

Later, Alexis watched from the upstairs bedroom at the B&B as Ryan walked home after seeing her safely inside. He seemed a solitary, somewhat lonely figure. Alexis knew Ryan would do what was best for everyone; he was that kind of guy. Her job was going to be harder because she needed to make sure Ryan also did what was best for him, and that included realizing they were good for each other. As he blended into the shadows of the night, she closed her eyes and whispered a prayer for a Christmas miracle.

Chapter Nine

Ryan had promised to drive Alexis around town and help set up her equipment, so although he had been on his feet since three and really needed a nap, he slugged down another cup of coffee instead. He was glad he had left her equipment and supplies loaded in the SUV.

Aunt Mary was at the bakery and would watch Emma once she woke. His daughter had wanted to go with them, but it was colder than normal today and Ryan didn't want her in the inclement weather. Besides, selfish or not, he wanted time alone with Alexis.

"Where do you want to go first?" He pulled onto Avenue A at the edge of the square.

"I know we already drove around, but I need to get a feel for the town -- how it's laid out; where the main facilities and highways are. It's not only about determining whether there's enough wind to support a field of wind turbines. It's finding the field, too."

"You know, I've never even seen one of those up close. It's not like you can put one in someone's back yard, can you?"

She laughed. "At least not the commercial size turbines Snow will need. To give you a comparison, the towers can be two hundred twelve feet high or more and your space shuttle is only one hundred twenty-two, nose to tail. The blades are one hundred sixteen feet in length so they wouldn't fit in the shuttle's cargo bay."

"Wow. I guess I never thought about the amount of space they would occupy – you know, because they're vertical."

"That's the mistake many people make. They figure if there's wind, they can have a wind farm and save all this money. But there are other considerations, and believe it or not, Snow isn't the only area of the country where controversy has arisen over the issue. Europe has harvested wind energy for years before the US got into it, and there are still political battles along with health and environmental concerns."

"And here I thought I had a good idea for Snow."

"It is, if done right."

Ryan had driven west of town, and now he parked by Piper Lake. "All of this is a state park. Even though this is where I saw the snow rollers, it probably wouldn't work for a city owned wind farm."

"It is beautiful," Alexis said, gazing out the window. "Look at all the trees and forest surrounding it; all the green, even in winter."

Ryan tried to see the area through her eyes. Evergreens rose in the background against the blue sky, a muted blend of colors because of the wide variety of Blue Spruce, Red Cedar and Eastern White Pine. The vivid colors offered by abundant Maple and Oak trees were gone now, but white barked Birch scattered throughout the landscape created a contrast in colors. "Quite a change from Houston, isn't it?"

Ryan enjoyed hearing her laugh; liked sharing his childhood with her. "When I was a kid, we'd ride our bikes out here and swim all day. The lifeguards knew all of us by name and when the phone rang, pretty soon you'd hear 'Diantelli, get your butt home'; or 'Georgie, your mom wants you right now.' We couldn't pretend like we hadn't heard them."

"It sounds like the ideal way to grow up." Her tone was wistful and Ryan realized that for the majority of their relationship, he and Alexis had focused on Emma. He knew her as an adult, but not much of her childhood; not the important things that fashioned a person into an adult.

"What about you?"

She gave a shrug. "Boarding schools; traveling to Europe in the summer; holidays with friends."

He could tell his eyes were wide, unbelieving of what she had said. "You don't sound too excited about all that luxury." Ryan had never considered himself poor, but there had certainly been some lean times.

"My parents died when I was too young to remember them. My grandparents raised me and while I know they loved me, they felt they were too old to raise another child and too young to want to stay home and do it."

"They shuffled you off to boarding schools?" He shook his head in disbelief. "I was only ten when my folks died, but Aunt Mary never questioned her responsibility to raise me, even though she'd never had any kids of her own."

"You were certainly very lucky."

Ryan now realized why Alexis had always been hesitant about holiday plans and why she had eagerly ventured north to see him and Emma. She had no family. He reached over and curled a hand behind her neck, tugging her forward as he leaned toward her. The kiss was gentle, but conveyed his hopes that he would be more than a holiday stop from now on. He felt her tentative response before lifting his head and gazing into her glittering green eyes.

"You're right. I am very, very lucky."

He pulled away from the lake and continued to drive around the outskirts of town, needlessly pointing out the mine that lay to the north. Smoke bellowed from tall stacks, meeting the cold winter air to form huge dark clouds that he knew were full of minute particles of coal. As they drove by Larsen's Orchard, Alexis asked him to stop. He turned into the parking by the side of the road.

He watched as she drew some sketches on the notepad she had in her lap. Pursing her lips, she surveyed the area and jotted notes beside her drawing.

"Problem?"

She gave a sigh. "Your little town is surrounded by mountains."

"And?"

"Weather systems in a valley like this are highly unpredictable."

"Does that mean there are no possibilities?" Ryan frowned, thinking of the hope he knew many people had, regardless of the miners' stand.

93

"Oh, no. In fact, sometimes in areas like this, wind comes right down the valley in a pattern called wind funneling. It's only going to take a lot more testing to gauge not only the wind speed, but the consistency." She looked over at him. "Ready to go to work?"

* * * *

Corin pushed open the door to the service station and when she didn't see Mitch, she walked around the counter, grabbed a candy bar and slipped through the door marked Danger – No Admittance. The combined sounds of rock and roll and the clanking of tools and an air compressor assaulted her ears.

There were two vehicles in the work bays but only one with the hood up and she suspected that was where she would find Mitch. Walking around the driver's side, she had to shout to be heard over the noise.

"Hey!"

Mitch's head came up and banged against the edge of the open hood.

"Ouch! Damnit!" He pressed a hand to the top of his head, covered with a ball cap so ratty looking she didn't even recognize the logo. He narrowed his gaze at her as she took another bite of chocolate. "That's eight-five cents, plus tax."

She shrugged. "Bill me." Undeterred by his grouchiness, she stepped to the side and turned down the radio, leaned her arms against the car's fender and looked at the engine. "Whatcha doing?"

"Working." He dropped a ratchet into the top of the tool box next to him and grabbed another.

Getting information out of Mitch was like playing twenty questions. Although he maintained the only full service gas station and garage within a hundred miles, he didn't spend any time at all chatting with his customers. They continued coming to him because he was an excellent mechanic, not because he passed the time of day while they waited for their vehicles to be repaired.

He hadn't always been like that. Corin remembered him in high school and for the few years after; until he had gone to war. She understood his reasons in the beginning, but that was fifteen years ago. He needed to get back to the land of the living, and that was one reason she was here. The other was more personal. She and Mitch had dated in high school and she still had a thing for him. He was tall, dark haired and when he smiled – which wasn't often enough – he was devastatingly handsome. He simply refused to give her more than the time of day.

"Working on what?"

He shot her a sidelong look.

"I know it's a car engine, but what are you doing to it?"

"Why do you want to know?"

Hmm, progress. Six words all at one time. "Maybe I'm thinking about becoming a mechanic. Give you a little competition."

He gave a snort and kept working.

Corin thought about standing there to see how long he maintained his silence but she didn't have a lot of time. She glanced at her watch. The children would be getting out of school at three-thirty and she had sent a notice to the school that practice for the pageant would start at four. She needed to be at the old theater to unlock the doors.

"Practice for the Christmas pageant starts this afternoon."

"No."

Well, so much for progress. "You don't even know what I want. How can you say no?"

He finally looked at her. "Corin, you want the same thing every year, and every year I tell you no. How about you quit asking?" He wiped his hands on a rag then put them on the top of the hood. "Look out."

She barely had time to step back before he lowered the hood with a bang and stomped off. She watched him go, his limp hardly noticeable anymore. If a person didn't know…She sighed. It was too bad he had basically healed on the outside but refused to let his heart do the same.

She thought about following and nagging him to sing this year, but knew from past experience it would do no good. Mitch had a voice like an angel, but part of him had died with Jerry and now he refused to sing. He would do penance the rest of his life, Corin thought, although Jerry would never have asked it.

Corin backed her car around by the gas island, shifted to drive and stomped on the gas as she pulled onto the highway. Sometimes she had to wonder about her own intelligence because she kept trying. Why couldn't she forget Mitch and his self-pity?

She backed off on the gas to turn the corner at Dogwood and slowed even further as she drove by the edge of the business district. She pulled into an empty parking place on Ash Street, turned off the car and fought to get rid of her annoyance before getting out. She thumped on the steering wheel with the heel of her hand.

"I refuse to believe the real Mitch Farley is gone forever." She repeated the sentence two more times before her anger dissolved. Now all she had to do was discover how to get him back.

She realized as she exited the car that she was late, but the kids didn't appear to mind. A group of girls stood on the sidewalk, huddled close to the building as they chatted away. The boys were trying to play King of the Mountain on a pile of snow.

The minute the girls saw her, they squealed and rushed her, all chattering at once. She knew them by name, as most came to the bookstore on a regular basis for the latest All American Girl books. She glanced past them to where one girl still stood.

"Emma. Hi." She quickly gave her a hug before opening the door to the building.

The boys tore past her, ignoring the girls who had started up the steps. "Charlie, turn on the lights and turn up the thermostat," she hollered at her son before turning back to Emma. "How did you get here?"

"Charlie told me about the practice so I talked Aunt Mary into letting me walk over here." She made a face.

"She only let me because it was sunny, even though it's right across the square."

"I am sorry. I didn't think…" She kept pace as Emma moved cautiously toward the steps.

"It's okay," she replied as she made the final step. "I hate being inside all day while I know the other kids are playing and building snow people. Besides, it'll be fun being in the pageant."

Corin held open the door. "Well, good, I'm very glad you came."

* * * *

After circling the town, Ryan and Alexis were back at Larsen's Orchard. There was little wind blowing today which Alexis explained would make it easier to launch the weather balloons. She opened a duffle bag and extracted a large latex balloon.

"It's a good thing I had some of this shipped to you in advance," she commented. "The instruments I wouldn't trust to have gotten here, but the helium tank I ordered to be delivered and the balloons would have been impossible to transport."

"Why don't you get readings from the National Weather Service instead of doing all this work?"

"I checked. Weather is recorded from Small Hill Resort and Topocane. Nothing is recorded directly here, which is what we need. You took Meteorology 101 – the wind doesn't blow in the same direction all over, nor at the same speed; or even the same direction and speed at different altitudes. In order to be as precise as possible, we need wind readings directly from the area where the wind farm is proposed.

"Knowing not only the wind speed, but also how much wind there actually is and how long the speeds last will be crucial in determining feasibility."

"Gotcha. Tell me what you need me to do." He watched her unwrap several small radiosondes from bubble wrap then she retrieved a spool of nylon cable and a small set of tools from the bag. "You come prepared."

She grinned. "Hey, a gal never knows when a pair of snips will come in handy." She looked around. "The meter box can go there, along the right of way. It's off the road but on public property. We'll have to remember to flag it in case the snow covers it. Wouldn't want a snow plow destroying government property."

Ryan grabbed one rope handle and dragged the large box out of the back of his truck. Once they leveled it on the ground, Alexis measured off a length of cable, wrapped it around a nearby tree and clamped it tight. She gave Ryan the tape measure.

"The rawinsonde has to be attached between two hundred eleven and two hundred twenty feet from the ground; the height for the blades of a turbine. The cable will have to be longer because we'll attach the balloon above that."

"Rawinsonde? I thought they were radiosondes."

She nodded. "A variation. Radiosondes measure atmospheric pressure, temperature and humidity; none of which concern us. Rawinsondes also measure wind speed and direction."

Ryan held the cable stretched between his hands and she clamped an instrument in-between.

"Now comes the tricky part." She dropped her snips back into the bag.

"What's that?"

"The balloon has to be attached, filled and clamped shut without lifting me right off the ground."

"That's why you brought me along – dead weight?"

"Muscle," she said with a smile.

Between the two of them, they inflated the two-foot diameter balloon to approximately six feet and launched it, the nylon cable slowly sliding through their gloved hands.

"Weather stations usually launch free floating balloons with expendable radiosondes. Since we want continuous readings from the same area, we'll anchor these." She nodded to where she had clamped the cable around the tree.

They watched the balloon clear the edge of the trees and continue to lift until it had stretched the cable tight.

Lexi flipped back the top of the wooden meter box and turned some knobs. Ryan heard a faint click-click.

"The rawinsonde will transmit data to this meter. I'll be able to download it directly to my computer."

"What are the rest of the knobs?"

"For the other five rawinsondes we're going to launch, all in different locations around the edges of town."

Ryan looked to where the balloon floated, barely moving. "What if there's no wind?"

"Every place has wind. It's a matter of whether there is enough to generate electricity. It doesn't have to be at the same speed all the time, but we need a minimum of thirteen miles per hour for the large turbines."

"Will the balloons stay inflated?"

"They should last. Helium loses about one percent of its lift capacity every twenty-four hours. These balloons are tested for seven pounds of lift capacity, and the rawinsondes are pretty light. Even including the nylon cable, there shouldn't be a problem."

"I should have let Emma come with us. This is a better science class than reading something from a book."

Alexis stepped close. "Well, if you want to invite me back for the next holiday, I can arrive early and we can bring the class out to collect data."

He bent to kiss her lips, cold from the air but warming quickly beneath his. "That's a date, but I don't know if I want to share you with a whole class of fifth graders."

She patted his cheek. "That's so sweet."

He scowled, but secretly enjoyed the compliment. "Why don't you stay here for the next month?" They climbed into the car and he started driving to the next location.

"Oh, Ryan, I would love to stay and see the snow festival and enjoy all the holiday activities, but I have some projects that need my attention."

Ryan thought about the Orion project specs that were half done on his computer. Alexis wasn't the only one with obligations. "The next time, let's plan on more than a couple of days on either side of the holiday, okay?"

She smiled, and it lit her eyes. "That sounds wonderful."

It took most of the afternoon to place the other five instruments around town in appropriate places. When that was finished, they returned to the meter box where Alexis set the dials to the required frequencies. She opened her laptop in the SUV and checked to make sure all six rawinsondes were transmitting.

"We're set." She snapped the screen shut.
****

Emma slowly followed Corin into the old theater. She heard the boys already horsing around on the stage. She had met several girls from school while they were waiting outside for Corin, and a few of them were friendly. The older girls, mostly seventh graders, were snooty and stayed in a group by themselves, but that was okay with her.

"All right, kids. Let's have all of you take seats down front; off the stage please." Corin called for everyone's attention. Instead of taking the stairs at the side of the stage, most of the boys jumped off the stage front, pushing each other around as they tried to get to the front row seats.

She watched Charlie acting up with his friends. She was glad he didn't act that way around her. She found a seat at the end of an aisle toward the back of the group where she could sit and keep her leg straight. As she laid her crutches on the floor beside her, she hoped when they went back to the doctor before Christmas she got her brace off. It would be wonderful to walk across the stage and stand and sing with the rest of the kids without everyone's attention focused on her crutches.

"My, I'm glad to see you all here," Corin said, her clear voice overriding the boys' boisterous noise. "I think there's more than last year, and I'm happy that some of our older kids decided to stick with us." She smiled at the older girls sitting in front of Emma. She reminded Emma of her teacher in Houston, who controlled classroom noise by the way she looked at them. By the time she's said three sentences, the entire theater was quiet.

"Since some of you have been performing in our Christmas pageant for several years, it gets harder and harder to find new programs to do. We've done the Grinch so many times I can't even eat anything green anymore."

The kids laughed at her joke. Emma liked Corin because she didn't talk down to kids like some adults. Besides, she was Charlie's mom.

Corin started handing out papers as she continued. "I've found a little play called The Toys' Christmas that I think you'll like, but we're not even going to read it today. It has some dialogue pieces and lots of good songs, but before we get to that part," she paused, looking around the group. "Did everyone get a paper?"

Emma took a page and handed the stack to the girl in the next row.

"Before we do anything, I want you to take a look at the list of characters and see what you'd like to be." Murmurs went through the group as kids talked back and forth. "Okay, I didn't mean right this minute. Take the papers home and talk to your parents because, as you know, there is no money for costumes for the Christmas Pageant, so everyone is responsible for their own. I don't want you telling your parents you have to have an expensive costume if you have something at home that will work."

Some of the boys in the front stood but Corin waved them to their seats again. "Also, there's a volunteer form at the bottom. If your parents would like to help build the set, make costumes or provide other props we need, have them fill that out and bring it back next week." Her voice rose as the boys raced to the back. "Practice starts at the same time next week."

The girls were quieter and slower leaving, talking in their little groups and Emma felt left out.

"Emma, please stay a minute? I need to ask your advice on something," Corin called to her as she got to her feet. Emma watched the other girls look at her speculatively.

"Sure." She shrugged. She made her way to the front as the girls left.

Corin collected a few stray papers that had been dropped. "I'll have some parent calling tonight wondering where the volunteer paper is, you hide and watch." She shook her head. "Sometimes I wonder why I do this every year."

"I think because you like it," Emma answered.

Corin laughed. "You're right. I look forward every year to this part of the holidays."

"Will it be the same this year?" Emma frowned, thinking of all the controversy over the costs of coal.

Corin shrugged. "I imagine we'll find some way to make it work. People in Snow have been making it work for over a hundred years. I don't suppose they'll stop now." She pulled on her coat. "Ready to go?"

"Why did you need to see me?" Emma almost forgot the original reason she had stayed.

"I wanted to apologize. I never thought about swinging by and getting you."

"That's okay."

"Well, the least I can do is give you a ride back home." Corin walked with her up the gently sloping aisle.

"It's only around the square to the other side."

"I know, but it's dark already and getting colder." Corin reached around the corner and switched off the lights, held the door open and when they had stepped through, turned and locked it.

Corin stopped her car in front of the bookstore a couple of minutes later. "I wonder if your dad is here. I want to ask him about helping build the set for the pageant. He should be good at that sort of thing."

Charlie had left with the boys and must have run clear across the square because he already had Wolf outside the bookstore. Emma hurriedly opened the door to say hi before turning back to look at Corin. "He and Alexis are putting out wind stuff, but I'll ask him. Thanks for the ride."

Chapter Ten

"I'm going to be a doll house." Emma burst into the apartment, her crutches clattering to the floor as she stood there arms outstretched, hopping on her good leg.

Alexis smiled as she watched Ryan's befuddled expression. She knew Emma was talking about the Christmas pageant because she had visited with Corin the day before at the bookstore. The little play she had found for the kids to perform sounded ideal, and Corin had said she would let the kids and their parents decide on costumes portraying toys. That would keep the cost down. Apparently Emma had already decided.

"That sounds like a great costume," she told Emma, hugging her tight when she hopped over and threw her arms around Alexis's waist.

She had grown to love this child as much as she did Ryan. When they had first met on a NASA project, he had made it clear that his first priority was Emma. Once Alexis found out everything the two of them had gone through, she had known he wouldn't want pity. She had offered him friendship, home cooked meals, and time alone while she and Emma got to know each other. It had been a good place to start, but now she wanted more. After Ryan's declaration that she should spend the month, she had hope that he wanted more than friendship, too.

Ryan shook his head. "I don't understand. How…and why…are you a doll house?"

Emma looked at Alexis and they shared a conspiratory wink. She sighed and hopped over to plop on the sofa, pulling her jeans at the knee to bring her foot up to the ottoman.

"Dad," Emma said and Alexis quickly turned back to the stove to hide her smile. She knew that exasperated tone of voice.

"Emma." He parroted her and they both burst into laughter. It was good to hear Ryan laugh. For the first two years she had known him, he had rarely smiled. She had worried about him moving back home because it meant he was taking that much more on himself. Now she knew Ryan had made the right choice.

Popping the casserole into the oven, she went to join them in the living room. "I think you need to give your dad a little more to go on, don't you?"

Emma wrinkled her nose. "But it's more fun making him guess."

Alexis gave her a mildly chiding look, but Ryan apparently knew how to play the game. He stood and went over to the fridge.

"Soda, Emma?" He arched his brows in question.

"Dad, don't you care?"

"Would you like a glass of wine, Alexis?" He ignored his daughter, pouring drinks and bringing them back with him.

"Okay fine, I'll tell you." Emma pouted.

Ryan winked and bent low to Alexis's ear. "Works every time."

She chuckled. "You are so mean."

Emma took a sip of soda before explaining. "We get to choose what toys we want to be for the Christmas pageant. I want to be a doll house – the big kind with all the rooms and little furniture." She gave him her best smile; the one Alexis knew melted his heart and his defenses. "Will you make my costume for me? Please?"

Ryan still looked a little lost. "Why not be a teddy bear, or a doll?"

A fleeting look of sadness crossed her features and was gone. "The teddy bears and dolls and the cowboys and balls all get to jump around and roll or do somersaults. Since I can't do that, I want to be something that always stays upright. Otherwise it won't look the same."

Alexis's heart ached for this little girl who was trying hard to fit in and not to let her handicap bother her.

"Well, if that's what you want to be, we'll figure out how to make it."

Emma struggled up from the couch and tucked her crutches under her arms. "Geez, Dad, you build space shuttles. How hard can it be to make a little doll house?" She walked away to wash for dinner.

Alexis snickered and when Ryan threw her a look, she laughed. "Oh, no, don't even give me that look. I have a plane to catch tomorrow afternoon, remember?"

"You're going to desert me?"

She patted his knee as she rose. "If you want a wind turbine in the back yard of your doll house, I'll whip one up for you."

"Funny. Ha, ha."

* * * *

It was a beautiful day. The sun was shining for the first time in days, and the four inches of new snow glittered brightly. Ryan had changed to a pair of sweats after church and now looked out the apartment window and smiled at the scene below. Numerous kids and several adults were shoveling the walks around the square. Instead of pushing the snow to the curb, it was being piled into wagons or on sleds and hauled across the street to where others were using it to create even more figures for the snow village. He smiled as he watched a couple of boys painting the corner policeman with blue colored water. For as far back as he could remember the whole town was transformed each year once the first snow fell. And even after the first group of figures began to appear, every snow brought more sculptors to create animals, people, and inanimate objects. There was never any theme – just each individual's imagination.

"Hey Emma, let's take a walk and see what new things are being created." He turned to where his daughter sat on the couch next to the small fireplace, her leg propped on a pillow on the coffee table.

"Charlie's coming over to get me pretty quick," she replied. "Don't you have cookies to bake?"

"It's Sunday."

"Yeah, but with the holiday coming, I know everybody is placing orders. Remember, you had me write orders at Doodles last Friday."

He did have orders. But still…

"Surely you can spare your dad a little time."

There was a knock at the door and he watched his daughter's face light up. He sighed. Somehow he thought he would have more than ten years before his daughter completely forgot he was alive.

"Hi, Mr. D," Charlie said politely.

"Where do you guys go every day?"

Charlie shot Emma a look that Ryan couldn't decipher.

"Just around," his daughter said.

"Around where?"

"Dad."

Charlie frowned as he looked at Emma. "We can tell him, can't we?"

"Charlie, I thought you said it was a secret."

"Okay, guys. Spill it," Ryan said sternly. "Charlie, I'm not risking my daughter's health if you're doing something that will make her sicker."

Another groan from his daughter.

Charlie pursed his lips for a moment and then caved, exactly like Ryan knew he would. "We're spying on Santa."

Ryan's mouth dropped open as he looked from one youngster to the other. "What?"

Emma shook her head. "I told you, Charlie."

"It's Mr. Nicholas who opened the toy store. He builds stuff and feeds reindeer in the forest."

Ryan turned toward the front windows and looked kitty-corner to the middle of the next block. As far as he knew, the store wasn't open and only the simply painted Toy Store in bright red letters on the window indicated what was to come later.

"Well, you won't have to go far to do your spying today. I see Mr. Nicholas walking into his store at this very minute." He grinned at the kids, wondering if he had ever had that much imagination. If he had, it was a very long time ago.

Emma tugged on her coat and wrapped her scarf around her neck. "He doesn't believe you, Charlie. Let's just go."

"You will be careful?" Ryan tugged Emma's hat lower on her forehead and she pushed it back up with a mittened hand.

"Dad, if something's going to happen to me, it might as well happen while I'm doing something fun instead of sitting around like a sick person."

She was a sick person, Ryan thought, even if she refused to be treated as such. And he knew she was right. Emma seemed to be getting stronger; almost to the point where he could forget she was sick. Her crutches click-clacked as she crossed to the door. Almost.

"One hour, no more."

Charlie jerked open the door. "Yes, sir."

Ryan walked down the stairs as Emma rode the chair lift, and watched as Charlie tucked blankets around her in the sleigh, the every faithful Wolf waiting patiently in a handmade harness. The two kids seemed to have an affinity for each other, and he guessed he didn't blame his daughter for wanting company her own age. It made the days go faster for her, even if it made Ryan worry even more. He listened to the bells – something new on Wolf's harness – as the kids moved down the alley and turned out of sight.

*****

They made their way on a circular route, stopping to talk to some of the kids in their class who were on the square. Charlie liked building the snow village but he knew Emma couldn't bend and carry snow and pack it into shapes. When she was with him, he pretended disinterest so she wouldn't feel left out.

"I can't believe you told him," Emma said as they stopped part way down the alley behind the east side of the square.

Charlie began stacking boxes against the wall so he could climb high enough to look in an overhead window.

"You said he wouldn't believe us, and he didn't. What's the big deal?" He climbed to the first level while Emma watched from the sleigh. He reached down to drag another box up to go higher. The box he stood on wobbled and he spread his feet for balance.

"If he thinks we're doing something bad, he won't let me go with you anymore." Emma gasped when he nearly fall, then she began coughing. She covered her mouth with her hands, smothering the sound. She looked extra pale today.

"Maybe we should go back," he said.

"Charlie, you promised." She managed to say without coughing.

When they had started their friendship, Emma had made him promise not to baby her, or tell her dad when she had problems – like today when she was coughing. For the most part, Charlie didn't have trouble keeping his promise because he knew how important "being normal" was to Emma. She had told him about her leg problem, even though he hadn't understood all the big words she had used. He only knew that she might have to wear that brace forever, so he had promised to help her have fun.

Making that promise was easy because he watched his mom and Mitch do the opposite every day. Ever since Mitch had come home from the army, he never smiled and never sang like he used to. Charlie didn't remember his own dad, and he didn't know if his mom was unhappy because his dad didn't live with them, or if it was because Mitch was her friend and he wasn't happy either. All Charlie knew was that he didn't want to grow up if it meant being sad all the time.

Now, he looked at Emma from his perch atop the boxes. Her cheeks were pink as she stared back at him.

"Are you all right now?"

She nodded.

Charlie turned and cautiously climbed onto the taller box he had stacked on the first one.

There was nothing to hold on to, so he got first to his knees then to his feet. He looked up, disappointed that he still wasn't tall enough to see in the window. With a sigh, he climbed back down, looking around for something else to stack on top to make it even taller.

"It looks wobbly." Emma scrunched up her face at his tower.

"I only need one more box," Charlie muttered before spying an empty plastic crate. He raced to get it. "This should make it tall enough." Since the crate was smaller than the boxes, he felt pretty sure it would all lean against the wall and not fall over with him on top. He set the crate on the first box, off to the side, leaving him room to climb up.

The second box was harder because he had to hang on to the crate and climb at the same time. Luckily he was a good climber. Once he was on the second box, he put the crate upside-down, one side against the wall. This time, he grabbed the window sill to help haul himself up. He got one knee on the crate, then the other. He felt the boxes shifting beneath him.

"Charlie, the snow's getting the box all wet. It's probably going to get soggy pretty quick," Emma whispered from below.

"I'm almost there." He huffed as he dragged himself up with the help of the window sill. "The window's all frosty," he reported to his co-conspirator. He scrubbed at the glass with a mittened hand, wiping away some of the grit and snow. He peered inside but he still wasn't tall enough to see down. He could only see across, but what he saw widened his eyes and made his heart beat faster.

"Whoa, Emma! You won't believe--" His sentence was cut off as the boxes shifted beneath him, one corner collapsing and throwing him away from the wall. He landed with a thud in a pile of snow at the side of the alley.

"Charlie!" Emma dragged herself out of the sleigh and shoved her crutches beneath her arms. She hobbled over to where Charlie laid, his eyes and mouth wide open. She reached down and hit him hard on the chest with her hand. "Charlie!"

He wheezed then started to cough...just as the back door to the toy shop was thrown open.

"What in the world?" Mr. Nicholas was clearly surprised to see them in his alley, and Emma bit her bottom lip to keep it from trembling. She had never talked to him, nor seen him up close for that matter, and he looked very tall and very big from her place by Charlie.

She turned when she felt Charlie moving beside her. He stood, dusting off his backside with a hand and bending over to retrieve his cap. Thank goodness he wasn't hurt.

"And who might you be?" Mr. Nicholas asked, his large hands sliding into the pockets at the front of the apron he wore over his huge belly. He was soft spoken and cheery looking as he smiled at them. His hair was certainly white, as was his beard, and his blue eyes twinkled at them. In fact, he actually looked, and acted, a lot like Emma thought Santa would, if she still believed in Santa.

Emma looked at Charlie who was staring, mouth open, at Mr. Nicholas.

"You really are Santa, aren't you?" he asked before she could stop him. He was constantly trying to convince her that Santa existed, but Emma was a non-believer and only went along with Charlie because he was her friend.

Mr. Nicholas laughed; a big, hearty, belly-shaking laugh. "Some people seem to think I may be. But that doesn't answer my question, does it?" Again, his sparkling eyes looked from one to the other.

"I...um...that is, we..." Charlie started.

"I'm Emma and this is Charlie." Emma cut Charlie off. "We were..." Now she was at a loss because she didn't want to lie.

Mr. Nicholas looked at the boxes and the old crate scattered now across the alley and it wasn't hard to guess what they had been doing. Instead of getting mad, he laughed again. "The toy store isn't opened yet, but why don't you two come by next Saturday and see me." He turned to go into the shop.

"Yes sir," Charlie and Emma said in unison, very happy not to be in trouble.

He stopped with his hand on the doorknob. "And when you do, you can come in the front door, like regular people, instead of trying to climb in the window. I wouldn't want to see either of you hurt."

Emma swore she didn't blink, but Mr. Nicholas was framed in the open door then in a split second he was gone. She heard a faint click as the door latched closed.

* * * *

The first weekend after the Thanksgiving holiday marked the more official start of the Snow Festival, but visitors had been coming to town since the first snow fall. Some would spend the weekend and get right in the middle of things; bringing their own shovels and wagons and helping create the sculptures. Others came back week after week to see the progress, and still others came dragging relatives and neighbors.

The Evergreen Gazette printed a twelve-page insert that was distributed through area newspapers and available at convenience stores all across the state. It contained ads from the local businesses, along with articles on the value of shopping hand-made. There were usually contests for visitors, like weekly drawings for who traveled the farthest; a voting ballot for the best sculpture, and all kinds of other promotions and give-aways. Emma had even written an article on the lights-out issue and Ryan heard several positive comments about the kids' efforts.

Ryan had asked all the shopkeepers to put out paper and pencil to collect addresses and emails. Not only would it help identify traffic patterns, but in the back of his mind he hoped the names would come in handy if they somehow convinced the city to get involved with wind energy.

On a positive note, the kids' lights-out campaign had garnered enough support that the city had reluctantly agreed to turn the lights on around the square, only during the weekend, and only from sunset to eight o'clock, assuming that was when the largest number of tourists visited.

"You need to take Emma outside to see it all," Aunt Mary had insisted the minute the lights came on that first Saturday evening. "It's something she's probably never experienced."

Ryan had driven her around a neighborhood in Houston to look at the lights, but it didn't come close to the display in Snow. He turned to find Emma already bundling up.

"We don't have Charlie's sleigh. Do you want me to carry you?"

She gave him an exasperated look that reminded him of his ex-wife, although he realized Emma had only facial features in common with her mother. Her temperament was entirely different.

"We won't be gone long," Ryan called over his shoulder as he opened the door, the bell jingling overhead in holiday welcome. The minute they were outside, childhood memories flooded him. Christmas carols played over an intercom system. Thousands upon thousands of colorful twinkling lights reflected in the snow sculptures dotting the landscape of the downtown area.

Ryan easily recalled his excitement as he and friends had competed to see who could create the most intricate snow sculptures. One year they had collaborated to construct a castle you could actually walk through, but the city had made them block the entrances because they were afraid it would collapse on someone.

Shoppers were everywhere and he stood for a minute enjoying the energy that radiated in the air around them. He smiled at the happy comments he heard as people passed.

"This is an annual outing for our family. The kids barely kept still in the car on the trip over."

"I've never been here before and it's positively wonderful – like a miniature fantasy land."

He nodded as people passed by and they returned his smile. In larger cities, people walked along the streets leery of the majority of others because they didn't know them. Here in Snow, there were no strangers. Perhaps it was the holiday season that made people's hearts lighter, but that

112

mood lasted well past Christmas day here in Snow. Anticipation that something magical might happen tapped you on the shoulder. From the looks of the crowds all around the square, he wasn't the only one who felt it.

"Dad, let's go across the street and see all the statues."

Ryan carefully guided Emma across the street, ever mindful of her slower pace. His boots and her crutches crunched the snow as they wandered along the shoveled path from one scene to the next. Sometimes entire families were depicted -- a snow mom with a bird's nest for a hat, a snow dad with a ratty scarf around his neck, little snow kids with coal eyes and buttons down the front of their round bellies.

Two boys were climbing onto the back of a snow horse, painted brown with large white spots. Their mom stood nearby, snapping a picture as the boys hooted and hollered.

In the middle of the square, all of which was called Center Park, was a large wooden gazebo. Pine trees stood sentinel to each side of the wide steps leading to the platform. The trees were decorated with lights and colored ribbons and each had an angel perched at the very top.

"They have band concerts here in the summer," he told Emma. "Everybody comes with their blankets and lawn chairs and you can lie under the stars and listen to the music."

"Did you think that was corny when you were a kid?"

Ryan thought about her question. "You know, I don't think I did. Of course, sometimes we spent more time horsing around than listening, but some of it must have soaked in. Still, there's something about hanging with friends and being outside that was…awesome."

"Awesome?" She looked at him, her mouth askew.

"Yeah. There's nothing like a small town where you can ride your bike all over, stopping to get a cold soda from the gas station, pedaling to the lake to go swimming on a hot day. Even stealing an apple from Mr. Larsen. We didn't have Wii and iPods and zillions of channels on TV. We had to make our own fun. It was a great place to grow up."

"Dad, look." Emma pointed as they rounded the gazebo. "An elephant! Oh, and a zebra and a tiger. Oh my gosh, they have a whole zoo."

Ryan laughed at his daughter's excitement. It was fascinating to see the artistic talent in the animals, objects, even people -- some larger than life -- all crafted from snow. Many of the residential streets had their own displays; some even had contests between blocks of residents. But the 'best of the best' usually appeared around the square.

"Let's take a picture and send to Alexis." He propped Emma on the back of a bear, but when he stood back to take a picture with his phone, someone tapped him on the shoulder.

"You get in there with your daughter. I'll take the picture," offered a smiling young man wearing a red and white striped hat right out of a Dr. Seuss book.

"Come on dad; get up here with me."

Ryan found climbing on the back of a cold, slippery black bear was not as easy as one would think. By the time he managed to get behind Emma, a small crowd of people were cheering him on, and the Dr. Seuss fan had snapped several pictures of Ryan's attempts.

Emma grabbed the phone before Ryan had a chance to erase the evidence. "Oh, yeah," she said, laughing as she looked through the pictures. "Lexi's going to love these." Ryan thanked the young man, who happily tipped his hat and moved on.

"Do you think Lexi's coming back?" Emma asked as they began the walk back to the bakery.

"Of course she is. She's collecting data from the instruments we launched and she'll have to make another presentation to the City Council."

"Is that the only reason she's coming back?"

Ryan had no trouble reading his daughter's mind.

"I miss her, too," Ryan said on a heartfelt sigh. The time Alexis had spent with them hadn't been near long enough. "We'll have to show her a good time when she comes back so she won't want to leave."

"I guess." She sounded as discouraged as Ryan felt.

Later that night, after he put Emma to bed, Ryan leaned his forehead against the cold window, watching as Mr. Pritchert pulled his pickup into the garage behind his store. His headlights were the only illumination in this section of town, and when the man lowered the garage door, the darkness was complete.

Even at night, there was usually some sound, some flicker of light in the distance; not this dark quiet with only the wind to keep him company. The inky night symbolized his loneliness. He told himself he wasn't alone; he had Emma, and Aunt Mary, and Alexis. But it was still his responsibility to take care of Emma; to stay positive, and keep praying that she would make a full recovery. Some days when he carried her to the bakery to keep him company he wanted to cry. Even though he made sure she ate, she weighed next to nothing; her arms and legs were thin and fragile. But when he would frown, she would put her hand against his cheek.

"Dad, don't worry. I'll be alright and then I can take care of you." And her bright smile got him through one more day.

Chapter Eleven

Once the festival began, many of the stores around the square were open all weekend with extended hours, so some were closed on Mondays, the Snickerdoodle Bakery included. Aunt Mary felt working six long days a week was more than enough. Besides, even though the store already had garland and bright Christmas decorations strung about, she had informed Emma it was time to decorate her house.

Of course, Ryan got recruited to shop for a tree. Emma chose the biggest one at the Lion's Club tree lot, and it had to be tied to the roof of the SUV to get it to Aunt Mary's. Once they had it set in the living room, he hauled boxes of decorations from the attic. He didn't mind because as Emma handed Aunt Mary each ornament, his aunt would tell her the story behind it and Ryan recalled all those same stories from his youth. He was glad his aunt was here to pass her history on to his daughter.

"Oh, my gosh. Is this Dad?" Emma held up a tissue paper wreath with a school picture glued in the middle. She started laughing. When Ryan tried to snatch it, she turned away. Digging into the box she retrieved another, this one with his face on an alphabet block.

"Don't say it," he warned her when she opened her mouth. "I can't believe you still have all those old school ornaments, Aunt Mary."

He watched her wrinkled hand lovingly touch his face in one of the pictures, and again felt the pain, lessened by passing years, but nonetheless still in a corner of his heart. The ornaments had been his mom's, made by Ryan in art class, one for every school year until he had come to live with Mary and Paul. It was one of the few things his aunt had kept when his parents' estate had been settled.

"This one says fifth grade," Emma said. "Where are the rest?"

Ryan glanced at his aunt, an apology forming for the grief he had put her through but she gave him a smile and walked over to add a hug, exactly as she had done all those years ago. Mary had wanted him to create an ornament that first Christmas he had lived with them but he had lashed out in anger, not against Mary but against God himself, for taking his parents away.

He hadn't wanted to celebrate Christmas; in fact, had refused the gifts Mary and Paul had bought for him. He also refused to go to church with them Christmas Eve, and generally had been a pain in the posterior. But Mary had never given up on him.

"Thank you," he said, his cheek against her soft white hair.

"Dad?"

"I think I probably outgrew making dorky ornaments," he answered her earlier question.

"They're not...well, yeah, they are pretty dorky," she replied, laughing as she hung another on the tree.

They had almost finished decorating when Emma pulled his cell phone from her pocket and Ryan wondered about getting her one for Christmas. Although he rarely used his anymore, with the landlines at the apartment and the bakery, he never seemed to have it on him when he needed it.

He watched her flip it open but she didn't say anything. Her lips twitched as she listened and she glanced at him with a sparkle in her eyes before handing him the phone. "It's for you."

Even before he put the phone to his ear he heard the laughter. He checked the caller ID.

"Alexis?"

Bursts of laughter came across the line, then she mumbled something but she was laughing so hard Ryan couldn't understand her. By this time Emma was whispering to Mary and the two of them began laughing. Apparently everyone knew the joke except him.

"You want to call me back?" He frowned.

"I'm sorry; truly I am. It's just so funny." She went off again, the sound muffled like she had the phone against her chest. When she finally gained some control, Ryan was let in on the joke.

"Emma sent me pictures of you sliding off the rump of a bear." She giggled again.

Ryan now smiled, but when he glanced toward his daughter, he gave her a mock frown and mouthed the words – you are in trouble – shaking a finger at her.

"They would have been funny enough," Alexis said, "but she added the caption 'Dad bear-ly hung on.'"

"I want you to remember there will still be plenty of snow by the time you get back here," he warned as he walked toward the kitchen to carry on a more private conversation.

As the door started to swing shut behind him, he heard Emma say, "Aunt Mary, if you have some construction paper, I think I know a great picture to put on an ornament for dad this year."

* * * *

"Hey, kiddo," Emma's dad said when she hobbled through the back door of the bakery Saturday morning. She took a deep breath, loving the smell of vanilla and cinnamon. Some days she thought she could actually taste the air around her.

She looked at her dad, already covered in flour. His dark hair looked almost gray and he had chocolate icing on the front of his apron. He liked to bake, and looked like he belonged here at the Snickerdoodle more than when he used to come home in dress shirts and ties when they lived in Houston.

"Are you happier baking cakes than working at NASA?"

He looked at her in surprise. "There are lots of jobs that can make a person happy, Emma, and they don't all have to be big and impressive. It's as important for someone to stock grocery shelves and pick up the

118

garbage…or bake cookies, as it is to run the government or build rockets."

"Geez, Dad, I only asked if you liked baking." She snitched a cookie from the counter and munched quietly, watching as he put another tray into the oven. She sometimes worried that he had…

"No, I'm not sorry I gave up NASA to bake cookies, if that's what you're wondering. And it had nothing to do with you. We both needed a change."

"Okay, that's too scary," she said because that was exactly what she had been thinking.

He grinned at her. "Besides, I'm still doing work for Lou." Sliding the last tray into the huge oven, he turned. "It's Saturday. What are you up to today?"

"Charlie and me have to…ah; we're going to help Mr. Nicholas at his shop."

"What did you do, Emma?" He had caught her slip and his tone warned Emma not to try and hedge. She did anyway.

"It wasn't me; it was Charlie."

Her dad had the same look Mr. Nicholas had when he caught them. She sighed, wondering if adults went to a special school to learn how to tell when kids did something wrong.

"We went to the back of the toy store, but it was Charlie who climbed on the boxes and tried to see inside. I didn't."

"I would hope not. Your leg is finally beginning to heal. I certainly don't want it broken again." She thought his tone held more worry than anger, so she explained the rest.

"The boxes sort of smushed under his weight and Charlie yelled when he fell in the snow. Mr. Nicholas came outside, but he didn't seem mad or anything. He told us if we wanted to see what he was doing, we should come on Saturday and help."

"So you get to be up close and personal with Santa." Her dad smiled.

She frowned. "I don't think he's Santa, only Charlie does. And besides, if he really was Santa, he wouldn't want us snooping around his workshop, would he?"

Her dad shrugged. "Maybe the magic only happens on Christmas Eve, or when all good little boys and girls are in their beds fast asleep."

"Yeah, right. You sound like Charlie." The bell over the bakery door jangled as Charlie came in.

"He sounds like me why?"

"Never mind," she said.

"Do you kids have time for an errand before you go see…Mr. Nicholas?"

Emma frowned over the way her dad said the man's name. She narrowed her gaze; surely he didn't still believe in Santa?

"Sure," Charlie answered. "Whatcha need?"

"Miss Vera and Miss Violet ordered cookies again for their bridge club, but I can't leave to deliver them and I don't want those two driving." Her dad looked outside as he spoke. It wasn't snowing, but it was cloudy and grey. "Would you two deliver their cookies?"

"Is it far?"

"Naw," Charlie answered. "It's only a couple of blocks off the square. I've taken stuff over there before for Mom. 'Sides, Emma, you gotta meet them. They're the oldest people ever – they've gotta be over a hundred."

"They're only in their eighties," her dad corrected, "but I suppose that is considered old when you're only ten. They were here during the depression. Maybe you can get them to tell you about the magic of Snow back when they were children." He looked at her and winked.

Emma didn't believe in magic. After all, how many times had she wished for her leg to get better and that hadn't happened. But she smiled and went along with the game. "They know the real story?"

"I'm sure they do." Her dad closed the lid on the box of cookies. She shrugged into her coat and hat, tugging on her mittens. Charlie already had Wolf harnessed to the sleigh and the dog waited patiently out front. The sleigh was actually Charlie's wagon tied onto an old plastic toboggan, but it worked great in the snow.

She and Charlie had figured an easy way for her to get into his wagon. He would slide one side out of the brackets that held it; she would back up, sit and swing her feet around. Once she had her crutches tucked in beside her, he would slide the wood rails back in place. Her dad sat the cookie box on her lap and bent to give her a kiss on the forehead. She rolled her eyes, wondering what Charlie would think.

"Stay out of trouble," he said waving them off.

Charlie whistled and Wolf started along the sidewalk, easily pulling Emma and the sleigh.

"I like your dad," Charlie said after they crossed the street and headed up Second Street. "He's cool."

"Yeah, I guess he's okay."

"Can I have one of those cookies? They'll never miss just one."

"No. Dad has them all lined up in neat rows. Anybody would notice if one was gone."

A dog barked and they turned to see Harley barreling down the street after them. When he got a little ahead of the sleigh, he started spinning in circles, bouncing all over and yipping and Emma laughed. Wolf ignored the smaller dog.

"Harley you'd better get home or old Mr. Pritchert may come after you with his bb gun," Charlie said. About that time, they heard the man yelling for Harley. The dog stopped spinning; his ears perked up, and he raced back the way he had come.

"He sure is a silly dog," Emma said. "Did Wolf do that when he was a puppy?"

"Yeah. He also peed all over the floor. Mom almost gave him back to the pound."

They rounded another corner and continued along the block until Wolf turned onto the sidewalk that led to a huge, red brick house. A porch ran all across the front, enclosed by a white, lattice-work railing and tall square pillars at the corners and in front by the steps. A porch swing hung to the left, swaying back and forth. Dark windows on the second floor, the shades half drawn, reminded Emma of a huge jack-o-lantern's eyes. She thought it all looked kind of spooky.

"This is it," Charlie said. "Miss Vera and Miss Violet have always lived in Snow. I think the house belonged to the old Mr. Carston. When he moved his family away, it was empty for a long time. One of the ladies was married to a banker or something and he bought it for her to live in. Then he died and the other sister moved in with her."

"And they live in it all by themselves?" The house was gigantic; too big for only two people.

Charlie shrugged. "I guess." He took the side off and Emma handed him the cookies so she could get out. "Wolf, you stay here." The dog immediately lay down on the sidewalk leading to the house.

"Can you get up the steps?"

Emma frowned at him. "I'm not crippled, Charlie." When he gave her a look, she added, "Not that way." And she showed him by reaching the porch first.

Charlie rang the bell. "They're slow; sometimes I have to ring the bell more than once." He waited a few minutes then pushed the buzzer again. Another minute went by before Emma heard the door unlock.

"Why Charlie Parker, what are you doing here?" A little old lady, not much taller than Emma, popped her white haired head out the door. Emma thought she looked like a little bird, her bright blue eyes wide and her mouth opened. Her hands fluttered about her little body like a baby bird's wings when they were learning to fly.

"We've brought your cookie order from the Snickerdoodle Bakery," Charlie said.

"What?" The lady pushed the storm door wider. She turned her head and said in a loud voice, "Vera, we've got visitors." When she turned back, she added, "Oh, dear, I'm afraid we weren't expecting company. We don't have any cookies to offer you, but come in, come in. Who's your friend?"

Emma looked at Charlie and he grinned back at her.

"This is Emma Diantelli. Her dad is Ryan Diantelli and he helps run the bakery." Charlie and Emma stepped inside and moved quickly to the side as the lady closed the door. He held out the box. "Here's your cookies."

Miss Violet looked totally surprised. "Why, aren't you clever to bring your own cookies for our visit?" She took the box and opened it as another old lady, dressed identically in a green plaid wool skirt and long sleeved white blouse, walked slowly with the aid of a cane through the door on the left. She wore a beautiful multicolored scarf over her shoulders and glasses perched on the end of her nose.

Emma looked from one to the other. Except for the glasses, they looked exactly alike with snow white hair curling around their heads, lots and lots of wrinkles on their faces, and blue veins spider-webbing along their thin hands. They both wore bright red lipstick and rouge and looked like their eyebrows were painted on with dark brown.

"Violet, dear, those cookies are for our bridge club, remember?" They even sounded alike, except Miss Vera was louder. Emma suspected that Miss Violet didn't hear very well.

Miss Vera patted her sister on the arm, then turned and smiled at Emma and Charlie. "How are you, my dears?" She didn't give them time to answer. "Charlie, did your mother send the book I ordered? Why, you look like your father," she said as she pushed her glasses up her nose and squinted at Emma. "I still remember when he came to live with Mary Decker."

Emma sometimes wondered what her dad had been like as a boy. Perhaps she should ask these ladies, but before she formed a question, both had turned and were leading the way into the living room.

Miss Vera waved them to a sofa and they had no sooner sat than Miss Violet was in front of them, the cookie box open. "Would you like a cookie?"

"Violet –"

Miss Violet tsked. "I know they're for the bridge club, sister, but heavens, those little birds can't eat all these. Just look at the bounty." She leaned close and whispered, "Sister thinks I'm dreadfully forgetful." She winked at Emma and Charlie then said loudly. "Besides, growing boys and girls need cookies, don't you?"

Charlie didn't hesitate. "Yes, ma'am." He reached into the box and grabbed two. Emma politely took one and thanked her, poking Charlie in the side with her elbow. He mumbled his thanks around a mouthful of frosted sugar cookie.

The two old ladies sat in high backed stuffed chairs on either side of a table. They each had a small footstool in front of their chair on which they rested their feet. Emma didn't think she knew any adults whose feet didn't reach the floor when they sat in a chair.

Their house was sort of like Aunt Mary's; full of old stuff, except these two ladies had even more stuff than Aunt Mary. They had lacy curtains on all the windows and heavy dark drapes held back by ties to let the light in. There were little white dollies on the tables under the lamps, along the back of the couch, and behind each of the ladies' heads as they perched in their chairs. Little figurines and china statues covered almost every available inch of table space.

"So Charlie Parker, about my book?" Miss Vera asked.

"What book is that?" Her sister looked over, eyes wide with curiosity.

"I asked Charlie if he had the book I ordered from his mother."

"Well, my heavens, sister. They brought us cookies. Why on earth would they also bring you a book?" Miss Violet shook her head and rolled her eyes.

Emma thought Miss Violet was extremely fascinated with the cookies. She took another from the box, which she kept on her lap. Emma didn't know when their bridge club was to meet, but if it wasn't today, she doubted there would be any cookies left. Or else her dad would get a call to make some more. Miss Violet daintily dabbed at her lips to avoid smearing her lipstick.

124

"I didn't know we'd be coming over here when I stopped to get Emma. I can call my mom, if you want."

Miss Vera waved a hand. "No need for that. I'm sure it will arrive in short order. What kind of grand adventure are you having on this fine snowy day? I see you have your dog with you." She glanced quickly at Emma's crutches, which she'd laid on the floor beside her feet. "It's a fine way to get around town when you have a bum leg, isn't it?" She gestured with her cane and Emma didn't feel quite so bad about her crutches.

Miss Violet piped up. "One day, I think I would like Charlie to take me for a ride in his dog sleigh. That would be such fun."

Her sister looked at her, eyes wide behind her glasses. "You would surely fall right out onto your head, Violet. And then where would you be? And where would I be without you, dear sister?"

"Well, there is that," Miss Violet answered. She turned to Charlie. "I'm afraid I'll have to forego riding in your grand sleigh behind your magnificent dog, but thank you kindly for the offer."

Charlie shrugged. "Sure."

Emma looked from him to the ladies and back. Charlie didn't seem to find anything at all strange about the conversation they were having. In the next minute she understood why.

"Before Emma's dad asked us to deliver your cookies, we were going to help Santa in his workshop."

"Charlie," she hissed.

"Santa is here in Snow?" Miss Violet gasped, forgetting she had a bite of cookie in her mouth. When Miss Vera shot her a glance, she clapped a hand over her mouth.

Emma felt like Alice in Wonderland.

"Well, Emma doesn't think he is, but he might be," Charlie defended.

"Of course, he could be," Miss Vera said. "After all, he has to work somewhere and what better place than in Snow. We already know there's magic here."

Miss Violet nodded in agreement, munching on her cookie.

Emma almost groaned because she knew that word would spark Charlie's interest.

"Tell us the story about Snow when there was magic," he said, scooting forward to the very edge of the couch. "Emma's dad said it happened a long time ago, but Emma doesn't believe it."

Both ladies looked at Emma and she felt her cheeks grow warm. "It's just that—"

"You don't have to explain, dear," Miss Vera said. Her eyes narrowed and she tipped her head to the side, still studying Emma. She brought her hand up, one bony, bent finger tapping her pursed red lips. "Sometimes it's hard to believe if the magic hasn't touched you, hmm?"

Emma's eyes grew wide. How did this old lady know what she was thinking?

"It was such a long time ago, and yet sometimes it seems like yesterday," Miss Violet said.

"Sister's right," Miss Vera added. "We were little children, maybe ten or so, and our father worked in the mines, as did almost everybody except the shopkeepers. And they were still mine employees, as everything in the town was bought and paid for by the mine." Her face took on a dreamy expression, and Emma leaned forward. She had read the story from a book, but wanted to hear it from someone who had been there.

"The town was called Carstonville at that time, even though for years before it was known as the snow festival town. Nobody knows exactly when or why it started, but like today, children and their parents would make snow people and forts and such and as word spread, people would drive from miles around to see what we had created."

"But then the awful depression hit," Miss Violet took over the story. "Even though coal was essential for electricity, there were shut downs and layoffs and Mr. Carston threatened to close the mine completely." She gave a heartfelt sigh. "As winter came on, supplies became scarce. I can remember Mama taking the last of her pennies to the company store to buy a soup bone. She made this big pot of soup that smelled heavenly – all spicy and tangy."

"It was actually no more than water," Miss Vera said, "with a little flavor. But she made it seem like the grandest meal on earth as we ate from her best, special occasion china she had brought over from Germany."

Emma thought perhaps she understood now why Miss Violet liked cookies so well. She couldn't imagine going without a treat now and again, much less having water soup for a meal.

"When the snow began that year, none of the adults wanted to create a fantasy world when their lives were so bleak, but all of us children decided that it might help make things seem better. Perhaps like Mama using the good china to serve us soup. We scooped and gathered snow and soon there were snow people on the corners, pretend houses, animals romping in the park. We'd find abandon birds' nests to put on the snowmen as hats, or a ratty old piece of material to wrap around their neck for a scarf. And of course, there was always coal for buttons and mouths and eyes."

"Don't forget the table," Miss Violet said. "That was the best thing of all. That was the real magic."

Miss Vera gave her sister an indulgent look. "It was all magic, but yes, you're right. The table was surely special."

"What about the table?" Charlie's eyes widened as he soaked in the story from long ago.

"Well, in the middle of the square, we made a huge pile of snow to look like a table. We put all manner of things on it – empty tins that had held vegetables and crackers or flour, mounds of snow to make pretend turkeys and hams. Anything we could find that resembled food was put on the table."

"And that was the day Mrs. Carston came to town in her big car with her own driver. When she got out of the car, we thought she was an angel; tall and beautiful with her huge hat and bright colored scarf." Miss Violet sighed again and closed her eyes.

"She asked what we were doing and we told her, not having the tact of adults, you see, that we had made a pretend Christmas table full of food because we had none; and pretend people wrapped in coats to keep them warm and even pretend puppies that we wanted to be real." The story swung back and forth between the two ladies, but perhaps because they had told it often and now remembered the times fondly, they didn't interrupt each other but simply picked up where the other paused. "She talked to all of us, asking questions, admiring our crude attempts at creating a happy holiday, and before she left, her driver handed each of us a stick of licorice."

"A whole piece," blurted Miss Violet. "Why, I never remember having a whole stick of candy any day in my life before that."

The women fell silent. Emma looked from one to the other and then to Charlie. "What's magic about getting a piece of licorice?" she whispered, but the two ladies heard her.

"Ah, the magic came Christmas Eve as we all spilled from the church after the annual Christmas pageant." Miss Vera's eyes twinkled. "For you see, in place of all the empty tins on the table were huge baskets of fresh fruit and breads; sugar plums and sweet treats. There were whole hams and turkeys and tins piled high of crackers and vegetables; flour and sugar. Our parents were very happy, of course, but that was not the end of the magic." She shook her head, tilting it just so as she smiled at them.

"The whole park had been transformed into something straight out of a fairy tale. All the snow people wore brand new real coats with scarves around their necks. There were sleds and ice skates and toys propped against the fences by our homes and scattered around the trees. That Christmas was the most magically of any to be remembered in Snow."

"Wow," Charlie said softly. "All those toys just appeared?"

Emma was thinking more about the coats and food. "How did it all get sorted out?"

Miss Violet chuckled. "Everyone shared in the bounty that had magically been left for us. We were all so pleased that no one thought to take it all."

"Now," Miss Vera put her hands on her knees and leaned forward. "Thank you for bringing our cookies, but I know you two young people don't want to spend your entire Saturday with a couple of old ladies." She slowly stood, gripping the arms of the chair before reaching for her cane. "Off you go on your adventure."

Charlie and Emma stood and followed her to the door. Emma looked back to say good bye to Miss Violet and saw that she was happily eating yet another cookie. She paused as Charlie opened the door. "Would you mind if I asked when your bridge club meets?" She wanted to make sure her dad made enough cookies.

Miss Vera smiled and patted Emma's cheek with one bony hand. "Such a sweet girl you are to ask. Bridge club isn't until next week, but sister tends to forget when she calls the bakery." She looked back into the sitting room. "Or perhaps she isn't as forgetful as she leads me to believe."

Emma didn't say anything as she climbed into Charlie's sleigh and they started down the sidewalk and turned back toward the center of town.

"It wasn't really magic and it wasn't Santa. It was Mrs. Carston, the lady in the car."

Charlie shrugged. "Probably, but it's still magic."

"What do you mean?"

"It was a person, doing good things for a lot of other people when they didn't have to. That's magic, isn't it? Like Mr. Nicholas is making toys for kids. Who's to say he isn't Santa Clause, or one of his helpers. Like the lady in the car might have been Santa's helper a long time ago. Nobody said they had to be elves, you know."

As they continued along the sidewalk, Wolf pulling her along in the sleigh and Charlie walking beside her, Emma thought about what he said. There was more to Charlie Parker than he let on.

He was polite to the old ladies, something that most boys their age wouldn't bother doing, unless it was their own grandparents. He didn't mind helping his mom or her dad, and he always brought her homework and got her papers back to Miss Michaels. He was a very good friend, and a very nice person…for a boy.

Chapter Twelve

Charlie and Emma stood in front of the toy store door and politely knocked. They both jumped when the shutter flew up and Mr. Nicholas peered out the window over wire rimmed spectacles, his head turning this way and that. He frowned before lowering his gaze to their height. Then he smiled, turned the lock and opened the door for them.

"I was expecting someone taller," he said, chuckling in a very ho, ho, ho way. Emma looked closer at him. He wasn't dressed at all like Santa, but instead wore a faded pair of jeans and a red plaid flannel shirt. Over the top of it all was an enormous apron with pockets across the front. She saw the handle of a hammer sticking out of one.

Instead of black boots, he had on a pair of tennis shoes, one of which was untied, and when he turned to walk away from them, she caught a glimpse of red and green striped socks. She bit her lip to keep from laughing.

Not that she believed in Santa, but Mr. Nicholas certainly didn't look like him. Well, except maybe in the way he laughed, all jolly like; or the way he had white hair and a beard; or—

"Emma?"

"Oh, I'm sorry. I was daydreaming." She felt her cheeks get hot and when she looked over at Charlie, he was laughing at her.

Mr. Nicholas laughed too, but she got the feeling he did that a lot and it wasn't at people. "Daydreaming is a fine thing to do. Why, I've had some of my best ideas for toys while daydreaming – like the hula-hoop, Ultraman, Bugaboo.

"Now let's see. What is it you're here for today?" He looked from one to the other, as though he didn't remember why he had told them to come. His eyes twinkled and, bending forward, he put his large hands on his knees, bringing him to their eye level. "Ah, yes. You thought perhaps you might see something special by peeking in the back windows." He raised a bushy white eyebrow.

"We thought…" Charlie started. She hoped he wasn't going to say they thought they were spying on Santa.

Mr. Nicholas straightened, waving a hand. "No need to explain. I was your age once, and probably as inquisitive."

"You were? Like a hundred years ago?" Charlie asked.

Emma rolled her eyes. "Nobody's that old."

Mr. Nicholas laughed, the sound taking up all the space around them and somehow sliding into Emma until she was laughing, too.

"Santa is," Charlie retorted, looking at Mr. Nicholas for confirmation.

He raised both brows at that. "Ho, ho, so you believe in Santa Clause?"

"Yes."

"No," Emma said at the same time.

Mr. Nicholas didn't say anything. Instead, he pursed his lips and looked thoughtful. "The store's not open yet, but I think you can still help me. I need someone to test the toys and put things together before we display them on the counters and shelves." He looked at them. "Would it be possible for the two of you to do that?"

"Sure." Charlie spun around and quickly flipped open the top of a huge box on the floor. "Oh, wow." He lifted out a bright red remote control car. "Do you have any Wii to try?"

"I'm afraid not," Mr. Nicholas replied. "That car is about as fancy as we get. We make more traditional toys." He lifted two boxes off a counter and put them on the floor by Emma.

"Here you go. You can sit right there and work on these boxes." He pointed to a chair, not saying anything about her crutches, which made Emma happy.

When she looked in one box she found little shoes and socks, pretty dresses, hats and bonnets. The other box contained dolls of all sizes. While Charlie played with little toy cars, making all kinds of racing car noises, she put pretty dresses on the dolls, then found shoes and hats that matched.

She tried to balance herself on her crutches as she carefully stood to put the last doll on a low shelf. Standing made her dizzy and she quickly sat again. She leaned to the side, resting her head on her folded arms on the table.

"Hey, are you all right?" Charlie touched her shoulder but she didn't lift her head. Funny; she ached everywhere except her leg.

"Do you want me to get your dad?" She heard concern in his voice.

She blindly reached out and grabbed his shirt so he wouldn't go tattle. It took her a minute before she could lift her head and turn to where he stood patiently waiting. "No," she whispered. When he finally nodded in agreement, her hand dropped to her lap. The dizziness had passed, but her stomach was still upset.

"Why don't you ask Santa for what it'll take to fix you?"

Emma scowled at him. "I don't believe in Santa. Besides, it's not like he can put the right type of blood in a box under the tree."

"Blood? Yuck!"

"I thought boys liked blood."

"Not me." Charlie gave an elaborate shiver, clear to his toes, then turned back to the train he was putting on a small circular track.

"Blood? Is someone hurt?" Mr. Nicholas glanced at the two of them as he walked in through a door at the back of the store.

"Naw. Emma needs--"

"Shut your mouth, Charlie Parker." Emma smacked him on the arm. His mouth dropped open in surprise before he grinned.

"Girly punch." But he rubbed his arm anyway.

She glared at him. Mr. Nicholas looked from one to the other.

"Do you want to tell me what this is all about?" Mr. Nicholas asked gently. She sighed. She didn't like talking about her illness, because people tended to pity her, thinking she was about ready to die. Or else, they looked scared, like they might catch something from her. Except Charlie, she thought, glancing his way. She had told him and he acted like it wasn't a big deal, like it wasn't any different from having a cold. That's why he was her friend.

She looked back to see Mr. Nicholas studying her.

"Well?"

She gave a careless shrug. "Osteomyelitis. My leg isn't healing right since it was broken. I need a special kind of blood so my bone marrow will start making red blood cells, but the doctors can't find anybody who has it. And all this makes my immune system weak, so I get colds and stuff easier."

He frowned. "Your parents?"

"Daddy has the same type as me -- AB positive -- but there's something else -- some antigen -- that makes blood compatible, and his blood doesn't have it. That's the problem."

Mr. Nicholas put a finger to his lips, tapping as he hummed. "Such big words from a little girl."

"If you had spent as much time as I have in the hospital, you'd have learned them because nobody tells you what's wrong."

Mr. Nicholas chuckled, his large belly shaking. "I suppose you're right, and mores the pity. Well, perhaps this will be the year for your miracle." He looked at her and winked. "If you believe, that is."

* * * *

Ryan sneaked back upstairs for a nap as soon as Aunt Mary got to the bakery at ten. With Greta gone, they were both keeping long hours. Mary had a few high school girls who helped at the register in the afternoons, but the baking was still up to the two of them. The three a.m. hours were getting to him. Emma had promised to do her homework and save any questions for later. Even though it was a week day, the traffic around the square was heavy as people came to shop and walk through Center Park to look at all the snow sculptures.

He pulled the shades in the apartment, hoping to block enough of the sun to sleep. For once, it was clear and although cold, the wind wasn't swirling the loose snow around. As he dragged on a pair of sweats, he wondered how Lexi's wind readings were going. He hadn't talked to her in a few days, which was unusual, but time had gotten away from him. Every afternoon he'd take Emma over to pageant practice, and he was usually in bed before nine; eight some days. He fell asleep dreaming of the few kisses they had shared and her promise to come back before Christmas and spend at least two weeks.

The ringing phone jerked him from sleep. He groggily slapped a hand along the bedside table. As he lifted the receiver, he squinted toward the window where a crack of sunlight split the two sections of curtain.

"'lo?"

"Ryan?"

"Alexis? I was dreaming about you."

"Dreaming? What are you doing sleeping in the middle of the day? Are you sick?"

Ryan rubbed a hand over his face, and glanced at the clock. He was not a catnap type person, and the two hours of sleep he had grabbed only made him more tired.

"I'm sorry; I shouldn't have disturbed you. I'll try to fix it from here, or I'll call you back later."

He padded to the kitchen for a glass of water. "No, I'm awake now and I'm not sick. Getting up in the middle of the night to start the bread dough is taking its toll."

Her velvety laugh further awakened Ryan. She had one of those pure, enjoying life types of laughs that made a person want to join in, even if they didn't know the joke. That was only one of the many reasons Ryan wanted Alexis in his life.

"Remember when you would stay up for thirty-six or more hours straight when there was a shuttle crisis?"

"I've aged considerably in the past three months, believe me. Tell me what's going on; what needs fixed?"

135

"I'm not getting any more readings from the rawinsondes. I don't know if it's the transmitters themselves or the meter box, but something has happened."

Ryan frowned. "I drove by the sites two days ago and all the balloons were still up."

He heard her sigh. "That's the problem with doing this remotely. Too many things can go wrong. Sometimes it's a loose screw or the meter box may have overcharged and kicked the breaker switch. In that case you'll have to reset it. Was the meter box covered with snow; or maybe it got dinged by a snow plow even though we flagged it?"

He had to chuckle. "You've only been gone a week and we're not buried to rooftop level with snow. It's not that bad here."

"I know, but it seemed like an awful lot of snow."

"I'll do a drive-by again and give you a call in about an hour, but this is going to cost you. The Department of Energy has got to have more money than NASA."

"How about a promise to cook when I come back?"

"Home-made or box?"

She tsked. "I do know how to use a recipe book. Are you feeding Emma something besides Mac and Cheese?"

"She likes that, especially with corndogs."

"You're Italian," Alexis countered. "I thought cooking was in your genes."

"Half Italian on my dad's side and he never learned to cook."

"It sounds like you're thoroughly awake now. I don't have to worry about you forgetting this conversation, do I?"

"Not at all. I'll grab Emma and we'll cruise around the town and see what's happening."

"Oh, speaking of, how's the doll house construction going?"

Ryan groaned. "Let's just say the architect and the contractor haven't quite reached agreement. She wants a ten room mansion with all this miniature furniture showing and I was thinking a framework of the outside only; maybe some shutters and a door painted on."

Again she laughed. "When you check my equipment and call me back, I'll talk to her. Maybe I can convince her that smaller is more energy efficient."

"Bless you. If you manage that, I'll help with the cooking."

"Deal. Let me know what you find."

Ryan hung up the phone and climbed into the shower, hoping the hard spray would finish clearing the cobwebs from his brain.

He had no trouble convincing Emma to take a ride with him, and as they cruised by the areas where Alexis had anchored the balloons, all were still floating above the trees. He used his binoculars and spotted the rawinsondes on each tether, although he had no idea whether they were transmitting.

"Well, the last one is over by Larsen's Orchard with the meter box." He handed the binoculars to Emma and pulled back onto the road.

"What happens if she can't get wind readings?" She peered through the lens. "Wow! Binoculars make things super close. I wonder if Charlie has a pair of these."

"You don't have to spy on Santa with binoculars if he's letting you help in his toy shop."

Emma put the binoculars in her lap and shrugged. "Charlie's the only one who thinks he's Santa. Besides, if he was, don't you think some of the other kids in town would think that too?"

"And they don't?"

She shook her head. "Nobody but Charlie."

"To answer your question, we'll have to ask Alexis about the wind readings. I suppose if all else fails, she can bring more equipment when she comes back at Christmas."

"She's coming back?" He heard the excitement in Emma's voice. "For keeps?"

Uh-oh. Ryan didn't know how to answer that, and then it was forgotten as he turned the corner and slowed the vehicle along the stretch of road by the orchard. "Well...nuts." That wasn't what he wanted to say, and only Emma's presence kept him from swearing a blue streak.

137

Splintered boards were scattered along the side of the road where the box had been. He slammed the car in park, got out and stomped across the road. The box housing the meter had been demolished, and there wasn't a dial on the meter that didn't have the glass smashed.

He swiveled his gaze to where the balloon should have been, but detected nothing in the sky. He walked toward the tree line, not remembering exactly where Alexis had cabled it. He tripped, one boot catching on a broken tree limb, he thought, until he looked down. Half buried under the latest snowfall was the cable.

He pulled, following it with his hands until it all lay coiled on top of the snow, the busted balloon sagging at the end. There was no rawinsonde anywhere along the cable, and he didn't see it lying on the ground. He looked into the trees, wondering if it had snagged on a branch when the balloon burst. When he didn't find it, he examined the cable closer, finding small notches where wire had apparently been cut. He began to suspect what had actually happened.

He climbed back into the car to get warm. "Got my cell phone?"

Emma dug in her pocket and handed him the phone, her frown mirroring his.

"Somebody broke Lexi's equipment, didn't they?"

"Looks that way. Hello, Sheriff Brown, this is Ryan Dinatelli. I'm at Larsen's Orchard and want to report some destruction of property."

"What was destroyed?" the sheriff asked but Ryan detected a note of boredom in his voice.

"The meter and box that Alexis Gray put out, along with a weather balloon. There's also theft because the rawinsonde is gone."

"The what?"

"Come out here alright? I'll show you."

"It might be awhile. I was going on my dinner hour."

Ryan didn't have any trouble guessing what side of the energy fence the sheriff was on, and he wasn't about to let him get by with anything. "That's fine, Sheriff. Since this is actually destruction of US government property, it's a federal issue anyway. I'll give the state police or the FBI a call instead."

"Diantelli, I've known your aunt all my life, and your uncle Paul too, when he worked in the mines. You don't want to cause this kind of trouble, son."

Ryan ground his teeth. "Sheriff, I'm not the one who caused the trouble. I'm the one who's going to put a stop to it if you don't." He hung up before the sheriff had a chance to spout more nonsense.

"It might be awhile," he told Emma. "Do you want me to take you back to Aunt Mary's?"

"Heck no. Are you really going to call the Feds?"

"You watch too much television."

"Man, I wish Charlie was here. Wait till I tell him what he missed."

Ryan glanced in his rear view mirror, actually surprised to see the sheriff's patrol car pull up behind him. When Emma grabbed the car handle, he caught her coat sleeve.

"You wait here, with the phone. You can call for back up if I get in trouble."

Her eyes grew round with wonder. "Are you serious?"

"Of course not. The sheriff and I are simply going to talk, but there may be words flying around that you don't need to hear. Besides, it's cold outside."

Her shoulders slumped. "It's not like I haven't heard those kinds of words before."

"Not from me, you haven't." Ryan stepped from the vehicle, wondering if he should be monitoring Emma's television viewing a little closer.

"Sheriff." He greeted the man with the respect due his position.

"Looks like an accident." Sheriff Brown had spent a whole thirty seconds surveying the scene. "Probably should have put a high wired fence around it."

"It had large signs stenciled on the top and side stating US government property. People don't go around smashing government property by accident." Ryan felt his anger growing at the man's ridiculous remark. He didn't bother explaining that a metal fence would have interfered with the radio waves.

"That may very well be, but this time of year there's too many outsiders in town."

Ryan snorted in disgust. "You're saying some tourist in town to see the snow festival came out here and smashed that box and the contents, pulled down and destroyed the weather balloon, and stole the radio transmitter?"

"All I'm saying is it will be hard to find any suspects."

Ryan threw his hands in the air. "Are you even going to look?"

Sheriff Brown narrowed his gaze. "Not if you keep up that attitude, I'm not." He stomped back to his vehicle, opened the door then leaned an arm across the door frame. "You want to file a report; you write it and bring it to the station. Then I'll see what I can discover, but since you don't own the equipment, I'm not legally bound to even take a report from you."

Ryan stood in the snow watching the sheriff drive off, sifting through the unspoken threats and innuendo. If he caused trouble over the broken equipment, the chasm between the miners and those in favor of alternative energy sources would grow wider, because he knew without a doubt that someone associated with Carston Mines had broken the equipment.

When he got back in the truck, Emma was on the phone. He held out his hand.

"Gotta go, Charlie. Yeah, you missed it but you should have seen my dad in action."

Ryan hung his head and closed his eyes. He felt the phone drop into his palm.

"Emma, in case you haven't already figured it out, news in this town spreads faster than a Texas wildfire. I do not want to find out that I beat up the sheriff."

"I didn't tell him that." She sounded offended. "Besides, you didn't even swear."

"And how would you know that? Did you roll down the windows?"

"You never swear, Dad. You hardly ever even get angry." Ryan wasn't sure if he heard pity or pride in her voice.

He punched in Alexis's number. "Hey, you're out of business. Someone smashed the box, the meter, and destroyed the weather balloon at the orchard."

"You're kidding. That's government property."

"Yeah, that's what I told the sheriff but he wasn't impressed."

"Did you find the rawinsonde?"

"Not the one here. The other five balloons are still floating, rawinsondes intact."

"I guess I can try to reprogram and access the rawinsondes directly to my computer instead of through the meter. I'll have to check with I-T and see if it can be done. Otherwise, there will be no readings."

"Ship another meter in an unmarked box. When it comes, you can talk me through programming it. This time I'll make sure it's safe." Ryan recalled the flat rooves on the buildings around the square. If he could lug the meter box to the roof, nobody would get to it; at least not without him hearing them from the apartment.

"You want to talk to Emma?" Even with the current problems, he didn't forget the costume issue.

Alexis chuckled. "You actually need me to do this? You're the dad."

"You promised. Talk to you tonight." He handed the phone to Emma and began the drive back to town, listening to his daughter chatter away.

Chapter Thirteen

Ryan signed for the UPS delivery and asked Matt, their regular driver, if there was any chance he would help Ryan carry the wooden box to the roof. Matt had laughed good naturedly and said only if that were the correct address and he had delivered it wrong, which of course he hadn't.

Now Ryan eyed the box, which they had shoved into a corner, and wondered how long he could wait before calling Aunt Mary to come to the bakery early. He was anxious to set the new meter box and call Alexis to program it.

Ryan realized it wasn't really about getting wind readings. It was more about the one-up-man-ship over whoever had smashed the first set of instruments. Whoever thought their handiwork would prevent progress in Snow had another think coming.

"I don't want you saying anything about the new equipment," he commented to Emma, who sat at the small table reading. He slid another cookie sheet into the oven. "The less said the better."

"Who am I going to tell?" she replied. "I hardly see anybody 'cept Charlie."

"Exactly."

"Charlie can keep a secret."

He raised a brow.

"Well, okay, just because he's the best PR man in getting out information on our project doesn't mean he can't keep quiet about other things." She studiously avoided his gaze, instead looking at the doodles she was making on her notebook paper.

"Is there something I need to know?" Emma was a good kid, and even if she wasn't hampered by her brace and crutches, he knew she would stay out of trouble.

Charlie on the other hand, was a boy and Ryan knew exactly how boys could be.

"Charlie has a huge imagination, that's all. Trust me; we're not doing anything wrong."

The timer went off and Ryan removed the cookie sheet from the oven, grabbed a spatula and scooted the cookies off and onto a cooling rack covered with a tee-towel.

"Well, nuts."

Emma came around the counter. "What happened?"

Ryan picked up a cookie crumble and handed it to her. She popped it into her mouth. "Wow, those are great."

He frowned at the pile of cookies that had all broken into small, thumb-sized pieces. "I tried a new recipe but they don't stick together. The first batch I let cool on the sheet and these I scooped off right away, but it doesn't make any difference." He gathered the corners of the towel. "I can't sell crumbs."

"Dad, wait." Emma reached for another piece. She chewed thoughtfully. "These really are good. Why don't you call them doodles and give them away?"

Emma reached under the counter and grabbed a plate. She held it and Ryan dumped the cookie bits onto it.

"I'll make a sign -- Free Doodles – and we'll put it beside the plate on the front counter."

"Now we're giving cookies away?"

"Dad, people will come in to try a free doodle and buy something else to take home. It's marketing."

"How do you know so much?"

"Because I'm a kid. They should be your primary target anyway because all kids like cookies and free stuff. Then they tell their parents, just like they did for Charlie's and my project."

"Do I need a Facebook page, too?" he teased.

She frowned. "I don't think Snow is ready for Facebook and My Space, although now that you mention it, maybe Charlie and I need to create a fan page for our project – you know, to tell other people so they can get their towns to conserve."

"I don't know much about those on-line places, but there are safeguards, aren't there? Against weirdoes?"

She laughed. "You're the only weirdo I know."

****

Ryan waited until after dark before lugging the meter box up the back fire escape to the roof. In a way it seemed ridiculous to engage in such subterfuge but he was taking no chances on anyone seeing him. Once he had the box positioned and the top of the crate opened, he called Alexis.

"Where did you place it?" she asked when he told her he was ready to program it.

"I can't tell you, in case my phone is tapped."

She laughed. "What is it with guys and spy games? I guess it doesn't matter, as long as we can receive the rawinsondes' transmissions. The balloons are still up, aren't they?"

"I did a quick loop around town earlier this afternoon and the five are still floating. I guess they figured without the meter box, they didn't have to worry about the rawinsondes."

She gave him the frequencies for each of the five remaining instruments, and he set each dial accordingly. The soft click-click of the meter was the only sound in the still night.

"It'll take a few minutes for my computer to pick up the signal," she said. "How are things going?"

Ryan tilted his head back and gazed around. "I think more people are using their fireplaces for heat because I can smell wood smoke up here. It reminds me of camp outs when I was a kid."

"Up here? You're in a tree somewhere?"

"No, but remind me to bring you here some night. There's no smog; no traffic noise. The sky is so clear you can see a trillion stars, and the rising moon casts a glow over the snow on the mountains."

"That sounds very romantic."

"I'm trying. We could huddle --" He was interrupted by a series of beeps from the box.

"What's happening?"

"My computer found the frequencies so you should have five green lights. You were saying?"

Ryan sighed. "Somehow it's not the same with Martian lights blinking at me. Besides, it's cold." Talking about what they would do only made it harder for him since she wasn't here. "It looks like you're all set."

"Ryan?"

He looked over the town, now seeing only the darkness and loneliness. "Hmm?"

"I'll be back in Snow before you know it." The soft spoken words were all he had for the moment.

* * * *

Corin was the last to arrive at the Holly Café. The bookstore had been extremely busy right at closing time, which suited her fine as sales had been slow all month. Everyone was feeling the economic crunch. If it weren't for the fact that her grandparents had owned the bookstore and the building and had given it to her when they retired to Arizona, she doubted she could make it. As it was, sales barely kept her and Charlie in the necessities.

She sighed as she opened the door to the sounds of laughter and the smells of spice and tamales. Friday was Mexican day at the Holly Café; one reason their group had decided to meet here instead of Butch's. When she had called Crissy about getting together, Crissy had said she would keep the café open after hours for the group, and that there would probably be enough food left in case anyone wanted dinner.

By the looks of it, everyone had wanted dinner. They had shoved three tables together that were loaded with chips and salsa and large drinks. She looked around to see if they needed a fourth table to make room for her.

"Hey, Corin, we thought you might not make it," called Janet, squished between Ryan and her husband, Steve.

"Does that mean there's no food left?" She glanced around the table, finally spying one last chair – next to

Mitch. She was mildly surprised to see him because he rarely interacted with people in town. She hesitated to sit beside him; not after their last fight where she had told him to get on with his life. In truth, it was none of her business but she simply hated to see him waste his talents.

Mitch pulled the coat from the back of the empty chair – his coat – and slid the chair out from the table. He didn't glance her way; didn't give any indication that he had actually saved the chair for her, but Corin's heart tripped a little anyway. They had so much history and some days she wondered if only…

Laughter erupted at the other end of the table, pulling Corin's thoughts away from what might have been. As she slid into the empty chair she looked around at the group; people who had been friends for as long as she could remember. It was yet another reason she loved living in Snow. Most people didn't move away and they carried on the traditions of their parents and sometimes, even their grandparents.

"Thanks," she said as Crissy put a plate of tamales, refried beans and a taco in front of her. Crissy was one such person. The Holly Café had been owned by her parents and now she ran it. She hadn't moved on, although her boyfriend had. Joe had left town the day of high school graduation, swearing his love for Crissy at the same time double swearing he would never work the mines like his father. Well, Corin guessed some people changed, but others didn't.

She dug into her meal, feeling a little guilty for having fixed Charlie a grilled cheese sandwich for dinner. As she ate she listened to several conversations going on at one time. Paige Michaels was talking about giving assessment tests in her elementary class before winter break; and Duane Potts was grudgingly admitting how great the food was at the Holly Café, even if it didn't quite reach the exalted levels of his bar-b-que. Duane was about the only older one in their crowd, but he was always fun. She didn't think of him being fifty.

146

"That's why it's never Bar-b-que night here. It's impossible to compete with you," Crissy said, sliding an extra chair to the table and plopping down. "Whew, what a day. It never stopped."

"That's good," Ryan commented and everyone agreed. Corin wasn't the only one feeling the money crunch and she wondered what would happen if things didn't work out for the holiday season.

"Did I miss the discussion on how to get our illustrious city council to leave the lights on all the time?" she asked around a bite of spicy tamale.

A collective groan echoed in the large room.

"We decided we weren't going to talk about that tonight," Toby Williams said, whose Dad had been on the City Council for probably a hundred years. Toby owned the Blitzen coffee shop and didn't always share his father's politics. Still Corin decided it was best not to discuss something that would make him take sides.

"I do want to say how well the kids' lights-out campaign is working," Paige said. "Emma and Charlie have decided we need another media blitz, so the class is designing posters in art." She looked over at Ryan. "Does she come up with these ideas on her own?"

"Afraid I can't take credit for any of it. Do you think I would have thought of doodles on my own?" Ryan smiled, referring to his daughter's latest idea.

"That was such a cute ad," Crissy said. "Free doodles at the Snickerdoodle. And I tried them – they're yummy. I'm thinking about copying the idea. You know, putting sprigs of holly on dinner plates. It's not like people eat the garnish when I use parsley anyway."

"Well, all I can say is this whole thing has totally taken over my class," Page commented. "We're tracking lights-out time for each student and they're actually trying to outdo each other. Emma emailed Ryan's friend, Alexis, and she's been sending us wind readings. She explained how to graph the results and said she'd even use our data at the next council meeting. The kids feel they're part of the town and are making a difference. And I'm getting math, science and language arts lesson plans without having to rack my brain."

"That's super. I know Charlie is enjoying it. He never was much for writing reports, but call it a newspaper article and he's all over it," Corin said. "Anything else exciting?" She looked from one face to the other.

"How are rehearsals going?" Janet asked.

Corin smiled. She loved working with the kids to create a Christmas pageant for the town. All ages participated and she had high school kids as well as elementary. That certainly helped when it came time to build the set and lift heavy props. The schools had long ago decided they wouldn't put on a winter program; they'd let her do it. Besides, the school had to be politically correct whereas Corin always had carols befitting the season, even if the theme was a fun one, like this year.

"Well, I don't want to give it all away, but I found this cute little play called The Toys' Christmas, where the toys in Santa's workshop come to life and sing. It has a lot of traditional carols and I think it'll be fun to have the audience participate." She turned to Mary Beth. "Will you play the piano for us again this year?"

Mary Beth beamed. "Of course I will. It wouldn't feel like Christmas if I wasn't involved in the pageant."

"Emma's sure excited about it," Ryan said. "Since she's not in the regular classroom, this is her chance to meet some of the other kids."

"How's she doing anyway?" Mary Beth asked.

Ryan nodded. "Good. Her last doctor's report showed the beginning of bone growth. I'm hoping soon she'll be able to go to school and climb stairs like a regular kid. She hates being on crutches."

Corin felt Mitch stiffen beside her and she forced herself not to look at him. She remembered those days when he first came home and before he got his prosthetic leg. He was so angry; even worse than now.

"There is one small problem with the stage at the Majestic," she piped up, changing the subject. "I'm hoping I can get the city to replace some of the boards. The other day when the bigger boys walked across it, I noticed some sag and heard a lot of squeaking."

"Good luck getting the city to do anything," Janet said. The others nodded their heads in agreement.

"It wouldn't take much…I don't think."

"You shouldn't be in that building anyway. It's old enough one of these days it's going to disintegrate." The low-pitched grumbling came from right next to her. Everyone stopped and stared at Mitch because until that moment, he'd be totally quiet.

"It's the only place we have for free," Corin answered, trying not to take his comment personally. "Besides, how long has it been since you were in it anyway?" So much for not being defensive.

"It used to be the movie theater when we were kids but I can remember my granddad reminiscing about going there to see the first talkie." Duane commented. "Mitch is right; it's really old, and since it's not being used, it's probably not been maintained."

Corin skewered him with a look. "You're not helping."

"It's all there is right now," Janet chimed in. "Corin and I are working on a grant to the state arts council to support a summer theatre program for the kids. Maybe we need to think about putting in some construction costs, too." Janet worked for an attorney in town; had kids Charlie's age and younger, and was as enthusiastic as Corin about the project. With her legal expertise, Corin hoped they had a good shot at getting a grant.

"In the meantime…?" Mitch groused.

What was with him anyway? Corin wondered. "In the meantime, we practice and give it our best shot. I don't want to even think about charging admission to help pay for repairs on a building we don't own. If it becomes a problem, I'll talk to Ron at the lumber yard and see if he has some scrap. Then I'll fix it myself."

"You don't need to be—"

"Wow, look at the time," Mary Beth interrupted Mitch, sliding her chair back to stand.

"Crissy, let us help with the dishes." Janet jumped up, too, stacking dishes to carry to the kitchen.

Corin glanced across the table at Ryan, who had a curious look. He had been gone; he didn't know about Mitch like the rest of them, and at the moment, Corin was too depressed to even think about explaining it.

* * * *

This time the trip to Pittsburgh sped by because of Emma's constant chatter – about everything from the festival to her homework to Alexis's arrival.

"You're glad she's coming to spend Christmas with us?" Ryan gave her a quick look.

"Oh, yes. You are, too, aren't you?"

"Definitely," he said with a grin.

Once they arrived at the doctor's office, Emma was put through the usual round of tests while Ryan waited impatiently. Finally Dr. Wesley came in, brandishing his laptop which he opened and studied.

"We don't do x-rays the traditional way anymore," he explained. "Everything's digital and immediately available." He tapped a key.

"Hmmm," he said; tapped another key and hummed again.

Ryan started to ask him what that meant, when he rolled on his stool over to the counter and pressed the intercom. "Pat, do we have a C-505 brace, left leg?"

Ryan watched Emma's face fall, her bottom lip trembling before she caught it between her teeth. He moved to stand closer.

Nurse Pat came in carrying a brace about half the size of the one Emma currently wore, and if Ryan wasn't mistaken, it was hinged at the knee, which would allow her more freedom of movement. He held his breath, not daring to hope or say anything before the doctor.

"Your bone density has improved greatly since your last visit, and everything I see indicates that you are finally healing. Your leg is five centimeters longer than the first

150

time I saw you. That might not seem like a lot, but in terms of recovery, it's a tremendous spurt.

"I believe you're ready for a little action, young lady." He held up the brace. "This brace is lighter weight, shorter and bends at the knee." He demonstrated and Ryan watched Emma's eyes open wide.

"I'll send the crutches home with you, but I want you to try and walk without them."

"No crutches?" Emma's voice was a soft whisper as though she feared he was teasing.

He shook his head. "If you get tired, or if your leg starts to hurt, you need to use the crutches. But for every minute you can walk without them, you'll be strengthening your leg and soon you probably won't even need the brace."

As he spoke, he opened a drawer and withdrew a screwdriver which he used on the old brace to remove it from her shoe. He slid the bottom el of the new brace through the sole and screwed it together on the other side.

He helped Emma put her shoe on, then adjusted the length so the hinge was at her knee. Instead of running almost to her hip bone, this brace stopped just above the knee; the curvature padded to fit next to Emma's thigh without rubbing. She was all smiles as she buckled it in place and Doctor Wesley helped her down from the exam table.

But when she tried to walk with him supporting her upper arm, her leg wouldn't bend.

"It won't work," she pouted.

"Your muscles have simply forgotten their job, that's all," the doctor said. "It will probably take a while, and you'll have to remind them sometimes, but soon it'll be like you never forgot."

Emma furrowed her brow in concentration and slowly bent her leg, taking a jerky step forward, then another.

The doctor cautioned her. "No running; only walking; and stairs only when necessary. Step up with your right leg; bring your other leg up to that step, then do it again. It'll take longer, but that way you're not putting extra pressure on your left leg as you push yourself up."

Emma smiled at Ryan. "I can go to school like the other kids."

Ryan felt as he had the day Emma was born – proud and so immediately in love to the point of bursting.

He held his hand out to Doctor Wesley. "I don't know how to thank you."

The man shook his head. "Modern medicine can't do what the human body can; if we simply let it. Emma's got a strong will and determination, and that sometimes makes all the difference." He looked over at Emma. "Remember, you decide how much you can do; but don't overdo it. And I want to see you again in three months."

Ryan held the crutches out but she refused to take them. "You heard him. I have to practice." She took another step or two and tottered. Ryan cautiously put out his hand, not sure how much he should offer to do. "Just until I get my balance," she said as she grabbed hold.

He smiled and winked at the doctor. "Of course."

Emma insisted on riding in front now that she could bend her knee. Ryan carefully lifted her to the front seat and she buckled herself in.

"I'll ride in the back after we pick up Lexi," she promised as they left the doctor's office and headed for the airport. "She'll want to ride in front with you." She gave him a grin and Ryan wondered what her devious ten-year-old mind was thinking.

* * * *

Emma scooted out of the car when he opened the door, and hesitantly took a few steps forward. "Look, Lexi. No crutches." The minute she was within reach, Emma wrapped her arms around Alexis's waist and hugged her close.

"Look at you," Alexis said, but she was gazing at Ryan over Emma's head, tears in her eyes. She handed him her portfolio as Emma continued to hang on her arm.

152

"Looks like you did your homework," Ryan said as he loaded her bags and they all piled in the car, Emma in the back seat this time.

"When you start talking lots of numbers, it's easier for people to understand a graph." She turned and put her arm across the back of the seat. "Now tell me what's happened in Snow since Thanksgiving."

* * * *

Aunt Mary had invited them for dinner and as usual, she had outdone herself, fixing a delicious pot roast with carrots and potatoes, gravy and her famous glorified rice salad.

"And there's apple pie for dessert," she said as she got up from the table to clear away the dishes.

"I'll do that." Ryan hurried around the table to take the dishes from her.

"I'll help," Alexis added.

"Oh, my goodness, no. You're company," Aunt Mary protested.

Alexis laughed. "I was company when I came for Thanksgiving, Mrs. Decker. You told me the second time I was to help myself."

Mary sat back in her chair. "Well, if that's the case, you surely can't continue to call me Mrs. Decker."

"You ladies sit and visit. Emma and I can handle this." He looked at his daughter, who was texting one of her friends. "Emma?"

"Dad, aren't I one of the ladies?"

"Not quite yet, you're not. Come on." Ryan took the stack of plates to the kitchen. He listened to his aunt and Alexis talk as he loaded dishes into the dishwasher. He loved the women in his life. Emma, of course, was his heart and soul. Aunt Mary had given him affection and showed him love was everywhere. He had given her plenty of worries when he first came to live with her and Uncle Paul. He had been angry and frightened and felt like his parents deserted him by dying but she hadn't given up on him.

153

He kissed the top of Emma's head as she hobbled over to the sink and handed him a single glass.

"My leg's getting tired," she groused and Ryan caved, like he usually did.

"Okay, go sit with the ladies, but mind your manners and stay off the phone."

She wrinkled her nose and left him the chore of cleaning up. She was a good kid and she helped as much as she was able. He had recently said her main job was to keep her school work completed and he'd worry about the rest. He knew she wanted to do more of the things other kids did, and he hoped she remembered saying that now that she no longer needed her crutches.

As he transferred the remainder of the roast to a storage container, he heard laughter from the other room. And then there was Alexis, he thought, adding her to his list of special females. Though sexy and as glamorous as any Hollywood model, there was nothing artificial about her. She was open and honest and grabbed life with both hands if she wasn't racing far ahead of it.

She had been the one who dragged Ryan from his self imposed solitude and self-incriminations and made him see he wasn't doing Emma any good if he was constantly beating up on himself. Their friendship had developed easily as she worked with NASA on a special energy project. Ryan didn't recall exactly when he had started thinking of Alexis as more than a friend. She probably knew the exact minute it had happened -- women had an uncanny ability to recall every little date and detail. He doubted she would rub his nose in the fact, but he knew better than to admit not remembering.

He hadn't realized how much he would miss her until he moved. As two highly skilled professionals dedicated to their work, he wasn't sure what the distance would do to their budding relationship.

"Dad." He heard Emma before she came rushing into the kitchen followed closely by Alexis and Aunt Mary. "Lexi has never had snow cream."

Chapter Fourteen

"I mentioned that I forgot to pick up ice cream for the apple pie," his aunt said.

"And I told her we could make snow cream but Lexi doesn't know what it is. Aunt Mary, we need a huge bowl and mixing spoon, and..." She kept rattling off items and Ryan looked over his daughter's head at Alexis's bemused expression.

He wondered if she had any idea what she was getting into by being involved with him. Emma was a good kid, but she did tend to get over zealous at times. He watched them pulling on coats and hats and realized they seemed to balance each other.

"How do you know about snow cream?" he asked his daughter.

"From Charlie, of course." She tugged her knit hat over her hair.

Charlie, of course. Why didn't that surprise him?

"I'll get the snow," he said, wiping his hands on a dish towel.

"No." Emma's reply was immediate. "Lexi has to do it herself. That's part of the initiation."

Ryan raised a brow at Alexis.

"I like initiations." She shrugged. "I think."

"At least you have fresh snow to scoop," he said handing over Mary's largest metal bowl and a couple of ladle-type cooking spoons. It had been snowing since noon and predictions were for more than four inches by morning. Of course, in Snow, the weather forecast was almost always met with cheers.

"Emma, hang on a second." He grabbed his coat from the wall peg by the back porch and shrugged into it. "Let me make sure the steps and walk are clear. I don't want you falling on your fanny."

"You know I won't fall; I'm used to it. But Lexi doesn't even have any boots."

Ryan looked at Alexis's slip-on flats. "Well, we'll definitely have to remedy that first thing tomorrow." Together they moved across the back porch, Ryan a step or two ahead to clear a path, being careful to shovel the snow only to one side so the other was clean enough to use for Emma's snow cream.

The evening air was cold and crisp, but they were protected from the wind by the house. Here, the snow fell in wet, fat flakes, quickly coating their shoulders in white. He chuckled at the girls, each trying to scoop snow into the bowl without stepping off the one shovel width clearing he had given them.

"We have to get lots because when we add the cream it all mushes down to nothing." Emma fired off instructions like a drill sergeant. "Over there – not too close to the house and make sure there's no…bird poop or anything on it."

Alexis leaned over a little too far and Ryan grabbed the back of her coat but not before she had taken a quick step forward to keep from falling.

"Augh! That's cold." She shook her foot, laughing. She handed Ryan the bowl then put one hand on his shoulder for balance as she slipped off her shoe and shook out the snow.

"Boots are definitely on the shopping list for tomorrow."

"Actually I do have boots," she replied, "but they're…"

"Let me guess – soft Italian leather with four inch heels."

"It's not like I spend a lot of time in hip deep snow."

"Those aren't boots; they're a fashion statement." He shook his head. "Besides, remember your last visit to town? A lot of the residents – ones who've been here forever and have strong ties to the coal mine – already see you as an outsider. It would be better if you dress like a local."

"Please tell me I don't have to wear one of those hats with ear flaps."

"Shame on you. That is so stereotyping." He turned to his daughter. "Emma, I think we have enough snow. Go in and make sure you have the cream and other ingredients on the counter. You know how fast this will melt. We'll be there in a minute."

After his daughter went into the house, Ryan set the bowl on the cold sidewalk and slid his arms around Alexis's waist, bringing her close. "I've missed you."

She looked at him, snowflakes landing on her eyelashes. "How much?"

In answer, he dipped his head, kissing one cold cheek then the other before settling on her mouth, which warmed quickly beneath his. It was a kiss of welcome, though Ryan realized he would like it to be more. All too soon their interlude was interrupted.

"Dad, are you two coming?"

Ryan sighed and Alexis giggled.

"Are you ready for this? Snow cream doesn't taste like real ice cream. It's simply something every kid who lives where it snows has to experience once in a lifetime." He picked up the bowl and led the way into the house.

The snow cream never did make it as topping on Aunt Mary's apple pie. With Emma giving Alexis instructions on adding just a few drops of vanilla and just a little bit of cream and Ryan sticking his finger in the bowl to taste test, they were all laughing hard enough that the snow almost melted. Emma wanted to put it in the freezer to see if it would harden, but instead they all got spoons and ate it right out of the bowl.

"This is very good." Alexis fought Ryan for the last spoonful. "Kind of a cross between a milkshake and a slurpy." She gave a little shiver and Ryan rubbed a hand across her back.

"Cold?"

"Eating snow cream after being out in the snow? Now why do you think that would make me cold?" she teased.

"You are such a warm weather woman. I don't see how you can even stand it in DC."

She wiggled her eyebrows. "I do a lot of field work and try to schedule my time there in the other three seasons."

"I didn't think I would like the snow, but I do. Especially when Charlie lets me ride in his sleigh with blankets on top," Emma said.

"Now that sounds like the way to get around town." Alexis nodded her head in agreement.

Emma giggled. "It's not like a real sleigh. He simply put his wagon onto an old toboggan and has his dog pull it. He said he asked Santa for a real sleigh, but..." She shrugged. "Like that's going to happen."

Ryan hadn't thought much about his little girl no longer believing in Santa. With all that had happened in the past couple of years, he honestly couldn't even remember if he had bought her a Santa present last year. This year would be different. It wasn't right that she didn't believe in the magic of the season or the wonders that were all around them.

"Now that you children are done making a mess in my kitchen," Aunt Mary peeked through the doorway, "are you ready for apple pie and coffee?"

Ryan put the bowl and spoons in the sink and joined them in the dining room for dessert. It wasn't until they were ready to leave that Mary protested. "Why should Alexis stay at the Poinsettia Bed & Breakfast when I have all this room right here?"

"I can't impose on you, Mary," Alexis said. "I have no idea how long I will have to stay this time."

"It's no imposition, dear."

Ryan gave his aunt a kiss on her weatherworn cheek. "Impartiality, Aunt Mary. Alexis is here to give results on the wind tests and explain whether it's feasible to build wind turbines for alternative energy. If she stays with you, everyone in town will think she's on the same side you are." He grinned at her. "And regardless of having been

158

married to a coal miner, we all know what side that would be, don't we?"

"It's no different than you driving her around town, dear boy," his aunt replied, but he caught a twinkle in her eyes. "I suppose it's alright for you to keep an eye on her."

"Good night, Aunt Mary." Ryan gave her another kiss and followed the girls to the car. His aunt was quite observant but he didn't mind at all if she thought he and Alexis were more than friends.

Emma fell asleep on the short drive across town, so Ryan left the car running as he walked Alexis to the front door of the B&B.

"It's good to have you here again," he whispered, wrapping his arms around her waist.

"I only hope I can live up to Emma's expectations. Do you know she asked me to go to school and talk to her class?"

Ryan laughed. "Sometimes she has so much energy, it's scary." He kissed her, a kiss of welcome and maybe something more. She returned the kiss with fervor.

"Wow, you've already met my expectations." He put his cheek next to hers. "Met and exceeded."

Alexis laughed; gave him another quick peck on the cheek and stepped back. "You'd better get Emma home to bed. I have a feeling we're all going to be very busy from now on."

* * * *

"Dad, I wanted room for furniture." Emma stood with her arms outstretched as Ryan slid the cardboard box frame up her arms. "This is just a box; it's not a doll house."

Personally, Ryan thought the costume for the Christmas pageant was quite good. It had taken a lot of hunting to find a box just a little wider than Emma's shoulders so her arms stuck through the sides without the cardboard cutting her. He had turned the box upside-down and cut arm holes and a head hole.

159

To make it easier to put on, he had slit open the back so the whole thing would wrap around her body with its four sides. It would only cover her from shoulder to hip, leaving her legs totally free at the bottom. She walked great without crutches now, but Ryan didn't want her legs tangled in a costume.

He had used the box flaps to fashion the roof, which would Velcro to the top of the house at both shoulders, peaking over her head. The front showed two floors of windows, a door and some shrubs along the front. He had even drawn curtains in the windows. All he had to do was paint it.

"Emma, if it's open on the front like a doll house, your belly will show." Designing efficient crew quarters and storage space on the space shuttle had required less work.

"I'll be a teddy bear and wear my feety pajamas instead. Then I can somersault."

She jerked her arms out of the holes, letting the box drop to the floor, then turned and walked away.

"You're not ready to somersault, young lady," he hollered after her as the bedroom door slammed.

"Hi. Bad time?" Alexis had knocked as she opened the door of the apartment. Ryan waved her in and she dragged off her fur hat and stomped her feet on the mat, closing the door behind her.

"I'm glad you're here." Ryan grabbed her hand, tugging her around the end of the couch.

"Ah, no."

He tried to look hurt. "You don't even know what I need."

"You were yelling and I believe that was Emma's door I heard. Besides the fact that I have a PhD and am fairly intelligent, I was also a ten year old girl...a very long time ago."

"But that's it, don't you see? You understand her; you can reason with her; make her see how hard..." Ryan's defense trailed to a stop as Alexis looped her arms around his neck and tugged him close for a kiss. He quickly forgot his daughter's tirade.

All too soon Alexis ended the kiss, tilting her head back, her green eyes twinkling with pleasure and mischief. "Didn't you ever learn the art of compromise?"

"I have that down to a science," he grinned then nipped her chin, "but what I have in mind for you certainly wouldn't work for a ten year old."

She laughed, letting him go. She picked up the box, not quite hiding her grimace. "I think in this case the compromise should be 'okay, Emma, whatever you want.'"

"That's not a compromise; that's caving."

"The definition of compromise is win-win, right?" At his nod, she continued. "If you do it Emma's way, she's happy, and you will be happy because she's happy."

"That's a lot of happies."

"'Tis the season," she responded flippantly as she walked to the kitchen for coffee.

****

"I so love having you here." Emma fairly bounced in her seat as Alexis put Ryan's SUV in gear and slowly drove down the alley before crossing Avenue A toward the highway.

"You know I can't interfere with you and your dad."

"I know, but convincing him to redesign the doll house costume makes me happy. And Dad is happy because you're here. So if you're happy, too…" she let the sentence trail off.

Alexis gave her a quick look. "You little sneak. You were listening."

Emma laughed, brushed her bangs from her eyes, then launched into Jingle Bells and Alexis sang with her. It was good to be back in Snow with Ryan and Emma. She and Ryan hadn't talked about the future, but she had some ideas. It wasn't the kind of present she could wrap and put under the tree, but she thought he'd like what she had in mind.

She and Emma drove to Seaton, singing Christmas songs along with the radio. Alexis had called This Little House and the owner, Charlotte Webb, had assured her they were open and had what they needed. Ryan had grinned when he tossed the car keys to her. Alexis thought he was probably afraid of another argument with Emma. He was a pushover where his daughter was concerned and while Emma was a good kid, she was also a normal ten year old, and used her wiles on her dad whenever possible.

"Are they going to build the wind turbines?" Emma asked a few minutes later.

"Well, all the results are good. There's enough consistent wind, but the city will have to decide if that's what they want. Even so, they'll have to vote on a bond issue to pay for it. If it passes, they build. If it doesn't, then the town will continue to depend on the coal mining."

"And the mine will still need people to work in it."

"That's right. Every business and industry needs workers."

"But why wouldn't they want to build a wind farm? I thought you said there was money from the government to help."

"There is, but it's like if you help pay for an IPod, you're more likely to take care of it and use it responsibly. If a city has to put some of its own money into the project, it's more likely to handle all the funds responsibly."

Alexis pulled into the parking lot at a small strip mall where the hobby center was located. When she and Emma got out of the car, Emma came around and tucked her hand into Alexis's.

"When school starts back after Christmas, I'm going to ask Miss Michaels if I can write another essay. This time to see if we can get people interested in the bond issue. I don't want to think that Charlie will have to work in a dark coal mine when he grows up."

Alexis squeezed her hand. "Charlie is very lucky to have a friend like you."

She and Emma had fun picking out miniature furniture to glue into her doll house, and she didn't have any problem keeping Emma from wanting to buy too much. Since the audience wouldn't be able to see it up close, they picked bright couches and beds that had colorful quilts, choosing larger pieces that would show from a distance.

Alexis watched Emma brush hair out of her eyes as she studied the assortment of furniture at the checkout counter.

"As long as we're having a girl's day, I have an idea," she said, turning to the cashier. "Is there a salon in the area that takes walk-ins?"

* * * *

"Dad, look." Emma hop-skipped across the apartment, dropping mittens, coat and scarf in her rush to get to her dad. Alexis followed more slowly, bringing in the bags and closing the door.

"Emma, pick up your things," Ryan gently reprimanded, but Alexis shook her head at him, knowing how Emma felt. After an afternoon getting haircuts, manicures and pedicures, she felt pretty excited herself.

Emma held her hands up in front of his face.

Ryan frowned. "You have ten fingers. I think that's the same number you left with, isn't it?"

Emma gave a long suffering sigh. Ryan threw Alexis a questioning look. She flicked her fingers, silently mouthing polish.

"Oh, polish. Very nice."

Alexis chuckled as she dipped a spoon to taste the spaghetti sauce Ryan had simmering on the stove. Guys just didn't get it. She waved her hand under his nose.

"You, too? What's the occasion?"

"Lexi said girls don't have to have a special reason to have a manicure and pedicure. It's simply to make us feel good."

"Pedicure too? You ladies are going to break me," he groused but he was smiling as he took out his wallet.

Lexi waved it aside. "It was my treat. I hope you don't mind, though, because I also had Emma's hair trimmed. Emma, show your dad."

Emma pulled off her stocking cap, the static electricity causing her new shorter bob to fly. Alexis reached over and smoothed it down. The style, just below her ears with raggedy bangs, made Emma look like the pixie she was.

"I like it and at least it doesn't match your pink nails," her dad teased.

Emma was already heading to her room. "Lexi says I can't dye my hair until I'm in high school. I wanted to change it to black, but I guess blonde is okay for now." Her voice faded.

"Black?" Ryan chocked.

"You might as well get used to it. Girls like to do things like color their hair and paint their toes."

He leaned forward to give her a kiss. "Thank you. I don't think about haircuts and stuff like that, but I know she has all her shots."

After dinner, Ryan showed Emma how he had altered the doll house costume. The front now had narrow cardboard floors splitting it into two levels with additional dividers for the rooms. Emma decided where the furniture would go and they glued each piece into place. By the time she went to bed, the costume was complete. Ryan was happy to have it done and Emma was ecstatic that it actually did look like a miniature doll house.

Alexis was probably the only one who worried, but not because of the costume. She crawled into bed that night knowing she had to find a way to keep from leaving Ryan and Emma when the holiday season was over. She hoped the plan forming in her mind was a way to have the best of both worlds, because as each day passed in Snow, she fell deeper in love with both Ryan and his daughter.

Chapter Fifteen

"Boo," Emma called as she slipped through the back door of the bakery. Her dad didn't even look up from where he was scooping cake batter into six round baking pans.

"It's hard to sneak up on someone when you stomp down the stairs from the apartment," he commented as he slid the cakes into the oven. He finally looked at her. "Don't you ever sit still anymore?"

164

Emma grinned. It felt so good to have the lighter brace on her leg and to be able to bend her knee that she didn't want to sit still. "I wasn't stomping." She recalled the doctor's warning about jumping around. But walking was different, and she wanted to do as much of it as possible.

"What's that?" Dad nodded to the notebook she had carried with her and now dumped on the small table in the front corner. "Homework?"

"Geez, no. Nobody gives homework the week before Christmas. Hey, am I going to school after the holidays?"

"Of course you are. You're only in fifth grade; you can't drop out yet."

He had been in a good mood for over a week, and Emma knew it was because Lexi was here. She had been thinking a lot about her dad lately, and knew he needed someone to keep him company. Someone different than her that is. She liked Lexi and hoped she would stay longer than the holiday.

"I mean really going to school."

He came over to where she stood. "I know what you mean, and yes, I think by the time the holidays are over, you'll be ready for that. But you'll have to make sure you don't—"

"I know. Don't jump; don't kick a soccer ball with my left foot; don't, don't, don't." A sigh escaped.

"Hey, you're getting better. That's what's important." They turned toward the door as the bell at the top jingled.

"Hi, Lexi." Emma had a plan. She had called Lexi from upstairs and asked her to go shopping.

"Good morning," Ryan said, leaning over and giving her a kiss on the cheek.

"Mmm, it always smells heavenly in here."

"Dad's a great cook." Emma smiled.

"I may be a good baker, but cooking is a whole different matter." Her dad reached around the counter and grabbed a sugar cookie, offering it to Lexi.

Lexi shook her head but laughed. "If I stick around here, I'll soon weigh two hundred pounds."

165

Emma frowned at the two adults. She was trying to help, and these two just weren't cooperating. She tugged her rubber boots on over her shoes. They were the latest style in bright splashes of colors, and her dad had bought a size larger than she needed so she could still wear the dumb brace that hooked under her clodhopper shoe. She couldn't wait to get it off and wear flip-flops – the kind with bright flowers on top of the toe pieces. In fact, she decided she would wear flip-flops all year round, even in the snow.

"Why the frown?" her dad asked.

"Huh, oh, nothing. Thinking about my shopping list." She quickly grabbed her coat.

"Ready to go, Lexi?" She tugged on her hat.

"You're going to leave me here while you go shopping?" He frowned but she knew he was teasing. His eyes still twinkled at Lexi.

"Emma insists on showing me the wonderland of shopping pleasures here in Snow." Lexi smiled.

"Do you need some money, squirt?"

"No, Mr. Nicholas has been paying Charlie and me to help at the store. Besides, I can't buy you a Christmas present with your own money."

"You have enough to buy me a new pickup truck?" He arched his brows and looked at her in surprise.

"As if."

He laughed and tugged her hat over her eyes. She reached a mittened hand to push it back and saw her dad sneaking a kiss with Lexi, right on the lips. She pretended not to notice, but grinned as she and Lexi exited the bakery. It was Wednesday and there weren't a lot of tourists in town, but Dad had said this weekend would be super busy since it was the last weekend before Christmas.

The sun was shining and the square looked pretty with garland wrapped around light poles, all the windows decorated, and snow sculptures everywhere. It was time to launch her plan.

"Snow looks pretty, doesn't it? Everybody decorates, you know."

166

"It does look very nice. Are you cold?" Lexi tugged her coat collar around her neck.

"No. It doesn't feel cold here with the sun shining." She had to remember her plan and that meant making Lexi fall in love with Snow…and her dad.

"Well, I don't know about that. The snow's not melting so it can't be real warm."

"Dad says once it starts snowing here the temperature stays…"

"Constant?" Lexi supplied.

"Yeah. Anyway, you get used to it real fast." She tucked her hand in Lexi's. "Here's the Wonderland Book Store. Corin owns that; you know, Charlie's mom." They came to the corner. "Over there is the Holly Café, right before the Poinsettia Bed & Breakfast where you're staying. Crissy owns both of them. Did you know her name is actually Christmas Carroll because she was born on Christmas?"

Lexi gave her a smile. "Hmm. Fascinating."

They carefully crossed the street and then turned to cross Lincoln Street and walked along the west side of the square, Emma pointing to each of the stores and said who owned them and if they had kids she knew.

"Why, I think you could work for the Snow Chamber of Commerce," Lexi said.

"We have to stop here. I know what I want to get Dad." Emma pulled open the door to Season's Greetings.

"Oh, smell, Lexi. It smells like Christmas." Warm fragrant air rushed around them as they entered the card and gift store. It was a different smell from the bakery, like pine trees and spices all mixed together. "I miss having a Christmas tree but Dad says there's no room. 'Sides, we put one up at Aunt Mary's and Dad says we'll spend Christmas Eve there."

"That sounds like a very nice plan."

"Well, hello there, Emma," Mrs. Oakes greeted them.

"Hi. This is my friend, Alexis Gray."

"Oh, we all know Miss Gray." Mrs. Oakes shook her hand. "We're one hundred percent behind building wind turbines; that we are. You can't stop progress."

Emma hadn't thought about all the grown up stuff going on in town when she had invited Lexi shopping. While she and Mrs. Oakes visited, Emma wandered over to look at the pens. She had spied the display weeks ago and had decided it was something her dad would like. Each one was handmade out of pretty pieces of wood. She couldn't decide between one made from Blue Box Elder and a dark brown one made out of Blackwood. She liked the pink ivory, too, but didn't think her dad was the pink type.

"Find something you like?" Lexi peeked over her shoulder.

Emma nodded. "I'm going to get Dad a pen. They're handmade; aren't they pretty?"

"Very."

Mrs. Oakes stood behind the counter. "You've been keeping your eye on those for a while now. Mr. Norris makes these at the Flying Hammer Woodshop. If you don't see one you like, he can probably make one special for you."

Emma looked sideways at Lexi. "Do you think he'd like the dark one or the blue one?"

"I think he'll love whichever one you pick, simply because it's from you."

"Yeah, you're right. I drew him a picture when I was three. I told him it was a cat, but it was pretty bad –just all these squiggles of color. He kept it on the refrigerator until I was eight." She made a face.

Lexi laughed. "Parents can be like that sometimes."

Emma decided on the Blackwood pen, and while Mrs. Oakes wrapped it in special Christmas paper, they wandered around the store, looking at cards and posters, ornaments and candles. Lexi bought some post cards – all with snow on them, of course. Emma got a small box of Christmas cards to send to her friends back in Houston.

"Oh, my, aren't these pretty?" Lexi touched a soft blue and green wool scarf with fringe on the ends. There were others on the table in a rainbow of colors; some square and some long rectangles, but all with fringe.

"You should get that one," Emma said. "It has green in it like the color of your eyes."

Lexi caressed the soft fabric. "You know you aren't supposed to buy anything for yourself when it gets close to Christmas. Otherwise, what will Santa bring you?"

Mrs. Oakes joined them. "The Woodley sisters make those, along with knitted mittens and long wrap-around scarves." She pointed to a rack with sets of matching mittens, caps and scarves.

Emma thought they looked familiar. "I remember seeing Miss Vera wearing a scarf on her shoulders when we were over there."

"I can't remember which one uses the loom and which one knits, but they keep us supplied in the winter. They love making things, and it gives them some income."

"You have a lot of cottage industries here in town, don't you?"

Mrs. Oakes nodded at Lexi's question. "We're not a Mecca for artists like some of your east coast towns, but we have our share of very artistic people. The small specialty shops are the reasons people like visiting Snow, rather than going to a big mall somewhere."

Lexi looked longingly at the table of scarves. "Well, you certainly have some very beautiful things. Are you ready to go, Emma?"

Emma nodded, thinking she would have to come back to Season's Greetings later to finish her Christmas shopping.

"Would you like a cup of hot chocolate?" Lexi asked as they stood on the sidewalk.

Emma nodded.

"Walk around or cut through the park?"

"I can walk okay now that I can bend my knee," Emma said, but her leg was a little achy. "But we can cut across the square and you can see all the snow sculptures."

"What's this?" Lexi pointed to one of the larger sculptures off to the right of the path they walked.

"Dad says every year one of the groups in town makes that to remind people of when the snow festival first started, a long time ago." They stopped before the frozen scene, which depicted a large table on which were lumps and shapes painted different colors. "I had read the story but Miss Vera and Miss Violet told it to Charlie and me again when we visited. They were kids back then; when the coal mine was shut down and the kids didn't even have any food. They still wanted the snow festival, so they made a table out of snow and put stuff on it – empty cans and stuff – to make it look like a huge table of food. Then Christmas Eve, when everybody was at church, someone came and put tons of real food on the table, enough for the whole town, and new coats on the snow people statues."

"Wow, that's quite a story. Do you think Santa did that?" They moved past more sculptures of snow people.

"I don't believe in Santa. I used to write him letters every year and all I wanted was for him to make my mom well and for my dad to be happy." Emma shrugged. "He brought me dolls instead."

Lexi put an arm around her shoulders and pulled her close. "Maybe things don't always work out exactly like we want, but that doesn't mean someone's not looking out for us."

Emma thought about how unhappy her dad had been when she had been sick and in the hospital so much. Now that she was getting better, and with Lexi here, her dad was much happier.

She looked at Lexi and grinned. "Maybe you're right."

Once they were settled in a booth at Blitzen's Coffee and Tea shop, Emma started back on her campaign.

"Isn't this great? Did you notice how most of the store names are like the holiday? There's Snowflake Glass and The Sleigh Antique store." She frowned, trying to think of more. "Oh, and the newspaper is called the Evergreen Gazette, but the flower shop is also called Evergreen's Greenhouse. I guess they must have run out of names. And it doesn't always snow here, even if that is the name. When we got here in October the trees were all pretty colors and it

170

was warm…well, sort of warm." She took a sip of hot chocolate. "And there's stuff to do here, too. Do you like to fish?"

"Well, I've never done it. I might like it."

"There's a lake here and they have a fishing tournament in the summer. You don't have to fish if you don't want. We can go swimming and have a picnic."

"Snow is certainly a wonderful place for children to grow up."

"Oh, it's not just for kids. There's adult stuff, too."

Lexi reached across the table and put her warm hand on Emma's. "What's this really all about?"

Emma looked at her hot chocolate. "I only thought…maybe you might like to live here."

"I have a home and a job in Houston, honey."

"I know, but Dad still does his job from here." Emma frowned. "Dad likes it when you're here. He smiles and goes around whistling." She looked across the table, pleading. "Won't you stay with us, please?"

Emma hadn't meant to blurt it out, and from the look on Lexi's face, she had caught her by surprise.

"Oh, my. I don't know quite what to say."

"Say you'll stay. Please?"

"Honey, that's not something you and I can decide."

"But I love you."

Lexi squeezed her hand. "And I love you, too."

"You and Dad can get married. Do you love him?"

Lexi smiled. "There are all kinds of love in the world, and when two people get married it's because they love each other very much."

Emma tried to interrupt but Lexi shook her head. "Loving someone enough to get married doesn't happen overnight and sometimes there are other things to figure out."

Emma scrunched down in her seat. "You don't love him."

Lexi gave a gentle laugh. "I didn't say that, but this is something between your father and me." She patted

Emma's hand. "Now, are you ready to show me the rest of your beautiful town?"

Emma took heart that at least Lexi hadn't said no. She realized that there was something she wanted for Christmas more than flip-flops.

* * * *

Charlie and Emma were once again at Mr. Nicholas's toy store, this time to decorate the store front. It had a deep display area and Charlie had climbed right in while she stood on the store floor by the edge of it and handed him ornaments for the small tree near the front of the window.

"None of the other kids know we're helping Mr. Nicholas," he said. "It's our secret."

"It can't be much of a secret if people come into the toy store to shop," she replied.

"Yes, but we're the only ones working here. And we're the only ones who know Mr. Nicholas' secret."

Emma shook her head. If Mr. Nicholas was Santa, why would he be in Snow, instead of at the North Pole?

"Mr. Nicholas," Charlie called, "we need more tinsel for around the edge, and more ornaments for the tree."

Near the back of the shop, Mr. Nicholas absent-mindedly glanced at them from a toy he was making. "Oh, my. More?" He looked over the top of his glasses and smiled. "That looks very nice. I should hire you two full time."

"Then we'd have to move to the North Pole," Charlie said.

"Charlie," Emma hissed, but Mr. Nicholas laughed.

"I think you may already live there, from the looks of the snow outside."

It had snowed again last night and Emma's dad almost hadn't let her come with Charlie. They had only talked him into it because it was right around the corner from the bakery. Having lived in Texas all her life, she had never seen so much snow except on TV. If it weren't for the festive snow sculptures scattered all over town, she thought

172

she might get very tired of snow. Instead, today she had seen a puppy that looked so real, she thought it would start barking any second as Wolf walked by. All the creations made her smile.

"I'll have to see if I have more decorations for you. There may be some upstairs."

"There's an upstairs here?" Charlie scooted across the window ledge and hopped to the floor. "I'll go."

"No, no." Mr. Nicholas jumped from his stool faster than Emma would have thought possible. "Have you decided what toys to put under the tree you're decorating in such grand style?"

Emma watched Mr. Nicholas closely. He seemed relieved that Charlie was easily distracted by his comment and had stopped in his tracks to look around at the shelves and display areas.

"We'll do that now," he said.

"Good, good," Mr. Nicholas murmured as he went through the back door of the shop and disappeared from view.

"Charlie, not so many boy toys." She turned her attention to her friend, who had his arms full of GI Joe's and trucks. She gathered some dolls and games from the shelves. "We need some of these. Help me."

"Sh. Do you hear that?" Charlie stopped in the middle of an aisle, his head cocked to the side. He dropped the toys he held and raced to the back where he turned down the Christmas music that had been playing rather loudly on an old fashioned radio.

Emma held her breath to listen. Above their heads, she heard scurrying, back and forth across the ceiling. She hunched her head into her shoulders, hoping it wasn't mice. "What is it?" Her voice was a faint whisper.

"It sounds like feet – lots of them – running back and forth." Charlie's face lit up, his eyes opening wide. "Elves! I wondered where he kept them." He darted straight to the back door and grabbed the knob.

"You can't go up there."

He kept tugging and tugging but the door wouldn't open.

"Charlie, get away from the door. We already got into trouble once."

The music from the radio suddenly blared and that's all Emma could hear. Charlie spun around from the door, eyes wild as if he thought Santa was going to appear out of thin air. He darted back to where he had dropped the toys and hurriedly started collecting them. He shoved a stuffed lion into Emma's arms and moved past her just as the back door opened and Mr. Nicholas reappeared with his arms full of shiny garland and three boxes of glass ornaments.

"This should be enough." Mr. Nicholas looked from one of them to the other and Emma wondered if she looked as guilty as Charlie, even though they hadn't done anything. "Is there something wrong?"

Emma shook her head as she stared at him. He had sawdust in his hair and on his plaid shirt, but she knew he hadn't been sawing down here.

"Uh, we were wondering how come there are so many toys," Charlie stammered. "Aren't you selling anything?"

Mr. Nicholas walked past them to set the ornaments on the edge of the display window. "Why, the toys are disappearing faster than we can keep up with orders."

Emma jerked her gaze to Charlie at Mr. Nicholas's use of the word we. Charlie looked at the ceiling then flashed a grin.

"Speaking of, have you two thought about what Santa can bring you for Christmas?" When he turned back and spoke to them, Emma swore his eyes were twinkling.

"I want a new sleigh for Wolf to pull," Charlie spoke right up. "For now, I took the wheels off my wagon and nailed it onto an old plastic toboggan. It works okay, but with a real sleigh, Wolf and I could give rides; or haul groceries for Miss Vera and Miss Violet." He stopped to take a breath and gazed up at Mr. Nicholas. "I drew a design for a new sleigh and sent it with my letter to Santa."

Emma thought Charlie had a great idea about using a sleigh to help people around town. It was too bad his letter would end up in the trash at some post office.

"And what about you, Emma?"

Emma shrugged. She had a secret wish; in fact two of them, but refused to say them out loud.

Mr. Nicholas pursed his lips in thought, quietly staring at her. When she remained silent, he winked. "I'm sure Santa can probably come up with a good surprise for you, too."

Chapter Sixteen

"I'm scared, Charlie." Emma buried her head under the blanket in the sleigh. It didn't make any difference that the blanket prevented her from seeing where they were going. The wind whipped around them in a swirling mass of cold, wet snow, coming so hard there was nothing to see except white all around them. When they had first entered the grove of trees, the branches had protected them and neither had realized how badly it had begun to snow. But now as they left the thicker stand of trees and ventured into the open, they realized a blizzard was raging.

It had only been cloudy when Charlie had stopped to see if she wanted to go with him as he followed Mr. Nicholas out to the reindeer again. She had left her dad a note but figured they'd be back before the city council meeting was over.

"We need to go back," she muttered, then repeated it louder to Charlie. The wind whipped her words away and she blindly reached out and grabbed his coat sleeve. She felt him tug on the rope that acted like a harness for Wolf. They came to a stop and for a minute, she thought the snow had stopped, too.

"I'm cold." She was bundled in her coat, hat and mittens, and sat beneath two blankets, but the wind blew through it all. She didn't know how Charlie stayed warm in only his coat and hat, but maybe it was because he had grown up here. Or maybe walking kept him warm.

She could barely see him through the snow. He had pulled his stocking hat over his face and all she saw were his eyes through the slit made in the hat. But what she saw made her stomach hurt. He was scared, too. Her lower lip trembled and she started to cry.

"Do you know where we are?"

"I think Mr. Larsen's shed is up ahead." His voice quivered and Emma knew they were in real trouble. What had started as another of their adventures had gone terribly wrong.

"I want my dad." The words spilled out before she pinched her lips together at the stricken expression that crossed Charlie's face.

"If Wolf can find the shed, we can get inside away from the storm." He tugged on the rope and Emma heard him say "apples" to Wolf as they started off again. Charlie had always said Wolf could see better and hear better than people and Emma hoped it was true.

****

"You haven't found out nothing, have you?" One of the miners shouted from the back of the city council room. "Even before your fancy equipment got broke."

Ryan started to stand but Aunt Mary put a restraining hand on his arm. "She can handle Pete," she whispered. Ryan leaned back in his chair but didn't relax.

Alexis stood at the front of the room, charts and graphs on easels to the side of her. She wore a chocolate colored turtle neck sweater and jeans tucked into fleece lined boots. She looked like any other resident of Snow, instead of a former professor at Harvard with a PhD in physics. As far as he was concerned, she deserved more respect.

Alexis pointed to one of the graphs. "Actually, we've learned a lot over the past month. Snow sits in a small pocket in the mountains that produces wind funneling. Most of the western third of the state is only rated marginal; however the wind resource potential here is rated as good with fifteen to sixteen mile per hour winds on a fairly consistent basis."

"Fairly consistent sounds like government words for you don't know," one of the hecklers jeered, but Alexis was unperturbed.

"Intermittent wind can be a problem, however using wind energy for the majority of the town's energy needs will greatly decrease dependency on coal, thereby making that fossil fuel last longer."

"I've been doing some research since you were here last," Carl Williams, the game warden, said. "There are all kinds of health problems happening in places they've put wind farms due to the noise and vibrations."

"I'm aware of the reports," Alexis replied, "and the Department of Energy is studying this issue very carefully. To date, the research is based solely on anecdotal reports, and we're already finding that if the wind turbines are placed as little as a mile and one-half from town or area farms, it is helping protect inhabitants from any related health problems."

Ryan had to give her credit; she didn't back down from the rude remarks and questions. He looked along the line of City Commissioners to where Sheriff Brown sat at the end. He wasn't real impressed with the guy, especially after having talked to him. Someone had destroyed United States government equipment, which was a felony, and the man had termed it "an unfortunate accident". And of course, there were no suspects.

"What about the costs?" The eventual question came from the back.

Ryan tried not to cringe. He and Alexis had talked about money and while they were accustomed to multibillion dollar budgets in their work, Snow was a small town.

"Estimates for a town the size of Snow consist of seven turbines costing twelve point six million dollars."

Even Ryan hadn't anticipated the roar that ensued.

The Mayor pounded his gavel to quiet the crowd. "We agreed to give Miss Gray time to do her tests. So that she doesn't think we're a bunch of back hills bumpkins, let her give her report."

Ryan's estimation of the man immediately rose.

"There are government grants, tax credits and increased government support for towns generating wind energy," Alexis told the group. "You might be interested to know that according to the American Wind Association, the 'payback time' for a large turbine is between three and eight months. That's the time it takes to generate enough electricity to make up for the energy consumed building and installing it. That's a pretty good turn-around."

She gave that a minute to soak in before continuing. "Snow is in the position of having the wind, therefore it makes sense for your town to apply for funds to create the wind farm. This will also allow the town to sell any overflow of power to other communities on the grid, through a process called net metering."

"All that's confusing."

"I know how government terms can sometimes be confusing, or even misleading." Alexis gave the group her smile and Ryan thought if that didn't soften some of the hard cores, nothing would. "You are already participating in time-of-use metering without ever realizing there was a label attached to it. Basically, the cost of producing electricity is highest during the daytime peak usage period and lowest at night, when usage is down. However, in winter when it gets dark earlier and is cold, usage doesn't always drop at night."

She pointed to another poster. "This is a graph the fifth grade class prepared on the lights-out campaign. You can see how reported usage has dropped during normally peak times and that's only data on a small group of residents. That's why your children's plan has such value. Lowering usage at night when it's normally high in the winter helps time-of-use metering."

Ryan heard the murmurs going through the crowd. One thing he had to say about the town of Snow, if it involved their children, there wasn't a person who said no.

"Well, you've certainly given us a lot to think about, Miss Gray," Mayor Cox said. "And we don't have to make any kind of decision right now, do we?"

Alexis barely had time to shake her head before he continued. "This matter is tabled until after the new year."

He gave the audience a smile that Ryan was sure had probably won him the mayoral election – sympathetic, encouraging and from Ryan's view, patently false. "In the meantime, Miss Parker asked that I remind all of you that the Christmas pageant is scheduled for next Thursday.

Don't forget." He pounded the gavel to end the meeting, but people were already leaving.

Ryan maneuvered his way to the front of the room. It only took a few minutes to help Alexis put her charts away. She had gone to a lot of work that, for the most part, went unnoticed by any of the people at the meeting.

"At least they didn't throw stones," she whispered as he picked up her portfolio.

"Yeah, but we haven't made it to the car yet." Ryan didn't actually expect any trouble. Snow was too small a town and even though factions had erupted over this particular issue, it wasn't like there hadn't been disagreements before. He remembered all the strikes over wages – then it had been the miners against the owners. Now it was the miners against progress. "God didn't make the world in a day," he said, taking Lexi's arm as they walked back to where Aunt Mary waited. "I don't suppose we can expect any kind of miracle when talking to third and fourth generation miners."

The wind and snow hit him square in the face when they walked out of city hall. "When did this start?" Aunt Mary pulled the hood of her coat over her head.

"Good thing I picked you up for the meeting," Ryan replied. "I don't want you driving home in this."

"Dear boy, you forget I've been driving in this for more years than you've been alive." She laughed, lifting her face upward. "I never get tired of the beauty of it."

Having lived in the south most of his adult life, Ryan was still getting used to winter. He felt Alexis shiver next to him. She had yet to acclimate, and he certainly hoped she could. It would help his plans if he didn't have to convince her to love him and the weather.

He tucked the women in his SUV and closed the doors. Sometime over the weeks that Alexis had been here, he had realized how much he wanted her in his life on a permanent basis. Emma loved her, too, and Ryan knew that was important.

He helped Aunt Mary to her door, promising to come over in the morning to shovel the walks. "No sense in doing it until this snow ends," she had told him, giving him a peck on the cheek.

Getting back in the car, he turned to Alexis. "It's early yet. Want to go for coffee?"

Before she could answer, Ryan's cell phone rang. "Hello, Charlie," he answered, seeing Charlie's name on the screen. That's what happens when your kid uses your phone more than you.

"No, this is Corin. I wanted you to tell Charlie I would come and get him. I don't want him trying to walk home in this storm."

"We're not at the apartment yet. I didn't know Charlie was coming over."

"Well, he's not here, so I assume he's with Emma. Those two are inseparable."

"Okay," Ryan replied, "but there's no sense in you getting back out in this. I'll bring him home."

"Thanks, Ryan. I appreciate it."

"No coffee?" Alexis asked.

Ryan shook his head, punching in the apartment number. He felt a frown form as the phone rang and rang but Emma didn't answer. That wasn't like her.

The apartment was dark when he and Alexis climbed the stairs and Ryan thought the kids were observing the lights-out rule even though it wasn't nine o'clock.

"Emma?" He flipped on the lights and realized in a glance that the kids weren't there. "Emma," he hollered, his heart beginning to pound and his stomach clutching. He rushed through the small living room to her bedroom only to find it empty.

"Ryan, there's a note." Alexis handed him a piece of paper.

He started to relax until he read what his daughter had written. "Oh, God," he groaned. "Come on." He grabbed Alexis's hand and practically dragged her down the stairs and back to the SUV. The back end fishtailed as he gunned the engine. The snow was coming so hard he could barely see. Letting his foot up on the accelerator, he put it in four wheel drive but still turned a half circle coming out of the alley.

"Ryan, what's wrong? What does this mean – we're going to see the reindeer?"

"Kids! They think the old man who runs the toy store is Santa. One day they followed him to the edge of town and saw him feeding his reindeer. Or so they say."

"Oh, no." He heard the anguish in her voice. "Surely they didn't go out in this blizzard?"

His hands clenched the steering wheel as the car slid around another corner. He managed to stop in front of the toy store when his tires hit the curb.

"I hope to the devil I'm wrong." He slammed the car in park and opened the door. "Call Corin. Tell her to start calling the other kids in the class and the program; see if anyone has seen them."

Ryan didn't expect Mr. Nicholas to still be at the toy store, but he pounded on the door anyway. He didn't know much about the man, but the kids always seem to have fun when they helped him, and he hadn't questioned it. This was Snow, for heaven's sake, not some big city where you have to worry about…he pounded again.

A light came on at the back of the store and Ryan saw Mr. Nicholas hurrying toward the front, pulling red suspenders over his shoulders.

"My goodness, what is wrong?" He opened the door and peered at Ryan over gold rimmed spectacles. "You're Emma's father, aren't—"

"Are Emma and Charlie here?" Ryan interrupted.

"Why, no. I only see them on the weekends."

"Where do you keep your reindeer?" Ryan asked, panic setting in, thinking of the kids out in this weather. He had no idea how long they'd been gone; what direction…God in heaven help him if he lost his little girl.

Mr. Nicholas looked at him strangely. "I don't have any—"

"The kids think you do and they've gone looking for them. If you go somewhere and feed any kind of deer, where is it?" His voice had risen almost to a shout. His hands reached out of their own volition, stopping short of grabbing the man's shirt front. It was the first time he'd seen him up close, and damned if he didn't look like Santa, with his white hair and beard, twinkling eyes and round belly. "Please, help me." His voice cracked.

"East of town, past the apple orchard. I'll get my boots and…"

Ryan raced back to the car.

"Corin called and no one has seen them." Lexi's worried frown met him as he stomped on the gas and the wheels spun away from the curb.

"Call back and tell her to call the mine and sound the alarm. Nicholas says they're probably at the edge of town between the forest and the apple orchard."

Alexis did as he asked, then turned toward him. "Why the mine?"

Ryan flipped on the radio instead of answering. As the mine whistle began to blow, the music on the station was interrupted. "For all those in the vicinity of Carston mine, this is not, I repeat, not a mine accident. We have two little kids missing, Emma Diantelli and Charlie Parker. They're believed to be in the area around Larsen's Orchard. We could sure use your help to find these youngsters before … well, before too long. Anyone with four wheel drive, head that way and let's get those kids out of the cold. Stay tuned to 101.5 for further details."

Ryan turned east at the next corner, and before they had gone two blocks, more and more car lights appeared, coming from all directions. He slowed to a crawl, just making out the red tail lights in front of him because the wind whipped the snow in all directions. By the time he edged to a stop on the road passing the orchard, twenty to thirty other cars were already there. All of them had parked angled toward the side of the road, the headlights still on. Snow swirled through the lights, creating a dizzying pattern of movement.

He reached in the seatback pocket for the flashlight he always kept there. "Stay in here where it's warm."

183

"No way. Emma's out there somewhere and I'm going with you." Alexis pulled her fur hat over her ears. "We're in this together."

When they came around to the front of the car, she slid her hand into his trembling one, squeezing. Her silent strength helped.

Crowds of people came forward, some faces familiar and others ones Ryan didn't know. He saw miners and businessmen; blue collar and white, and for now, there were no lines dividing them. They looked to him for instructions, but all Ryan could do was shrug, his throat thick with tears.

It was Pete, the same crusty miner who had harassed Alexis less than an hour ago who finally spoke up. "We're going to spread out, but everyone needs to stay in two's. Don't want nobody else getting lost in this whiteout. Let's go straight east, away from the car lights. Call out three times then everybody be quiet. If'n everybody's calling all the time, we ain't going to hear them yelling back."

"Ryan, Ryan!" Corin stumbled through snow up to her thighs. She fell forward but quickly scrambled to her feet and kept moving, grabbing his sleeve when he reached for her. "Oh, please…"

He saw the despair in her eyes; heard the heartbreak in her voice but he had no way to console her; he was as frantic.

Alexis took over. "Corin, honey. You stay with us. We're going to find them with everybody looking." She reached for Corin's hand. "Come on; take my hand so Ryan can use the flashlight."

Corin sobbed, then seemed to realize what they needed to do. She grabbed Alexis's hand and the three of them started forward, shuffling their way through over a foot of new snow that had fallen since early evening. Cold slithered down Ryan's back as the wind worked its way beneath the upturned collar of his coat. His hands already felt icy inside his gloves. The snow soon obscured any light from the cars, leaving them in eerie darkness with only flashlights breaking the gloom.

"Look for tracks," he heard Pete holler over the wind, but Ryan knew with the wind blowing, any tracks would have disappeared within minutes.

The calls began; first Emma's name then Charlie's. The silence about killed Ryan, his heart pounding so hard he wondered if he would even be able to hear if the kids answered. Reaching the partial shelter of the trees made walking harder because here the snow was even deeper, drifting almost to his hips in places.

Every step Ryan took drew the panic closer. He clearly recalled all the trips to the hospital; the surgeries; how he had sat by his daughter's bedside, holding her hand in recovery. Each and every time had cracked his heart a little more. This time he was terrified that it would be broken beyond repair.

He tried to call with the others, but his voice wavered. Tears blocked his vision, the moisture freezing on his eyelashes before it could fall. "Please, God," he whispered over and over, "give me this one miracle. I'll never ask for another thing in this lifetime."

"Quiet!" Someone shouted. Almost as one, the human line stopped in silence. In the distance, Ryan heard a yelp, then another, this time a little louder.

"Wolf!" Corin yelled. "Here, boy!"

A shadow loomed out of the darkness, bounding his way over drifts as high as his back. Wolf raced straight to Corin, but wouldn't get close enough for her to catch his collar. He turned in tight circles, barking, and then raced back the way he had come, stopping at the edge of light from Ryan's flashlight. Once again he spun in a circle, yipping at them.

"He wants us to follow," Corin said, tugging Ryan and Alexis forward. "He knows where they are. He'd never leave Charlie." She let loose of Alexis's arm and started running, floundering in the snow.

Ryan was right behind her, the others shining lights into almost a single beam as everyone followed Wolf, who stayed enough ahead to keep them all moving.

They hadn't gone more than thirty yards when the dog stopped in front of a wood shed that Ryan realized was Mr. Larsen's summer roadside stand. In the snow everything became disoriented and he hadn't even thought to look there first.

"Emma!" he yelled, jerking at the door to get it open past the snow.

"Daddy!"

Ryan fell to his knees in front of the two shivering children, hugging them both tightly to his chest. Corin pushed right in beside him, snatching Charlie and kissing him until he weakly protested. Ryan knew he was crying, but didn't care in the least if the entire town saw him.

"Are you alright?" He placed his hands on Emma's cheeks.

She nodded, her lower lip trembling. "Wolf found the shed. Charlie said he could see, even in a blizzard."

"Let's get you guys bundled up and back to the car." Ryan gathered Emma in one of the blankets from the sleigh they had been wise enough to bring into the shed with them. He lifted her in his arms, backing out of the shed.

"I can walk, Mom." He heard Charlie protest Corin's insistence that she get one of the men to carry him.

"Charlie Parker, I love you, but you are in so much trouble."

"It wasn't his fault," Emma said over Ryan's shoulder.

"Missy, I think both of you are in a lot of trouble." Ryan said the words, but then she put her arms around his neck and hugged him tight. He took a calming breath, then another, as the adrenalin seeped from his system, leaving his hands shaking and his head pounding.

By the time they got to the car, someone had called the mine office and the whistle had shut down. Everyone in town would know the emergency was over, and would turn to the radio station for the update. He knew he owed something more to these people who had braved a whiteout to help him.

Emotionally exhausted, Ryan still took time to shake every single person's hand and individually thank them all.

They all waved it away like it was an ordinary happening. For Ryan, who lived in a city where some people looked right past the homeless as though they didn't exist, it was anything but ordinary. It wasn't simply because of the children. People in Snow took care of each other. Squabbling like siblings, they would still stand together in a crisis.

****

Alexis insisted on coming upstairs with them to make sure Emma got a warm bath. Ryan hadn't wanted to let his daughter out of his sight until Alexis quietly reminded him that even though she was his daughter, she was ten.

It took a minute for Ryan to understand her meaning and he was again glad that she was there. Later, after he had tucked Emma into bed, they sat together on the sofa.

"If tonight is any indication, how am I ever going to get through the teenage years and all that goes with raising a daughter?" He rubbed his hand over itchy, tired eyes.

Alexis curled close, reaching an arm around to rub his neck. "You're doing a wonderful job and you know it."

He shook his head. "I was so afraid I had lost her tonight. After everything we've already been through in the last two years, I…" He couldn't finish.

She placed her hand on his cheek, turning his head toward her.

"I love you, Ryan Diantelli. You are the gentlest man I have ever known, but with so much inner strength. You've taken on the world for the sake of your daughter and that kind of love is very rare."

"Emma will always be…"

Alexis put a finger to his lips before he finished, her eyes glittering with unshed tears. "I know. I wasn't asking for a declaration."

He kissed her finger before taking her wrist and placing her palm on his chest, right over his heart. He smiled. "You women always think you know what a man is thinking."

Her eyes widened. "But we don't?"

"Not in this case. Emma will always be the light of my life. She's my daughter. But I love her in a different way." He gazed solemnly into her eyes. "I have plenty of room for a grown up type of love. Would you consider sharing my heart?"

Chapter Seventeen

Emma was none the worse for wear the next morning, not even a sore throat, for which Ryan was very thankful. He had called Corin earlier and Charlie was doing okay, too.

"We need to talk about what you did," he told Emma when he put a bowl of cereal in front of her.

"We've gone there before," she said, her eyes on the spoon as she poked her Cheerios into the milk.

"That's not the point."

"I know we shouldn't have gone without permission," she said softly.

"That's part of it," he replied. Ever since Emma had been old enough to reason, he had tried to talk through situations with her instead of using the old parent stand-by *because I said so*. It wasn't that he didn't think she would make mistakes; he only hoped she would remember the lesson longer and not repeat them.

"Knock, knock." Alexis opened the apartment door.

"Hi, Lexi!" Emma's head swiveled and she gave her a bright smile.

Alexis looked from her to Ryan. "Whoops, have I interrupted something?"

"Yes." Ryan said.

"No." Emma answered at the same time.

"We were discussing yesterday," Ryan clarified.

"Ah." Alexis nodded as she removed her coat and hung it on the hall tree. "That was pretty scary, wasn't it?" She addressed her question to Emma, who looked immediately repentant.

Ryan was glad Alexis hadn't said he was scared. Dads weren't supposed to be afraid of anything.

"You haven't been through a winter in Snow, Emma, and I don't think you realize how quickly the weather can change," he stated. "In Houston, remember times when the sun would shine and the next minute it would rain?"

"But it wasn't snowing when we left."

"That's what I'm trying to tell you. The weather can change in a second. When the snow comes down as hard as it did yesterday and the wind blows, it's called a whiteout because everything looks white and blocks out everything. You can't tell what direction you're going, or what lies ahead. What would you have done if you hadn't found the shed?"

"Wolf found the shed," she said softly, "and he stayed with us until…he must have heard everybody yelling. All of a sudden his ears pricked up and he started scratching at the door and whining." She looked from one adult to the other, hesitating before she went on. "Charlie thought he had to go out to…potty."

"Speaking of Charlie, I think I'm going to have to restrict you from going in his sleigh for a while."

Emma looked crestfallen. As happy as Ryan was that neither child had been hurt, or worse, he knew he had to punish her.

"That's okay," she finally said. "Charlie called and said he and Wolf are grounded for the rest of their lives."

Ryan had to turn away to hide his smile. Corin must still be pretty mad.

"Dad?"

He poured Alexis a cup of coffee and they both sat at the table with Emma. "Yes?"

"Remember when the mine whistle blew and we went out there and everybody was there – the whole town, even if they weren't miners?"

He nodded.

She pursed her lips, wiggling her mouth back and forth as she thought about what she wanted to say. "Did they come out in the snow last night; for Charlie and me?"

"As a matter of fact, many of them did. A lot of people helped us search for you."

"Could I…can Charlie and me write a thank you letter?"

Ryan felt his heart overflow with pride that his daughter thought of others. "I think that would be very nice. I'm sure Mrs. Hall would run it in the Evergreen Gazette for you."

That seemed to satisfy Emma and she finally dug into her soggy cereal. Ryan looked over at Alexis, hoping his love shone in his eyes. She smiled and put her hand over his.

"Dad?" Emma was half way to the sink with her empty bowl when she turned. "How did you guys know where to look for us?"

"Mr. Nicholas told me where he fed the reindeer."

Her eyes widened to the size of saucers. "You're kidding, right? He told you he had reindeer?"

Ryan recalled his near assault on the man to get information from him. "You do know he's not really Santa Clause, don't you?"

Emma made a noise that sounded much like a snort. "Just because he makes toys doesn't mean he's Santa. Even if Charlie thinks he is." She gave him a look that was too grown up for a ten year old. "I know there's no real Santa, but I don't tell Charlie that. He thought he heard sleigh bells last night when we were in the shed, and that Santa was watching out for us because the shed didn't seem too cold. But I know it was Wolf keeping us warm."

Her comment nudged a memory from last night. Ryan had been so distraught over Emma's disappearance, then ecstatic when they found her, that he hadn't given it much consideration. At the time, he had thought the glow he saw around the shed had been caused by the number of flashlights reflecting off the swirling, blowing snow. But now when he envisioned the scene, no snow had been falling in the vicinity of the shed, and he clearly remembered the calm that surrounded him as he approached the small wooden building.

He shook his head. It was simply a unique set of circumstances that had him imagining things that hadn't actually happened. Still, when he considered all the people helping them search, he wondered if perhaps Emma and

191

Charlie had been used by a higher being to help bring the town together. After all, the conflict over wind energy was far less important than human life – especially a child.

He opened his arms. "Give me a hug, then go get dressed. I have to help Alexis collect her equipment, and you might as well ride along and learn about wind and temperature."

She scrunched up her face, though she didn't look all that unhappy. "Is this one of those lessons you want me to learn so I won't make the same mistake twice?"

Ryan laughed. "How did you get so smart?"

She kissed him on the cheek. "I have a smart daddy." She rubbed noses. "Thanks."

Ryan fell silent after she left the room. Slowly he turned to look at Alexis, who was smiling. "Remember what I said last night, about not surviving her teen years?"

"Uh-huh."

He sighed. "When she acts like that – all grown up – I think I have it made."

"Oh, I don't think you should get too comfortable."

He looked at her in surprise. "Why? I handled that pretty well."

She chuckled. "You have so much to learn." She leaned over and gave him a kiss. "About both of us."

Ryan dropped his chin to his chest with a groan.

* * * *

Ryan thought Shelby Hall did an excellent job writing up the City Council meeting. She not only had some judicious quotes from the council members, but she had interviewed Alexis for additional information on her findings. The two women had spent some time transferring Alexis's data to a format the newspaper could reproduce. Shelby wanted to make sure the residents knew all the facts, not simply what the recorder for the Council would report in her official minutes.

Now, the day after the Gazette was published, Alexis's cell was ringing constantly. It was a good thing it was Ryan's turn to cook.

"Why does Lexi have to work while she's here on vacation?" Emma helped him clear the table after dinner while Alexis took yet another call.

"You should be glad she answers her phone," Ryan replied. "She's not talking to people in Houston or DC. Most of the calls are from people right here in town. She allowed Shelby to put her number in the article for people to call. Going to the source -- which in this case is Alexis-- is better than people talking among themselves and starting rumors. This way, she can give them the correct information to consider."

"She even mentioned my class's graph in the article." Emma laid the Scrabble® board on the clean table.

"Did Miss Michaels give you and Charlie extra credit for all your work?"

Emma shrugged. "I don't need extra credit. I do my work. Charlie is a different story. Do all boys act like him?"

Ryan loved these types of conversations with his daughter. "Act how?"

"You know."

"Honey, it's been a lot of years since I was a kid. Give me a hint."

"Like he's all nice one minute then acts like a dork the next. He goofs off with the boys at pageant practice and doesn't even listen to his mother very well."

"But he doesn't act badly around you, does he?"

"Not most of the time."

Ryan nodded. "Boys always want their friends to think they're hot stuff."

Emma shook her head. "That doesn't make any sense. I'm his friend and he doesn't do that around me."

"That's the best part about having a girl for your friend. You don't have to pretend you're hot stuff. You can be yourself."

"Boys are weird."

Ryan laughed and gave her a hug. "I'll let you in on a secret. Boys think girls are weird too, until they turn about thirteen."

"Boys are weird well beyond the age of thirteen." Alexis joined the conversation. "Sometimes they stay that way well into their thirties." She made a face at Ryan.

"Yuck. You guys give me a lot to look forward to."

Ryan drew his seven letter tiles for the game and sorted them on the tray. They had been having game night for several weeks, and he enjoyed this special time with Emma, and now Alexis. He had never had – or most likely never taken –time in Houston just to talk. The time spent with his daughter always seemed to have been in a hospital.

"I get to go first," he said, laying his tiles across the star in the middle.

"That's not the rules," Emma argued.

"Yeah, but since I'm the dad, and I'm also a boy, I get to be weird, remember." Was it coincidence that the tiles he laid on the board spelled w-e-i-r-d?

* * * *

"Dad, Dad!" Emma double hopped into the bakery early the next morning. She didn't need her crutches any more, but if she was in a hurry and she knew better than to run, she did this funny skip-hop. She stopped in front of the counter and held out his cell phone. "Miss Michaels called and there's big news."

He took the phone and held it to his ear. "Hello?"

Emma shook her head and sighed. "She called upstairs. I gave her this number and told her to call in two min—"

The ringing phone interrupted her. Ryan had to smile at his daughter's mathematical brain. She had known exactly how long it would take to reach him from the apartment upstairs.

She hopped up and down. "Answer it."

"Quit jumping; you'll hurt yourself," he said before punching the on button. "Hello, Paige?"

"You knew it was me?"

"Emma said two minutes."

"How does she do that? I want her tested right after the holidays. There's got to be a way for her to accelerate through high school math and start on college level Algebra."

"That's your news?"

She laughed. "No. Sorry, it's simply that I've never had a student with her gift before."

"I know. I used to let her figure launch and re-entry time tables for the Shuttle, but when my boss found out, he made me stop."

"You're kidding, right?"

"Of course. How can I help you?"

"I received a call from WKUP in Pittsburgh and they want to come and do a story on our class project. I told them it had started with Emma and they want to interview her."

"Wow." Ryan looked at Emma, who hung over the counter, grinning.

"Since she's a minor, I have to get your approval."

"Ask her about Charlie," Emma hissed.

"What about Charlie?" Ryan was asking Emma, but Paige answered.

"That's exactly what Emma said. She refuses to take full credit for this, even though it started with her essay. I'll give Corin a call and see what she thinks."

Ryan knew how loyal Emma was to Charlie. "I doubt Emma will do it without him." He was rewarded with a huge smile and two thumbs up from his daughter.

"Well, we'll have two TV celebrities in Snow then. I'll get back to you."

Ryan tossed the phone back to his daughter. "Are you and Charlie going to want stars on your doors after this is over?"

"Dad." In an instant her face went from glowing to misery. "Oh, no."

"What; are you nervous already?"

"Not me; Charlie. Remember how we talked about him doing stupid stuff?"

He nodded, but she didn't see it as she had started pacing in front of the counter.

"How am I going to get Charlie to promise not to talk about Santa being here in Snow?"

"The television crew is coming about the lights-out effort; not about Santa."

"Dad, you're not helping. I know that and you know that, but Charlie will think Mr. Nicholas is a bigger story."

"What makes the difference if Charlie talks about Mr. Nicholas and the toy shop? Maybe it will be good for business."

"I know." She snapped her fingers, totally ignoring his comments. "I'll tell Charlie that he can't say Mr. Nicholas is Santa because so many people will come and pester him that he won't be able to finish all the toys he has to make for Christmas."

"Emma, I don't think you need to go to extremes."

"He's not Santa, Dad, and I don't want Charlie to look bad on TV."

He had to give her credit. She was not only loyal to her friends; she had their best interests at heart.

* * * *

Corin opened the door and all the kids rushed passed her. It didn't feel like the heat was on in the old theater as she had requested and she shook her head in resignation. The city was so concerned about the power that they couldn't even heat a building for a couple of hours for the kids? She was going to have a talk with Mayor Cox first thing in the morning, if she didn't call him at home tonight.

"Tommy, stay off the stage until we're all ready. You know the rules." The boys always wanted to run and jump off the edge, which was only a few feet from the floor, but she worried that someone would get hurt.

"Mom, when are we going to have dress rehearsal?" Charlie stuck his head out of Santa's sack, which was actually a large red paper circle with a slit in the middle that Corin had pinned to an opening in the curtain. All the

196

children, representing toys in the play, would come through that opening as though they were climbing out of Santa's bag. At least she hoped that's what it would look like to the audience.

"Charlie, don't be jerking the curtain open. I don't want the paper torn before we even do the play. And get down here. If Tommy and the others can't be there yet, you shouldn't be either."

As Charlie bounded across the stage to where she stood below it, boards squeaked from his weight. Yet another thing to discuss with the Mayor. Someone was supposed to fix that.

"Okay, kids, we only have a week before the pageant. Does everybody have their costume done? Any moms need ideas or help? Tuesday I want to have dress rehearsal to make sure everything works."

Becky raised her hand. "Mom wants to know if I can wear feety pajamas with a pillow stuffed inside for my teddy bear costume. She's going to make ears to go on a headband and put makeup on my face."

"That will work great. Remember, I don't want your parents spending money on costumes. Tommy, how's your mom doing with the soldier costumes?"

Tommy shrugged. "I don't know."

Corin knew Lisa Stuart would probably have something outstanding; she usually did. She jotted a note to call her, just in case.

"Mary Beth will be here tomorrow to play the piano for the songs. Since they're traditional Christmas songs, I'm sure you already know the words. Today, we'll run through the rest of the play, and pause where the songs will be. Everybody ready?"

It was a mad scramble up the stairs at the side of the stage. Corin followed to see if they were in order. "No, Susie, the dolls come after the wrapped presents." She moved two of the girls around. "Emma, you'll be next. How's your dad coming on your costume?"

Emma grinned. "Lexi and I finally got him to make it right, with little furniture and everything. Dad said it was harder than building the space shuttle."

"I can't wait to see it." Corin had enjoyed getting to know Alexis Gray, and felt she was good for Ryan. She sighed. At least one of them was finding the right person to have in his life.

Once all the kids were in the proper order, Corin went to sit on the fifth row of the auditorium. She wanted to make sure she could hear the kids from a distance. "Ready?" she called loud enough for the chatter to die. She nodded to Sheri, an eighth grader who would give the introduction.

"Once upon a time, the day before Christmas Eve, Santa turned off the lights to the workshop and left for the night. All was quiet, until suddenly…"

That was the cue for the children to chatter.

"Where are my chattering toys?" Corin's question was immediately answered by a chorus of yelling. With a sigh, she climbed the stage steps. "I will be back here for the play," she patiently explained for the umpteenth time, "but I can't see what's going on during rehearsal. Who can tell me what you're supposed to do?"

Susie raised her hand. "When Sheri says suddenly, we're supposed to chatter for five seconds…" She put up her fingers one at a time. "Then we're quiet."

Corin looked at the group. "Got it?" Heads nodded. "Let's try it again." She returned to her seat and gave Sheri the cue.

"Once upon a time, the day before Christmas Eve, Santa turned off the lights to the workshop and left for the night. All was quiet, until suddenly…"

Chatter rose from behind the curtain. Corin silently counted…to seven. Close enough.

"…a wondrous, magical thing happened." Sheri concluded as Troy and Dale, who would be elves, sneaked around the far side curtain, tiptoeing across the stage toward Santa's sack. The second grade twins were cute as buttons and acted up just enough to be believable.

The stage floor squeaked again and Corin frowned.

"Let's see what Santa has in his sack," Troy said. They held open the sides of the sack and curtains and the toys started walking through.

"No, wait." Corin stopped them again. "Remember we talked about how you'd come out?" She hurried up to the stage. "Come over here." Once all the kids stood along the back of the stage, she continued. "Soldiers, how should you climb from Santa's bag?"

Tommy and his cronies straightened their shoulders and marched in place, arms and legs stiff.

"Good. Now, wrapped presents, you won't be able to tumble about, but you're not stiff like the soldiers." The little girls nodded. "The rest of you – vary the way you come out of Santa's bag. Skip, jump...dolls, you can twirl around. You don't have to be in a hurry, but remember, you're toys that have come to life and you're all excited."

Some of the kids still looked dubious. "Justin, you're a ball. Here, let me show you..."

She went behind the curtain and poked her head through the opening, eyes wide as she looked this way and that. Putting her hands on the floor, she turned a somersault then another toward the center of the stage.

As her head came over her feet the second time, a loud crack echoed in her ears and the floor trembled under her. Wood splintered beneath her feet, several boards giving way under her weight.

"Mom!" Charlie yelled, starting forward.

"Stay back!" Corin found herself suspended – her legs and torso dangling below the stage floor. She wiggled her legs around but found no cross beams to support her. The only thing that kept her from falling straight through was her outstretched arms. She knew the room beneath the stage, originally used for costume changes, had a good six to eight foot ceiling, and she didn't exactly want to drop into whatever was lying around on the floor.

Some of the smaller girls started crying.

Corin surprised herself by staying calm. "Sheri, help everyone get off the stage. Go down the stairs, don't walk towards the front."

"Mom, Tommy and I can pull you out." Charlie scooted closer on hands and knees, grabbing one of her outstretched hands. When he tugged, splintered wood dug into her armpit.

"I called Dad," Emma said from the front of the stage. "He'll be right here."

Corin groaned. Although the hole wasn't large, her arms already ached from supporting her weight. She thought about all the times she had promised herself to exercise. When she wiggled, another board poked painfully into her back. She dropped her head forward and closed her eyes.

Not more than a minute later, although it seemed infinitely longer, she heard the doors burst open.

"Hurry Dad!" Emma shouted.

"Mitch, help!" Charlie hollered at the same time.

Mitch? Corin didn't want to open her eyes.

"You boys join the others," Ryan instructed as he came onto the stage. "We don't know how much weight this stage will support."

"Not much, apparently," Mitch commented and Corin swore she heard amusement in his voice. A second later he laughed out loud, huge guffaws that rolled across her in waves.

She jerked her head up to find him bent in half laughing so hard tears rolled down his cheeks.

"Mitchell Farley, I swear—"

"Save the threats for later," Ryan said, poking around her with one hand before continuing to Mitch. "We're going to have to lift her straight up. If we drag her, she'll have splinters everywhere."

Ryan grabbed her upper arm. "Ready?"

"I hope she's not as heavy as a car engine." Mitch snorted, swallowing more laughter when Corin scowled at him.

He reached for her arm and Corin jerked away, her anger overriding the tenuous circumstances. She squealed as she listed to the side, slipping further into the hole.

"Suck it in, Corin!" Mitch grunted, grabbing her arm.

She flew upward, the strength of the two good sized men effortlessly pulling her free.

They shuffled her to the far edge of the stage before lowering her to her feet. She wobbled, her legs numb, and Mitch caught her around the waist. When he started laughing again, she smacked his chest and straightened.

"You are such a –"

"Tut, tut; the children." He grinned at her.

Corin looked over to where Alexis, whom she hadn't known was there, had all the children corralled and was busy calling parents on a cell phone.

"Can you walk down the steps?" Ryan cradled her elbow in one hand.

"I think I can. Oh," Corin grimaced as she straightened her sweater and felt pinpoints of pain across her back. "I think I have splinters."

"Want me to take a look?" Mitch smirked at her.

It suddenly hit her. She hadn't seen Mitch smile since he returned home, much less laugh out loud as he had done tonight. She tilted her head to look at him but under her scrutiny, he sobered.

"Oh, no you don't," she said. "Now that you've laughed, even if it was at my expense, you are not going back to before!"

He shrugged his wide shoulders and turned away. "Whatever."

Her shoulders dropped. Ryan cupped her elbow and they followed Mitch. "Give him time," he whispered.

"How many years, exactly?"

"Well, I was surprised when he stopped by the bakery and asked me to help him fix the stage..." Ryan hesitated and looked behind him. "That was a start, even if it's not an option now."

"Oh, what are we going to do about the pageant?" Corin moaned.

"Leave it for tomorrow. Let's get you over to the apartment and have Alexis check your back. I'm sorry if we were a little rough pulling you out but I didn't know how long the rest of the flooring would last."

"At least the children weren't hurt."

"That's the last call," Alexis said when they came to stand by her. "All the parents are on the way. I didn't give a lot of details, but I did tell them what happened. Otherwise, I was afraid the children would embellish the tale so much it would make the daily paper."

Ryan laughed. "If we had a daily paper. As it is, the story won't appear until next week."

Corin groaned at the thought but then brightened. "Maybe the publicity will help."

"Would you two gals take Corin over to the apartment?" Ryan asked. "I'll stay here with the kids until all the parents show up."

Emma tugged on her coat. "She did a great somersault, Dad."

Corin laughed and shook her head. "No more gymnastics for me, kiddo." Charlie was hovering close to her side, at the age where he didn't want to be labeled a mama's boy, but clearly concerned. She ruffled his hair. "Stay here with Ryan and Mitch?" She had noticed that Mitch was still leaning negligently against the stage front, arms crossed over his chest. When he nodded, indicating he would look after Charlie, she shrugged into her coat with Alexis's help, and left.

Chapter Eighteen

Ryan could smell coffee as he and Mitch climbed the stairs, Charlie close behind. On the way across the square he had explained to Charlie that he probably shouldn't say anything about the accident unless his mom brought it up. When Charlie asked why, Mitch had smirked, giving Ryan a look that said yeah, why? Having a daughter had given Ryan marginal insight into the workings of the female mind.

"Women do not like to be reminded of embarrassing incidents."

"She's my mom. She's always embarrassing me with hugs and junk," Charlie protested.

"That's different," Ryan said, although he wasn't sure exactly how.

"Why?" Charlie repeated.

"It just is," Mitch chimed in, "so behave yourself."

The gals were gathered around the small kitchen table drinking coffee and talking quietly. Emma jumped up and came around the table. She gave him a hug, all smiles. "It was like a Superman movie," she said. "You and Mitch are heroes."

"Well, I don't know about that," he replied, but inside his heart always expanded when his daughter looked at him like she was now, making him feel ten feet tall.

She limped back over to where Alexis was sitting. "Did you hurt your leg?" he asked before he thought about her response with others present. And here he had been lecturing Charlie.

"I wasn't doing jumping jacks, Dad. I was just walking. The doctor said I needed to exercise it."

"But not overdo it," he reminded her quietly.

"I don't know about you, but I could stand to put my feet up," Mitch said.

Ryan shifted his gaze to Corin, who had stopped talking in midsentence to stare at Mitch. He didn't think Mitch ever spoke about his injury and now he was doing it for Emma's sake. He hurriedly slid the love seat halfway around so they could sit and still talk to the girls. Before he sat, he poured coffee for him and Mitch while Alexis made Charlie a cup of hot chocolate.

"Now what are we going to do about the program?" Emma asked the question on everyone's mind. "Can we have it at the school?"

Corin shook her head. "Every year I ask and every year they say no. Because of the religious nature of the songs, and sometimes the program, even though the school's not the one sponsoring it, they worry about someone objecting and causing trouble."

"Who does sponsor it exactly?" Ryan asked.

Corin looked off to the side but he noticed a slight blush had risen in her cheeks.

"Corin does it on her own," Mitch answered. "And just like this fool town and its festivals, she refuses to charge admission or collect money to help with costumes, advertising, or getting somewhere safe to have it."

Concern etched Mitch's voice rather than mockery but Corin skewered him with a look. Ryan wondered why those two didn't see what was right in front of their noses. He sat back to watch the fireworks.

"Not everything in this town has to have a price tag attached to it," Corin sputtered.

"When it benefits the town, the town should pay for it," Mitch shot back.

"Like they're doing with the lighting around the square?"

"Don't lay that on me, Corin. I'm not on the City Council."

"Right. You live here, you work here, but you act like you don't belong."

"Oh-kay," Ryan interrupted when he saw Charlie and his daughter exchange looks.

"Sorry," Corin apologized, "I shouldn't have…" she waved a hand negligently as her sentence trailed off. Ryan felt Mitch relax back against the sofa.

"I guess in addition to talking to the Mayor about the broken stage, now I'll have to nicely ask if we can use the city council room for practice." Corin sighed. "But there's not enough room there to actually hold the pageant."

Emma came over and leaned her elbow on Ryan's shoulder. "Dad, you work for NASA. Call Uncle Lou."

He circled her small waist with his arm. "Honey, this isn't a problem Lou can fix."

"But someone has to. Uncle Lou always comes to you when there's a problem. What do you do when something doesn't work?"

He didn't know how to make her understand the two things were worlds apart. He looked around at the people watching him expectantly – some very dear to him and others having become special in the short time he'd been in Snow. As he watched Emma walk – without crutches -- to where Alexis sat, he realized that one miracle had already happened this holiday season. Why not help make another?

* * * *

The next day, Alexis was helping Corin on decorations and the printed program and had taken Emma with her. The two of them had become inseparable, and that made Ryan very happy. He had hopes that Alexis would stay in Snow with them after the holidays. In fact, he hoped she would become a permanent part of their lives.

He thought about proposing on Christmas Eve, but hadn't even had time to shop for a ring. Needless to say, if he bought one in Snow the whole town would know before Alexis did. Of course, the first thing to do was to get her to accept a proposal because there were some pretty hefty logistics to work out. They loved each other; that wasn't the problem.

Ryan supposed they could move wherever Alexis's job took her, although Emma liked Snow and appeared to be fitting in quite well with kids her age. He liked the idea of Emma growing up in a small town and making friends she'd have for a lifetime. That wouldn't happen if they moved all over or lived in a big city with hundreds of students in each grade at school.

His job wasn't a problem at all, because he'd continue doing consulting work, but had no plans to go back to the rat race.

"Good afternoon, Mrs. Potts," he greeted his former teacher. "Glad it's almost time for vacation?"

"I enjoy my job, Ryan."

"I'm sure you do, but everybody needs a holiday once in a while." He smiled as he boxed her order of holiday pies.

She sighed. "You're right, of course. I always worry that if I say I'm glad, people will think I don't like being in education."

"Mrs. Potts, if you lived through the class I was in and stayed in education after that, no one can say you're not dedicated."

She smiled. "Every class has its own unique character, but your group..." She shook her head at the memory. "And yet look at all of you now. Not a loser among you."

He laughed. "All because of your gentle influence." He handed her the bag, took her money and rang up the sale.

"I don't see Emma. How is she doing?"

Ryan beamed. "The doctor gave us good news. Emma's bones are healing and she's walking without crutches. As long as she's careful, she should be able to go to school full time after the holiday."

"Oh, that is good news. Tell her to enjoy vacation and I expect to see her bright and early next year." She tugged on her gloves and collected her purchases. "Have a very Merry Christmas, Ryan."

"And you too, Mrs. Potts."

Ryan flipped the sign to closed and locked the front door. Although the bakery would be open until mid-day Christmas Eve, they'd advertised shorter hours several days

206

this week. Aunt Mary had parties and teas with several of her social and church groups, and he still had things to do.

He began whistling Jingle Bells as he bundled up and went out back to start his car. He had told Alexis to make sure she kept Emma busy until after five because he had yet to finish his shopping and if she were home she'd want to tag along.

He smiled as he drove around the block to the hardware store. Emma had done without for so long because of her leg, it was hard not to buy her roller skates, a skateboard and a bike, but he'd settled for just the bike – a sparkling red ten speed. He needed to pick it up and hide it over at Aunt Mary's, where they'd celebrate Christmas.

He already had Aunt Mary's present. He'd made arrangements with Mary's good friend, Ellie Payne, to go on an Alaskan cruise with his aunt next summer. Ellie had agreed that if Ryan asked her what she wanted, Mary would say nothing but another year of good health. Ellie confided that the two of them had talked about taking a cruise one day, but hadn't gotten around to it. Ryan figured there was no reason to put it off any longer.

That left Alexis. As he came out of the hardware store, he walked by the gum ball machines lined up along the inside glass windows. He stopped, backed up and looked again. Only one actually held giant gum balls. Another displayed neon colored super balls. The rest contained a variety of small, clear plastic eggs, each with a prize inside. He grinned, fishing in his pocket for change, dropping two quarters in a machine that had a glittery pink sticker on the front advertising princess rings.

* * * *

Corin looked around at the sea of faces; the number of parents crammed into the City Council chambers rapidly raising the temperature of the room. A glimpse toward the back and she spied Ryan who gave her a thumbs up signal. He had once again become her good friend.

She glanced at her notes but jerked her head back up as her peripheral vision caught a late comer sliding in the back door. She stared at Mitch's tall profile as he skulked along the back wall before sidling up next to Ryan. She didn't have a clue as to why he was there, and only hoped it wasn't to make fun of her for falling through the stage floor.

"Thank you all for coming tonight," she said above the buzz of voices. "I'll try not to keep you very long. As you know, we've lost the use of the Majestic Theater for our Christmas pageant."

Soft laughter echoed through the crowd. She smiled. "Believe me; it wasn't that funny at the time."

"Can't we use one of the school auditoriums?" a parent from the back asked.

Corin shook her head. "Every year we try and are turned down."

"We pay taxes and school fees; why can't we use it when it's closed anyway?" This from another father, followed by more murmurs.

"Please, we already have enough going on in Snow at the moment; there's no sense in trying to make bigger waves over this. As you know, I've been holding practice here, but again, it's not big enough for the program. Ryan Diantelli came up with an idea and I talked to the children and they agreed. We're going to have the program at Center Park, in the gazebo."

"It's winter. And it'll probably snow."

Corin sometimes wondered at the logic of people. "You're right. Chances are pretty good that it will snow...in Snow." Some laughter met her comment and eased the tension. "Look, the kids are very excited about it, and the program's not that long. I've already talked to Mary Beth and she said she would pre-record the music. That way we only need an electrical source instead of the actual piano."

Ryan spoke from the back of the room. "I'll visit with Harold Carston about providing a generator."

"Good luck with that!"

"Diantelli's new in town. He doesn't know any better."

"Why do we need a generator out in the snow anyway?"

The comments and questions flew, and Corin wished she had a gavel; even a whistle would do. A second later an ear-splitting whistle rent the air. If wishes were fishes. It seemed a lifetime since she had heard that whistle below her bedroom window.

Mitch lowered his hand from his mouth. "Listen you mor—" he stopped when Ryan nudged him sharply with an elbow. Corin watched Mitch close his eyes for a second and she knew by the deep breath he took he was gathering his patience. The fact that he was even here amazed her; his speaking to a group of people was a miracle.

"Corin is trying her…darnedest to have your Christmas program, just like she does every year. It would help if you listened and agreed instead of arguing; like there isn't already enough of that going on in this town." His voice was deep and rough and it still had the ability to send shivers down Corin's spine. More astonishing, the people in the room shut up and listened.

"Since the city is being stingy with its electricity," Mitch continued, "we'll need light around the gazebo. I have a friend who has some floodlights. If Diantelli manages to get that generator, we can hook them up."

Corin could hardly believe that not only was Mitch standing up for her; he was volunteering to help, at least in a small way. Now if he would only sing.

Ron Morton, whose daughter, Susie, was in the program, jumped up from where he sat near the front. "I store the trash barrels for the lake and parks in winter when they're not in use. How about if I bring in half a dozen barrels, with plenty of wood in them to create a little heat, and place them strategically around the area? It would add to the light effect and be enough to keep people from freezing while they watch the program."

Corin lost control of the meeting as everybody talked at once about what they could do to make this work. When she glanced to where Mitch leaned against the back wall, arms crossed over his chest, she raised a brow. He returned her unspoken question with a shrug of his wide shoulders.

"There is one more thing to consider," she finally managed when the various conversations died down. "Since the children will be outside for the program, they'll need to wear their coats and boots. It would work well if their coats fit underneath their costumes. That way the audience can still see what they are supposed to be. I think most of the costumes are being designed to wear over clothes anyway." She thought through the list of toys – soldiers, balls, a race car; baby dolls and teddy bears; presents and games. "If you have any questions or concerns, let me know or give Lisa Stuart a call since she's our resident costume designer." She smiled at Lisa, who always went overboard helping with the pageant.

The meeting concluded and Corin allowed her shoulders to sag in relief. At least the parents hadn't balked at the idea of doing the program outside. The more she thought about all the snow sculptures around the square, the more appropriate it seemed. She wove her way through the chairs toward the back door. It wasn't a bad thing, she knew, to let others help, but what if they couldn't follow through? Like Ryan.

"How in the world are you ever going to convince Carston to loan us a generator?" she asked him when she got to the back of the room.

He grinned. "I'll appeal to his better nature."

Mitch snorted. "You might as well offer him a ride on the space shuttle – both impossibilities."

Corin turned to Mitch. "Thank you for standing up for me."

He scowled, apparently not wanting to be reminded that he was a nice guy, at times.

"Have you reconsidered—?"

"The answer's the same as the last time you asked," he interrupted to say. He turned and pushed open the door. "Diantelli, call me when you manage your miracle." The door swung shut behind him.

Corin sighed.

"Want to get a cup of coffee?" Ryan held the door open for her.

"Don't you need to get home? I know Alexis is here."

"They're playing Monopoly and I always lose my houses first, anyway."

She gave a short laugh. "Seriously, Ryan, how are you going to talk Harold Carston into lending a generator?"

Ryan shrugged. "I have no idea, but since I don't know all the history behind the town and the mine, having been gone all these years, you see, maybe he'll cave if only to get rid of me." He tried to give her a wide eyed innocent stare, but Corin wasn't buying it, and knew Carston wouldn't either.

"You can't have lived in Snow any time at all and not know about the constant friction. Besides, did you forget you're the one who brought the Department of Energy into town?"

He smiled. "You think he knows that?"

She rolled her eyes but had to laugh. "Why didn't I fall for you in high school when you were hot and available?"

They walked along the north side of the square. The holiday lights weren't on; the darkness only broken periodically by small puddles of light from every other streetlight.

"I love this town. It hasn't changed much in my entire life, but I feel something slipping away." Corin blew a cloud of breath into the frosty air. "Something intangible, yet as necessary to the town as the air we breathe."

"It's the spirit of Snow," Ryan said. "It lives in the history of the mine; the people who have lived and died here; the dreams of the future."

They walked into Blitzen's, fragrant smells of coffee and spice mixing in the warm air.

"Hi, Toby," Ryan called. "Bring us a couple of cappuccinos, please?" He and Corin settled into a booth toward the back.

"I think that's one of the reasons I wanted to bring Emma back here," Ryan continued his earlier thoughts. "Big cities don't have that same spirit. There's too many

211

people; too many different cultures and diversity. While that's not a bad thing, and I'm all for Emma understanding the world around her, I also want her to have a sense of community and family."

She grinned. "Try using that speech on Carston; maybe it'll soften him up. I mean, he can't want the town to die before his coal supply does."

They sipped their drinks in companionable silence but Corin could see Ryan's brain working. Still, she was surprised when he spoke.

"You thought I was hot in school?"

She felt her cheeks grow warm. "Every girl thought you were hot when you first showed up in fifth grade. You had that dark Italian hair and eyes, but you kept to yourself. Nobody could read you."

"That first year was tough after my parents died."

"I don't think anybody knew why you had come to live with your aunt and uncle. Some thought you were on probation, or a runaway. There was even talk that Mary wasn't actually your aunt and you were in the witness protection program. All that just added to your mysteriousness."

"You're kidding, right?"

She shook her head. "Nope. All kinds of rumors floated around that first year, then you sort of blended in and became one of us."

"Why didn't we date in high school? Other than the senior prom, that is."

She smiled in memory. "You were too nice." When his brow arched in question, she continued. "I was a wild child; gave my parents fits. I ran with the crowd that had fast cars; smoked, did a little drinking and partied hard."

She saw when things started to click.

"That would have been Mitch Farley and Jerry Hall among others. It certainly wasn't me."

She agreed. "No, you were in National Honor Society and had plans to leave Snow and become something great. I just figured on graduating, getting married and having babies." She shrugged. "Small town dreams."

"There's nothing wrong with that."

He leaned back in his chair. "What happened between you and Mitch? The sparks fly like the fourth of July whenever the two of you are together." He watched her cheeks darken in a blush.

"He was the reason I was always in trouble with my folks. He was an original bad boy – fast car, handsome as sin, always riding right on the edge of the law."

"It's funny I don't remember a lot about him."

"He was three years older than us, and suspended from school almost as much as he was there. The only reason he managed to graduate was because Miss Christiansen, the music teacher, kept going to bat for him. He can sing like a dream, and was solo medalist at state all four years of high school." She knew she sounded smitten. "We'd go to the lake at night, sneak past the barricades and lay on the beach and he'd sing to me. He liked the old stuff – Elvis, the Beatles."

"You're both still living in Snow; why didn't you get married?"

"This is where the love story becomes a soap opera." Corin sighed. "Right after Mitch graduated, he pushed the limit a little too far and got caught street racing with some kids from Seaton, over east. The judge decided to give him a choice – jail time and probation or the army."

"Mitch doesn't appear to be the sort to do well with authority."

"That's the funny thing. He chose the Army and actually liked it. His best friend Jerry, even though he didn't get caught racing, joined with him and they managed to go through basic and get stationed together."

Ryan looked thoughtful. "And because you would have only been…what? Fifteen? Your parents wouldn't let you get married and go with him."

She grimaced. "Right. Not that Mitch asked. He just up and left one day without even a good-bye."

"Ouch."

Corin looked at her watch, realizing how late it was. "I'd better get home. No telling what Charlie is up to."

Ryan put his hand over hers. "No way are you going until you finish the story."

"Not much left to tell. Mitch and Jerry left; I married Tom Parker when I finished beautician school, but the minute I got pregnant he left us. I never once heard from Mitch, but I avidly read about him in the Gazette. He was a mechanic and drove a General's jeep – saved the man's life more than once, I guess. I never saw him until he returned to Snow, wounded."

"And Jerry Hall died?"

"Mitch thinks it's his fault; that if Jerry hadn't enlisted with him, he'd still be alive. It happened in December, within weeks of when they were to be rotated stateside. That's why Mitch gets especially moody this time of year." She gave a brittle laugh. "Not that he's much better at other times. Anyway, he refuses to actually have a life."

She stood. "I have to go. Thanks for the support tonight. Next time, you'll have to tell me your story – single dad raising a daughter; being friends with a beautiful lady."

Ryan helped her into her coat. "Ha. It's a soap opera that would rival yours for a daytime Emmy, believe me."

* * * *

Ryan thought about Corin's story as he walked home, snow crunching under his boots the only sound in the night. It seemed a waste that Corin waited for Mitch to come to his senses, and although Ryan couldn't begin to imagine how Mitch felt, there were similarities in their circumstances. It had been extremely difficult for him to get past his own guilt when it came to his wife.

As he climbed the steps to the apartment, he heard girlish laughter. Unlike Mitch, who refused to let go of his past, Ryan now knew what he wanted his future to look like.

"I'm taking Alexis to the roof," he said the minute he opened the door. He grabbed her coat off the hall tree and held it out for her.

She gave him a quizzical look but when he didn't say more, she came over and slid her arms into her coat.

"I'll go with you." Emma jumped up from the table where they had been playing a game.

"You weren't invited," Ryan replied. Both females looked at him in surprise, before he saw Emma's eyes widen and she smiled.

"Oh-kay," she acquiesced quickly. "But you have to come back in time for the news. We're supposed to be live at ten," she mimicked the commercial. She came over and gave him a kiss and an extra hard hug, whispering in his ear. "Do it right, okay?" The little minx knew exactly what Ryan intended.

Alexis didn't chastise him as they climbed the outside stairs to the roof. She no doubt longed for some quiet time as much as Ryan did. She'd had additional meetings with the individual members of the City Council and Ryan hoped for some good news for the town of Snow. But when she wasn't working on her wind data, she and Emma were helping Corin or running errands for Aunt Mary.

Ryan had grabbed a flashlight but when they stepped off the last metal stair onto the flat roof, he switched it off, enclosing them in darkness. There was no moon and yet the snow that covered the entire town glowed with a soft luminous light.

He stood behind Alexis, wrapping his arms around her. "Look up."

She tilted her head back against his shoulder and together they gazed into the farthest reaches of heaven, millions of twinkling stars baring evidence that all was good in his world.

"Oh, Ryan, it's breathtakingly beautiful here."

There was no need to say anything. The night surrounded them in serene silence. The small plastic egg felt like a lead weight in Ryan's pocket. Now, the idea of giving Alexis an adjustable ring with a plastic stone seemed ludicrous. Recalling Emma's threat, he wondered exactly how he was supposed to 'do it right'. Then Alexis gave him the opening he needed.

"I wonder what will happen here. I've talked and talked, but I have no idea whether your city council will accept my recommendations."

Ryan's heart hammered. "You could stick around and find out." He held up the plastic egg.

Alexis stepped away and turned to face him. "What is this?" She took off her mittens, tucked them in her pockets and took the egg, popping it open. "A princess….ring?" The last word was a gasp.

Ryan started rambling. "I wanted to get a real one but you know this town. Everybody would know before you. I should have waited to give it to you on Friday; it's your present after all, but I never was able to wait for Christmas Day when it was something I truly wanted."

She stopped his mutterings with a kiss, and he wrapped her shivering body close. Regardless of what people said, love the second time around was not less explosive. His discovery that he loved Alexis sort of burst upon him one day. But this time, because they had started as friends, he realized their love was a lot more enduring, and comfortable. With everything that had gone on in his life, it still totally amazed him that he had found Alexis.

"Does Emma know?" Alexis asked. "Oh, nuts." Her hands were shaking and the ring dropped into the snow.

Ryan pulled the flashlight from his pocket and dropped to one knee, sifting snow through his gloves until the light caught and glittered against the ring. He fumbled until he finally had to take off his glove and stick his hand into the snow. When he looked at Alexis's anxious face, he decided he might as well do this right.

Taking her hand, he slid the ring onto her finger. "Alexis Gray, will you marry Emma and me?"

She gave him such a tender smile, Ryan's heart soared. "How can I possibly say no to a two-for-one bargain with a genuine princess ring thrown in for good measure?"

"Even if it means living in Snow, at least for a while?"

"Get up; your jeans are going to be all wet. And what; you propose then try to talk me out of it?"

Ryan stood, brushed off the knee of his pants and wrapped his arms around her. "I just want you to know what you're getting into."

"There's no doubt about it; you're trying to renege. Well, forget it because it's my Christmas present and you can't take it back." She curled her fingers into the lapels of his coat, tugged him close, and kissed his chin. "More than that, I asked for a Christmas miracle and you gave it to me."

Ryan hugged her tight. "Snow is known for its miracles, you know."

Chapter Nineteen

"Dad, you're going to miss it!"

Their moment was interrupted by Emma's shout from the window, so they hurried back downstairs in time to see the news reporter standing in front of Emma's class at the school library. He was talking in general terms about the cost of electricity as the kids waved to the camera from behind him. Ryan and Alexis sat on the couch bracketing Emma as the reporter asked Miss Michaels a question about the project.

"When will he get to us?" Emma bounced, unable to sit still. The camera cut to the graph the class had made, then to a close-up of Emma.

She squealed.

"Hush," Ryan said as she pounded on his leg.

"…and if everyone tries, even for an hour a day like we did in Snow, the savings can help your town and the coal industry." Emma's sincerity came clearly across the television screen. Her pixie smile cinched it.

A commercial popped onto the screen.

"That's it?" Obviously disappointed with her fifteen seconds of fame, she stood, turning to face them, arms spread wide. "What about the interviews with the other kids? What about Charlie?"

"Honey, they always take lots more footage than they know they're going to use. When they go back to the station, they have to edit the piece to fit the news broadcast. Unfortunately, your time was probably pre-empted by bank failures and the ongoing conflict overseas."

Emma looked down and frowned. "I suppose, and at least Charlie didn't talk about—" She squealed again, this time grabbing Alexis's wrist and pulling her hand close. Ryan would have given anything for a camera to catch the comical expression on her face.

"You gave her a plastic princess ring?"

Alexis held up her left hand, turning it this way and that. "I rather like it."

"But Dad," his daughter protested on Alexis's behalf. "You can afford—"

"She said yes, Emma. That's more important, don't you think?"

Total quiet reigned as Emma looked from one adult to the other.

"I said yes when he told me I got you in the bargain." Alexis patted Emma's cheek.

Emma emitted yet another squeal as she launched herself at them, one arm around each of their necks, laughing and jabbering about how much she loved them, about Christmas miracles, and how this was much better than being on TV anyway.

* * * *

The only thing to go right Wednesday was that it hadn't started snowing…yet. Ryan mopped his brow with his sleeve and reset his hat. Even in thirty degree weather, he, Mitch and Ron were working without coats as they positioned barrels around the park.

Ron had loaded the barrels full of scrap lumber onto his flatbed with the help of a forklift at the lumber yard. The guys had found them too heavy to unload, so had to dump the wood, unload the barrels and roll them into position, before refilling them with lumber.

Mitch had wanted to get Charlie and his friends to help but Ryan convinced him not to interrupt Corin's practice at the gazebo. Personally, he figured Mitch simply liked to hassle Corin. Those two acted like a couple of teenagers just discovering their hormones.

Now, hours later, the floodlights weren't any easier to get positioned and connected. The park was so full of snow sculptures it was difficult to find enough open space to set the tripods without being right in the area reserved for the audience. In addition, because of the recent television coverage, the square was crowded with spectators and last minute shoppers. To keep people from possibly tripping, they strung the electrical cords overhead to the generator, which took more time and more electrical wire. Of course, the generator had to be set at the far corner of the square so the noise wouldn't interfere with the program. The logistics of the whole thing were more complicated than Ryan's work at NASA.

He took a break while Mitch and Ron left to collect more extension cords. Mitch was a wizard when it came to things electrical, but even more so in the actual acquisition of whatever they needed. It had all been donated for the program, unlike Ryan's negotiations with Carston. He began to think he had been bamboozled into getting the generator.

It had taken several phone calls before Ryan had secured Carston's agreement to loan the town a generator for the program. Agreement at a price, but it didn't matter and no one would ever know. Ryan would do whatever was necessary for the kids to have their program.

He now smiled as the kids marched and tumbled and skipped and jumped through the red curtain at the edge of the gazebo then across the make shift stage. The setting was minimal, but with all the decorated trees in the park and the snow sculptures, there wasn't a need for more.

He caught sight of Alexis as she herded Toby across the street with two large carafes while she carried a bakery box and a stack of paper cups. This was what Christmas truly meant. More than the decorations and commercialism – even though he was in business – the holiday was a time for family and community and belonging.

He wanted his daughter to have that sense of belonging, just as he had during his youth in Snow. He knew now that he and Emma could have made it work in Houston, especially with Alexis's help. He had used Emma's illness as an excuse to come home and he was very happy he had. Emma was thriving, and Snow had given him a sense of contentment. Well, that and Alexis agreeing to marry him. Aunt Mary had been thrilled and

Corin was already ordering bridal magazines at the bookstore.

Emma saw him and waved then quickly got back in place as music started and the kids sang "Old Saint Nick." Without conscious thought, his gaze shifted across the street to the toy store.

Something about Mr. Nicholas nudged a long forgotten memory from his youth. The last Christmas his parents were alive, when he was about Emma's age, Ryan had sworn he saw Santa outside their house on Christmas Eve. His parents had smiled, not believing him for a minute. That mental snapshot – the two of them standing together smiling – was how he remembered them to this day.

All the recent incidents – Emma and Charlie getting lost, Corin's accident on the stage, even Alexis coming to discuss wind energy – made Ryan wonder about the possibility of some unseen force behind it all. Just look at how all those separate events had brought the town folk closer; working together for common goals. Was it the sense of peace and goodwill that always came with the Christmas season, or was it the magic of Snow?

"The music's not loud enough," Mitch yelled from behind him.

Ryan scrunched his shoulders at the bellow. Leave it to Mitch to intrude on his happy thoughts. He turned to see him, Ron and another man he didn't know, moving ladders to string another set of light cords.

"You can't hear the kids from here either," Mitch hollered above the music.

Mary Beth shut off the CD player. Corin waved her arms to quiet the kids and they immediately raced off the stage to where Alexis and Toby handed out hot chocolate and cookies. Corin turned with hands on hips to glare at Mitch. Ryan was glad to be standing to the side as the darts flew. She didn't say a word, but something passed between them.

"I'll call the school and go get microphones and speakers," Mitch said. Ryan looked at him in surprise because he didn't detect any grumbling in his voice.

"We're going to need a switch box and an electrician's license if you keep finding things to plug in," Ryan called after him. He wasn't worried about the generator; it could probably light up the entire town.

"Got it," Mitch threw over his shoulder with a wave. Ryan figured it didn't matter what he referred to, Mitch was finally becoming part of Snow again.

* * * *

Ryan had been afraid the day before Christmas would drag and Emma would pester him about anything and everything, but she had disappeared – with Charlie, of course – shortly after breakfast.

Considering Charlie's imagination and the fact it was Christmas Eve, he had elicited a promise before they had left the bakery. "Don't leave town on Santa's sleigh, okay?" he had asked as Emma bundled up at the door.

"Oh, wow, that would be too cool!" Charlie had exclaimed, but Emma just gave him one of her eye rolls and a kiss good bye.

He had helped Aunt Mary as everyone came in for last minute holiday goodies and when Alexis came over later in the morning, Ryan had loaded his SUV to make the home deliveries.

After the holidays he knew they'd have to talk about getting Mary some help. These past three months had made Ryan realize how much work was involved running the business. It wasn't that he was afraid of hard work or the physical aspects of the job. He'd even adjusted to a severe lack of sleep and he felt better at the moment than when he had sat at a desk eight hours a day.

But he and Alexis hadn't talked about where they would live in the long run, and he knew it was a discussion they had to have. As much as he wanted Emma to grow up in Snow, he couldn't ask Alexis to give up her career.

Myriad thoughts raced through his brain as he now waited for Emma to get ready for the Christmas pageant.

"Are you almost ready?" he hollered at her from the living room.

"Dad, it's right across the street," she hollered back.

"How long does it take to put on a doll house costume?" He turned to Alexis.

She laughed and patted the couch beside her. "I told you that you had a lot to learn about females; especially when they're getting ready to go out for the evening."

"She's only ten. It's not like she's going on a date."

He turned when he heard Emma. "You don't even have your costume on." She was dressed in slacks and a sweater, and carried her costume. He took the oversized box from her.

"It's too hard to walk in, especially down the stairs. Besides, I have to put my coat on first." Instead of going toward the door, she turned and stood in front of Alexis. Ryan noticed she held a small package behind her back.

"Dad used to let me open one present on Christmas Eve," she said. "I know you already got your present from him," she looked at him over her shoulder, "even if it wasn't a real ring." Emma held out the brightly wrapped present. "Since you live in Houston, this won't work there, so I thought you might as well have it to wear tonight."

Ryan knew they hadn't discussed living arrangements, other than when he had mentioned staying in Snow a little longer. In fact, they hadn't even discussed when they would marry. Yet Emma sensed the importance of Alexis's job and hadn't assumed she would stay in Snow.

Alexis took the package, but set it in her lap instead of opening it. "Well, as for living in Houston…" She looked at him. "I guess you get your present now, too, although it's not something you can actually unwrap." She scooted to the front of the couch and circled Emma's waist with her arm but kept her gaze on him. "I've talked to my boss, and if the town of Snow decides to invest in wind turbines, I'm going to take a leave of absence from the Department of Energy and become a consultant for the project."

"In Snow?" Emma squeaked.

Ryan felt a grin split his face.

"In Snow," Alexis confirmed.

"Then you'll definitely need that." Emma pointed to her present.

Alexis tore open the paper to reveal a long woolen scarf in a bright pattern of color with fringe on the ends. "It's one of Miss Vera's scarves," she said as she caressed the soft wool.

Emma nodded. "The one you looked at when we were shopping for Dad's present." She turned to him. "You don't get that present until tomorrow."

"It's beautiful. Thank you, Emma." Alexis kissed her cheek then stood and wrapped the scarf around her neck.

Ryan used it to tug her close for a quick kiss. "Do you think you'll be able to handle winters in Snow now?"

"I can handle winter wherever my family is." She included Emma in their embrace.

"Can we go now?" Emma groused, although she was smiling.

"Don't you want a present to open?"

His daughter shook her head. "I already got two presents – you're happy and we've got Alexis."

"What about a present from Santa?"

"You sound like Charlie," Emma said as she stomped into her rubber boots and put on her coat. "He was so disappointed today when we went to the toy store and there was a big sign on the door saying closed to make deliveries. Then he said of course Santa would have to leave early if he went all around the world in a single day."

She shook her head. "He just doesn't get it. Everybody closed early today. It's Christmas Eve."

"Well, you can't blame Charlie for still believing in miracles," Ryan said as he ushered his own two miracles out of the apartment and closed the door behind him, the bells on the wreath ringing merrily.

* * * *

Floodlights brightened the area around the gazebo, creating a surreal scene as the sky overhead was dark; the streetlights were out, and as had been the norm, the Christmas lights were off. No one seemed to mind the dark or the cold as they chatted gaily making their way from parked cars to the area left open for the program's audience. Some carried folding chairs and others stood near the burning barrels. Ryan noticed Mitch and his crew had managed to appropriate several rows of wooden chairs to line the area in front of the stage. He wondered if the City Council members would recognize them.

He deposited Alexis and Aunt Mary in the second row then walked with Emma around the back of the stage, carrying her costume.

"Are you warm enough?" He helped her slide her arms into the costume holes, turned her around and secured the Velcro across the back.

She turned and wiggled a mittened hand, urging him closer. When he bent to her level, she kissed his cheek. "I love you, Dad." Then she turned and hurried off to join her friends as Corin put them in line.

The play was cute, all the kids performing their lines loudly, although the microphones helped amplify some of the young children's voices. Carols were interspersed between groups of dialogue and the audience was encouraged to sing along.

As Ryan sang traditional Christmas carols he knew by heart, he thought about all the Christmases of his life – back when his parents were alive; when he had first come to live with Aunt Mary and Uncle Paul; Emma's first Christmas as a baby. Each holiday had been special in its own way, yet as he looked back, it seemed they had all been leading him to this day in Snow.

Before the last song, some of the older boys passed out small candles and one by one, people lit theirs from a friend or neighbor. Someone turned the floodlights off and a shiver of anticipation raced through Ryan, just as it had for all the Christmas Eves of his past.

The children began singing O Come All Ye Faithful and gradually more voices rose in song. Ryan lifted his gaze toward heaven as snowflakes floated down in the night and the church bells began to ring.

Every year had been like this, and yet every year appeared like a new miracle as the people of Snow converged to praise the Lord and give thanks for all they had received. Struggles and disagreements were forgotten, just as they had been all those years ago during the depression when children had kept the faith and had reminded the town what faith was all about.

He glanced at Emma, who had certainly done that for him this year. Emma had a goodness within that shone like a beacon and had at times been his support rather than the other way around. She was an inspiration to him, and she had definitely gotten the people of Snow motivated. He knew the conflict over alternative energy wasn't over, and they still had a battle on their hands. After all, Snow was a coal mining town and always had been. But for tonight, there really was joy to the world.

Ryan realized how right his life was as they walked to the corner and waited for Emma after the program. Aunt Mary held his arm on the left and Alexis was on his right. His daughter came running – running –to where they stood.

"Dad, look!" Emma grabbed her dad's hand as they turned back toward Center Park. Light by light, section by section, the entire square came alive in shimmering color. The tallest tree in the center glittered in the night as the star at the very top winked and twinkled. O Holy Night played over the loud speakers. People stopped to stare, then began laughing and singing as they made their way to cars or walked home.

"How did you manage that?" her dad asked Mitch as he, Corin and Charlie met them.

Mitch shook his head. "Not me."

"Maybe it's the magic of Snow," Aunt Mary whispered.

"Do you hear that?" Charlie piped up. He tilted his head to the side. "Sleigh bells!" He started across the street then turned back. "Emma, come on!"

She shook her head in resignation, but followed in her friend's wake.

"It's deserted," she said when they stood in front of the toy store. It did seem strange. Only yesterday there had been toys and decorations in the windows; things she and Charlie had put there. The words for the shop had been painted in bright red on the window. Now the store was dark and empty; the paint on the window faded and peeling.

Charlie turned the handle on the door and with a squeak, it actually opened. A piece of paper fluttered to the ground at his feet. He picked it up and Emma saw their names printed on the folded note.

He handed it to her. She frowned then slowly unfolded the paper.

"Always believe." She looked at Charlie. "That's all it says."

Charlie nodded solemnly, turned around and walked into the toy store. The lights didn't work, but for once there was enough light outside to shine through the windows. The place was much as it had been the first time Charlie had brought her here – empty except for some scraps of wood and a couple cans of paint, turned on their sides.

"Oh, yeah!" Charlie hollered and raced toward the back of the store, his boot heels echoing eerily in the vacant shop.

Emma came more slowly.

"It's just like the drawing I sent him! Just exactly!" Charlie hopped around, waving his hands and dancing in a circle. It wasn't until he moved to the side that Emma saw what stood on the toy store floor.

A sleigh; exactly the right size for Wolf to pull. A sleigh, with beautifully carved wooden sides and real metal runners instead of a plastic toboggan; and real leather harness instead of mismatched pieces of rope.

"Even if you don't need to anymore, I'll give you a ride." Charlie's voice was full of excitement. "I'll get Wolf and we'll take you for a ride. Get in." He picked up a small blanket that had been laid on the wooden seat of the sleigh.

"Huh? Santa must have left these for you."

He turned and handed Emma a pair of pink flip-flops; the kind with the floppy plastic flowers across the toes.

The End

Barbara Baldwin books also published by Books We Love

Lost Knight of Arabia
Spinning Through Time
Christmas Wishes

Keep Reading for an Excerpt from Barbara Baldwin's Christmas Wishes

Christmas Wishes
Chapter 1

Chanti drove her Lexus along the winding road, taking note of the late autumn foliage, the harvest decorations still adorning porches and around mailboxes. Pretty soon, snowmen and Santa Clauses would replace fall leaves and scarecrows. No one in town wanted to be the last to get their decorations out, so almost like magic, they would all appear at the same time. She frowned, thinking so many things in her life were as predictable as the Hattiesville decorating. Lately, that predictability was leaving her unsettled. Wasn't there supposed to be more to life?

She turned the corner onto the two-mile private drive that led to her house. She took a deep breath as the house came into view, consciously making herself relax. Things were great, so why was she so anxious?

Coming home always made her smile, and regardless of her previous thoughts, she could now feel the corners of her mouth lift. The house had belonged to her parents and it was two tall stories with pillars at the front porch steps. The wings were each a single story and curved almost in a semicircle, like arms spreading wide to welcome her home. When she was young, riding up front in the limo with George while her father rode in back with his cell phone and computer, she had told George the house talked to her.

"You don't say," George would reply good-naturedly. "And what might the grand lady be chatting about today?"

"She's happy to see us – see how her arms are open wide for us?"

"Mmmm," was all he would say, always agreeing with her.

"And she says Wilma has made us the bestest dinner, and, oh look George, she's wearing a beautiful hat today!"

Chanti remembered that day, much like today, when the weather had turned cold but there was still a late afternoon sun slanting across the lawn. She slowed to a stop in the drive, just before it began to circle around the fountain to the front door. The lady was once again wearing a hat and she smiled at the memory.

The trees that surrounded the house on three sides and shaded it on the hottest days were in full fall array, their colors every shade of yellow to brown, orange to red. Even though it was late November, the weather had been mild until recently, so the trees had only just turned. The way the huge oaks and maples towered over the house had always made it look like they were crowning it, or in the case of a six year old's imagination, making a hat for the house-lady to wear.

She noticed there were a few stray branches sticking out at odd angles, and thought perhaps George should trim them.

No, George was too old to be climbing the house to the roof to get at the trees. Besides, she thought whimsically, they looked like feathers, giving the grand lady a ta-ta haughty look.

She closed the door to the car, a genuine smile on her face at last. Being home always did that, whether she had been at her office in Chicago or on one of the many whirlwind tours of Europe where her cosmetic line had launched this past year.

The front chandelier flickered on as Chanti opened the door, dropping her keys in the tray on the side table and her briefcase on the matching antique chair. She shuffled through the mail, nothing catching her interest but knowing she had to go through it every day or it would be overwhelming. Besides, it was the end of the month and there were bills to pay. She knew she could just let Nelson handle the household accounts as he did her business, but she preferred knowing where her money went. And she didn't want any one else knowing what it took to keep this house up. If it weren't for the memories, she should probably sell it and move to a condo in the city, if for no other reason than proximity to work.

"Hi, sweet pea. You're home early," Wilma called to her from the kitchen.

Chanti smiled. Wilma and her husband, George, were just two more reasons to keep the house, even if the maintenance overwhelmed her at times. They were long past retirement age, and her father had left them well off when he died, but they refused to leave Red Rock Quay. Said they would leave when she did, but where would they go? She couldn't see George in a retirement home, and Wilma would just try to take over management of the kitchen. So there you had it. She was thirty-two years old and stuck with still being called sweet pea.

Chanti walked through the gigantic dining room, used only on occasion when she was forced to have dinner parties, and pushed the swinging door open to the kitchen, warm and fragrant as always. She reached above the counter to one of the glass-fronted cupboards, pulling out two wine glasses. Getting the bottle of white wine from the fridge, she poured herself and Wilma a glass.

"And how was your day, dear?" she asked facetiously as she sat on one of the bar stools, reaching over to place a wine glass near Wilma, who stirred something delicious smelling on the stove.

She considered her housekeeper and her husband friends rather than employees. They ate together in the cozy kitchen instead of the cold, formal dining room. Chanti still helped clean up and dry dishes and Wilma still scolded her if she talked with her mouth full.

"I've been better," Wilma answered her question.

"Your shoulder again?" Chanti asked, getting up to go around the cooking island to help.

"You just sit down and drink your wine." Wilma waved a spoon at her. "You worked hard all day."

Chanti snorted. "Sitting at my desk on a computer and talking on the phone is not hard work. Did you ever call Merry Maids housecleaning service to get someone to help around here?"

"Those young girls don't know how to clean. I've told you that before, now just leave it. George helps out more than enough."

"George is older than you and both of you should have retired years ago."

Wilma narrowed her eyes at Chanti, and she knew it was a losing argument. The same argument they had almost weekly.

George came in and gave his wife a hug, a wet smacking kiss on the cheek, and pinched her butt.

Wilma swatted at him and Chanti laughed. She wondered sometimes if there was anyone out there for her like Wilma had George, but she quickly squelched the thought. She had too much money for most men to actually love her, and she had too much education and business savvy for the rest. Any song about "a good ole boy's girl" was never going to be sung to her. She'd have to content herself with the occasional affair, usually while traveling. That way, she didn't have to worry about some guy stalking her when he found out she was rich.

"Frost in the air," George commented as he helped set the table for three in the window nook.

"Hmm?" Chanti set aside her daydreams. "Well, since it's the end of November and we live outside of Chicago by Lake Michigan, I would say frost is always a possibility."

"You always were a smart one," George responded.

Smarty-pants, rich bitch--Chanti had been called both and more throughout her life although she knew George didn't mean it in a derogatory way. She couldn't help it if her family had been well off and now her cosmetics company was skyrocketing into prominence. She frowned, twirling her wine glass by the stem. She should be happy; delighted; ecstatic. Her newest line, Chantilly Frost, was set to launch in the Chicago area with major advertising on television and in all the area newspapers -- the Sun-Times, Tribune, and Chicago Magazine. She had even purchased space on the new internet format -- Digital City Chicago.

So why was she suddenly so bored with her life?

"I'm going to Charlie's," she said suddenly, getting up from the table and leaving without another word.

* * *

232

AJ glanced around the dim interior of the bar. It was early evening, just barely past quitting time, but already the place was packed. Men in jeans and flannel shirts, women in pants and sweaters all joined to bring the volume of the place to one decibel below deafening. It appeared that Charlie's was a place for the working man; not the executive, stuffed shirt, martini and cosmopolitan types that frequented the bars in the city. Of course, some people considered Hattiesville part of Chicago since it sat right at the end of the Metra commuter rail line, but for the residents, like his friend Charlie, the small town was an entity of its own and they liked it that way.

He took a swig of beer, letting the cool malt slide down his throat, wishing he were back in Texas where he belonged. Unfortunately, business had brought him north, and for a while at least, his address was the America Inn two blocks over. Charlie had offered him the use of his spare room, but AJ kept odd hours and didn't want to be in a position to have to carry on polite conversation over a dinner table. Even with his college roommate and long time friend, Charlie Brown.

He started to speak with Charlie when the door opened, letting in a blast of cold November air. Wishing again for Texas, he shivered and thought about moving further down the bar, away from the portal to the North Pole. Instead, his gaze went to the latest arrival and he forgot all about being cold.

A tumble of long blonde hair fell around her shoulders when she pulled off a brightly striped stocking cap. Knee high boots clicked against the wood floor as she ate up the distance to the bar. She pulled off her mittens, stuffed them into her hat and snagged the buttons of her leather coat as she hopped onto the bar stool right next to him. As she tugged her coat off, AJ couldn't help but admire the way her sweater curved snuggly over a great figure.

"Allow me, ma'am." He reached for the back of her coat to help her and touched the nape of her neck. Perhaps it was the static electricity from her leather and wool, but AJ could have sworn he felt a current pass between them.

"Oh, God, Charlie. Tell me he didn't just call me ma'am," she groaned, talking to the bartender but turning her head to gaze at him, her green eyes twinkling and her full, dark pink lips curved in a smile. He just knew if he kissed her, she'd taste like champagne.

Even though he was pretty sure she was teasing, he felt the need to defend himself. "Where I come from, it's only polite to call females over the age…uh, grown women, that is, ma'am. At least until we're properly introduced." Since she apparently knew Charlie, AJ glanced that way, hoping his friend would take the hint.

She narrowed her gaze at his near slip about age, but then shrugged it off. "Around here, only school teachers, the minister's wife and your grandma would be called that. And all of them are well over the age of…uh…" She mimicked him, but let the rest of the sentence trail off.

"Hey, Tilly, give the guy a break." Charlie grinned as he took down a wine glass and poured her a drink.

He knew her all right, AJ thought, and she must be a regular if he also knew her drink without asking. He watched as she wrinkled her nose and pursed lusciously glossed lips.

"We are not in third grade any more, Charlie. I have no braids for you to pull, and you do not call me that awful name."

"Why not, you call me Charlie."

"You would rather I call you Alfred?"

AJ spewed a mouthful of beer across the bar as he burst out laughing. "That's why you always signed your name A. Charles Brown?"

"Better than Andrew Jackson, you damned cowboy," Charlie shot right back. It had been a continuing argument their four years as college roommates. They had called each other cowboy and city slicker, but had forged a bond stronger than he had with his brothers.

"Who's your friend?" the woman asked, her gaze running appreciatively up, then back down AJ and he could feel himself respond.

"AJ," he introduced himself. "And I take it your real name isn't Tilly?" He stuck out his hand.

"Chanti," she replied as she slid her slim hand into his. The slight jolt he had felt when helping her with her coat turned to a bolt of electricity, shooting from her fingers up his arm.

"Chant-Tilly," he put the two pieces together. "As in Chantilly Lace, a pretty face?" It was a favorite old country song. From the warmth and energy in her handshake, some instinct told him she would be like so many of the other songs on his truck radio – good woman and good loving.

Charlie snorted. "More like Chantilly—"

"Just Chanti," she said.

When he released her hand, reluctantly, she casually placed it on the arm he had bent to the bar. "Ignore Charlie. He gets mad because the girls are always on this side of the bar." She took a sip of wine. "Want to dance?" She swung her legs around to face him, her knees bumping his hip.

When she smiled at him, the sun came out on this cold northland and AJ thought maybe his time here in Hattiesville might have an upside after all. As he put an arm around her waist and swung her into the rhythm of the music, she looped both arms around his neck and snuggled closer. Oh, yeah, a dance was just the beginning.

* * *

Chanti knew she was living dangerously. Not in being at Charlie's, for it was the neighborhood of her childhood and regardless of how times had changed, some things had not. The bar had belonged to Charlie's uncle, and now Charlie. She lived in her parents' house, and Marvin over there playing pool, had been a plumber assistant with his dad and now ran the business.

No, the danger lay in the stranger with the soft southern drawl, faded jeans and boots who kept her

235

swirling around the dance floor, pausing in-between jukebox songs just long enough to swallow some beer. He had chucked quarters into the machine, rapidly punching numbers before she had a chance to review the song labels, and now she knew why. All the songs he'd picked were slow dances, and every slow dance brought them closer and closer.

"How long have you known Charlie?" he asked now, slowing his steps until they were simply rocking to and fro.

"Forever," she murmured the response, more interested in the way his dark hair curled behind his ears and along his nape. She slid one hand along his shoulder until her fingers touched the silky locks. No short buzz cut for this cowboy, she thought, and yet the style suited him.

"Your accent says Texas and Charlie called you a cowboy. Do you really have cows?" She twirled a finger, capturing a lock and tugging ever so slightly.

"There's a romantic song on the jukebox, I have a beautiful woman in my arms and she wants to talk livestock?" He gave a dramatic sigh. "I must be losing my touch."

Chanti felt his hand slide slightly south to pull her hips closer to his. "Oh, I wouldn't say that."

"Did you date?" he asked and she knew he was really asking if she and Charlie had slept together.

"Charlie?" She made a face.

He responded by turning her in a sweeping circle and she squealed as she clung to his neck. When he slowed, she tilted back to capture his gaze. She had gathered AJ and Charlie were friends, and most men didn't poach, especially on friends. So AJ must be interested. Normally she would tell a man her personal life was none of his business, but in this case, he got the truth. Because she was interested, too.

"When he finally grew up and quit pulling my braids, yeah, we dated, but decided we were better off as friends."

"Friends? Men and women are business associates or lovers, not friends."

Chanti stopped dead in her tracks, her hands dropping to her sides. "You have got to be kidding me." She stared in amazement, then turned and walked away from him to the bar where she'd left her glass of wine. He was only a step or two behind her.

"What did I say?" he asked, sounding genuinely perplexed.

"Charlie, your friend is a moron."

Charlie shrugged. "I know, but what can I say?" When Chanti heard AJ give a whispered help me out here, Charlie added, "I suppose he gave you the friends or lovers speech?"

She narrowed her gaze at him. "Yeah, and you'd better not tell me you believe that crap." She and Charlie were friends and he knew all her secrets.

"You have to remember he's from Texas, where they protect their women and horses with equal fervor."

Out of the corner of her eye she saw AJ drop his head to his hands. "You're not helping here," he said in a strangled voice.

Chanti laughed, she just couldn't help it. She liked Charlie's friend; in fact there was chemistry between them she had never felt before. She wasn't normally one to pick up guys at a bar. To say the least it was a dangerous proposition in this day and age, even at Charlie's small hometown place. But there had been a just right feel to his arms around her when they danced and an unfamiliar but exciting sizzle when he had nuzzled the side of her neck.

She watched as he downed the last of his beer, his throat muscles contracting as he swallowed. Her stomach pitched as she wondered what he would taste like if she licked a path down his throat or sank her teeth into the skin right where his crew neck sweater circled his thick neck. But then he tossed some bills on the counter and stood up.

"Gotta go," he said to Charlie but Chanti wondered if there was a little hesitancy in his voice. Did he want her to ask him to stay? Usually men came on to her and she was in control of the situation, determining whether the relationship advanced or was nipped in the bud. She wasn't sure how to go about this turn of the tables. How embarrassing if she asked and he said no.

"Nice to meet you, Miss Chantilly Lace." He set his hat on his head then touched the brim. Of course he wore a cowboy hat.

"Don't your ears get cold in the winter?" she asked the idiotic question, if only to keep him there just a little longer.

He grinned. "It's not cold in Texas," he said and walked past her toward the door. Chanti started to swivel to watch him leave when she felt his warm breath at her ear. "But you can come with me now and find out how they fare in Hattiesville."

When she spun around, his back was to her, his long strides taking him quickly to the door. He was letting her choose, but in a way neither would lose face since chances were they would never see each other again. She turned back to Charlie, her gaze searching her friend's face for the answer even before she asked the question.

"Is he an okay guy?"

Charlie didn't answer right away, his gaze on the departing AJ. When he finally turned her way, his eyes were serious but a hint of a smile lifted the corners of his mouth. "Yeah, silly-Tilly. I think he might be just what you need."

She didn't stop to analyze his words. She grabbed her coat off the back of her chair, tugging it on as she hurried through the crowd that suddenly seemed intent on blocking her path.

About The Author

Barbara was born in California and now resides in the midwest. She loves to travel and explore new places, which usually means each of her novels is set in a different locale. She has been published in formats from poetry and short stories to full-length fiction. She wrote and co-produced a documentary on state history which won state and national awards, but she really loves writing romance, whether it be contemporary, historical or time travel. Just for fun, each year she writes a Christmas short story for family and friends—some heartfelt and others whimsical — but always a gift from her heart. She has an MA in Communication, has taught at the college level and has made over 100 presentations at state and national conferences. She also loves to create art through pottery and fused glass, candles, baskets and quilts. Visit her website at http://www.authorsden.com/barbarajbaldwin.